# The Ties That Bind

# Peter Crussell

NEW REPORT PUBLISHING

Write to: enquiries@newreportpublishing.co.uk

First published in paperback by New Report Publishing in 2020

Paperback ISBN: 978-1-9999096-5-9

NEW REPORT

PUBLISHING

NEW REPORT PUBLISHING

*Also available by Peter Crussell*

Children's Book Series:
*TALES FROM THE ENCHANTED FOREST*
Summer Holidays
Brownie Pack Holiday
The Tooth Fairy
Autumn Adventures

The Enchanted Forest Colouring and Activity Book

# The Hilliard Family Tree

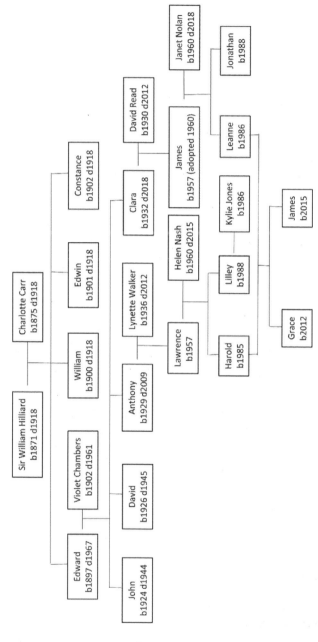

# Chapter One
## Cause and Effect

I am writing this account because you told me it would be good for me.

You said that it would help my recovery. You convinced me that, by writing a full account of events, it would exorcize the trauma from my mind.

"It'll be like a confession," you said, "by writing it down you'll release it and it'll be out there, in the open. It will no longer have a hold on you. You can move on."

Maybe you're right.

Already, as I complete these first few sentences, I can feel a weight lifting from my mind like the mist rising from a field on a warm spring morning. Perhaps it's just the power of suggestion but it's like I'm going through a catharsis. It's as though my mind is beginning to make sense of everything and the events of the last eight months, or should that be the last one hundred years, are coming into sharp focus. The clarity is alarming and yet, at the same time, exhilarating.

Larry thinks so too.

As I look back on the events, I think I can see a pattern. I begin to see what they call 'cause and effect', and the question that keeps coming to my mind is: what if?

What if the event that triggered it all hadn't happened?

The event that triggered it all was death. Whether it was the deaths that happened eight months ago or the deaths that happened one hundred years ago, that is for you to decide, but it was certainly death that set a chain of events in motion so I shall start my story with the day that my life changed irrevocably and the first 'what if'.

What if ... the A34 between Didcot and Oxford hadn't been jammed that morning forcing my wife, Janet, to take the A4016 into Oxford instead?

What if ... the Estonian driver of the articulated lorry, driving in the UK for the first time, hadn't been searching playlists on his MP3 player instead of concentrating on the unfamiliar road as he rounded the sudden sharp bend?

What if ... he hadn't been driving too fast to be able to control his vehicle?

What if ... he hadn't been driving on the wrong side of the road?

The answer to all the above is simple; Janet and my mother would still be alive today and, as a result, I wouldn't have had my breakdown. I also wouldn't have been staying with Larry at Rosehip Hall in Downham Fen in Cambridgeshire instead of being at my own home in Sutton Courtney in Oxfordshire.

And if I hadn't been staying with Larry at Rosehip Hall then the events that I am about to recount would never have happened and things might have been very different.

And I would not have discovered who I am.

That's what if!

Would you say that was fate? Serendipity? Or chance?


For those of you who are interested in knowing every detail I'll offer you this to start with. Larry is my cousin and best friend.

When I say he's my cousin that's not entirely true. He *is* my cousin, but I was adopted so, in a sense he isn't. I was adopted by his Aunt Clara and her husband David, in 1960, just before my third birthday. David was the vicar in Sutton Courtney and he and Clara had been unable to have children of their own, so they adopted me, and everyone was happy.

Clara and David were, in every respect other than by birth, my mum and dad. In all honesty I couldn't have asked for a better childhood. I wanted for nothing, I was spoiled by my mum and I was loved, unconditionally, by them both. In fact, I didn't even know I was adopted until I decided to get married when I was in my mid-twenties and had to produce my birth certificate and then, as it turned out, my adoption papers too because the name on my birth certificate was different from the name I was known by. My birth name was James Walters, and my adopted name was James Read. James is for formal stuff, like passports and birth certificates. You can call me Jim like my friends do.

Admittedly, finding out I was adopted did come as a bit of a shock. I really had no idea and, as I very quickly discovered, I actually didn't care that much. Clara and David were, unequivocally, my mum and dad. I loved them both dearly. To my mind, whoever and wherever they might be, my birth parents had given up any rights over me the moment they gave me up for adoption. They clearly weren't interested in me so why should I be interested in them? I owed them nothing so why should I care? How interesting our view on life can be when we are young. I wasn't even interested back then in finding out who they were and, as it turned out, it was really quite important.

I was brought up by my parents in Sutton Courtney, a quiet village south of Oxford. Every summer, during the school holidays, my mum would take me to stay with my grandad, Edward Hilliard, a World War One veteran who had fought for his country in the trenches.

My cousin Larry would join us so we could play together. We were typical boys growing up in the nineteen-sixties. We watched Crackerjack and Blue Peter on the television; we read Enid Blyton, C.S. Lewis and Ian Fleming; we played with Action Man, Lego and Scalextric and had the latest toys for boys like Johnny Seven and Secret Sam.

Grandad had lived in a huge old house called Rosehip Hall, which he inherited at the beginning of 1919 after his father, Sir William Hilliard, was murdered by local villager, Seth Chambers at the end of the previous year. By all accounts, Chambers had been a ruffian and a drunk and had thought our great grandfather was having an affair with his wife, Beth. He had killed them both after a drinking binge in our local village pub, The Three Horseshoes. Beth Chambers had been the housekeeper at the Hall for over a decade when her husband embarked on his drunken rampage. They never found her body, but the shooting of Sir William was seen by more than half the village. Chambers was detained and hanged the following year.

The Hall had been built by one of our ancestors in the 18th Century some years after they had drained the Cambridgeshire fens. The ancestor had been an engineer and had made his fortune by designing and building the sluice gates that controlled the fenland waterways. Generations later Rosehip Hall remains in the family and is where Larry now lives.

And where my story takes place.

Set in fifteen acres, the land consists of woodland, paddocks, wildflower meadows, various outhouses and barns. It even has its own chapel, which Seth Chambers had tried to burn down in his drunken rampage. In the 18th Century the country was still bitterly divided by religious persecution and division and many country houses and stately homes had their own places of worship. Set near to the house, the tiny chapel still stood, with no outward signs of the fire. Inside was very different. The only things that remain undamaged from its ravishes were some memorial stones in the blackened walls and on the floor and a large heavy altar stone along the far wall, opposite the entrance. I imagine that, in its time, there would have been benches or chairs for the family and servants to sit on during Sunday service but, ever since I can remember, it was an empty building, used for storage rather than worship.

During the mid-sixties Larry and I discovered an icehouse in the woods about a hundred metres from the back of the house. It sat about three metres deep beneath a mound of earth about five metres from the path and, to two seven-year-old boys, it was the best discovery we made. It became our secret place and when we were in our early teens, we used the icehouse to store our contraband like cigarettes, alcohol and copies of Playboy magazine. It hadn't been used for decades when we found it and Larry and I had had to dig out the entrance, and then bury it again to keep it hidden. We had sequestered a ladder from Grandad's shed to make it easier to get in and out.

So now you know a little bit about me I'll get on with my story.

Where were we?

Ah, yes, the trigger event. The 'cause' in 'cause and effect'.


The last thing I remember saying to Janet as I leant in through the window of her Fiat 500 to kiss her goodbye was "Drive safely, darling."

She laughed. She always had a beautiful laugh.

"I'm only going to Oxford, darling. We'll be back for dinner."

The 'we' was Janet and my mother, who was then in her eighty-seventh year and was physically fit and as bright as a button. She looked up at me from the passenger seat as she was fastening her seatbelt and said, "Stop fussing, you silly boy," – she often called me a silly boy, even though I am sixty-one years old – "Janet's been driving for nearly 40 years and never had an accident; you don't need to keep telling her to drive safely."

I waved and made silly faces at them as Janet backed the car down the drive and they set off on their shopping day in Oxford.

That was the last time I saw either of them alive.

The local travel news had announced earlier that there was a major traffic jam on the A34 into Oxford and drivers could expect delays of up to two hours, so Janet took the A4016 instead and that's where she died.

The police estimated that the lorry had been travelling about sixty miles an hour on impact and it didn't even try to stop. The cab of the lorry was fitted with CCTV which, to my horror, was shown on the national news. It showed the driver searching playlists on his MP3 player; it showed the lorry veering across the road and driving on the wrong side; it showed Janet's car coming towards it as it rounded the bend. That was as much of the footage as they showed on television.

With no time for either driver to take evasive action the CCTV showed the cab as first it jolted, and then bounced and bumped, as Janet's car disappeared beneath it. The film footage then showed the driver being thrown through his windshield and landing on the road in front like a discarded doll before the cab tipped over and careered along the road on its side before coming to a halt, half in the neighbouring field and blocking the road completely.

The only consolation was that mum and Janet died instantly and probably knew nothing about it. That may have made the television viewers feel a little better, but it was no consolation to me.

I remember the knock on the door later that afternoon. I had been working on a picture. Since taking early retirement a year previously I had taken up art as a hobby and I was trying to finish a portrait of my mum in time for her birthday.

I remember how my heart missed a beat when I saw the two policemen standing on my doorstep in their fluorescent jackets, holding their hats in their hands and looking sombre. I remember feeling totally numb as they informed me of my loss. My head was spinning as they spoke; but their voices, soft and sympathetic, faded to become just background noise.

I found myself trying to picture Janet's and mum's faces and found I couldn't.

For the next few hours I worked on autopilot as I phoned my children, Leanne and Jonathan. Leanne is married to Larry's son, Harry and they lived, with their two children, Grace and James, in Milton Keynes. My son Jonathan had emigrated to Australia some years ago and now lives in Sydney. I woke him up; it was about 4am where he was.

Two hours later, having taken the children out of school early, Leanne was sitting with me on the sofa, holding onto me as I tried to comfort her. The children were out in the garden playing. She wept for her mother and grandmother and made my shirt wet.

I didn't cry, I couldn't.

I wouldn't.

It was my role to be strong for Leanne and the grandchildren. I was of the generation that didn't show emotion; it wasn't expected, and it wasn't welcome. Quite the opposite, in fact. Stiff upper lip and all that. I always remember what Grandad Edward would tell us if ever he saw Larry or me crying when we were children; "Do you think anyone saw me crying in the trenches? Of course they didn't, it's not the done thing. Now, run along and remember boy, stiff upper lip and all that, eh."

So, I didn't cry even though I felt as though someone had ripped my heart from my breast and was squeezing the life from it. I felt cold; as though my own life had ended with Janet's death.

In many respects, it had.

Leanne cried for nearly two hours. It started despairingly; inconsolable, body shaking, snot pouring, wet cheeked wailing. I held her close, unable to speak the words of comfort she needed; hoping that, by wrapping my arms tightly around her, I was comforting her.

Eventually her crying subsided to sobbing, punctuated by a series of rapid intakes of breath. Over the next hour it became softer and at times I thought she may have fallen asleep but then she would let out another sob.

At last, exhausted, she stopped. She was all cried out for the moment. The tears would return, of course, although without the force and raw emotion of the tears she had just cried.

"I'm sorry, daddy," she said, raising her head and seeing the wet patch of her snot mixed with tears that had spread over the front of my shirt.

"No," I said, forcing a smile, "let it out, let it all out. Cry as much as you need." I kissed her forehead.

"Besides," I added, "I've got plenty more shirts," and she laughed.

Having her and the children there gave me something to do and I was grateful for the distraction.

While Leanne had been crying the children had come running in from the garden. They saw their mother in her state and had put their little arms around her, to try and make her feel better. James, who was only three, cried too, not really knowing why. After a while though, either because they were uncomfortable or bored, Grace, who was six, took James into the dining room to do some drawing.

They each drew a picture of their grandmother and great-grandmother. James had drawn a pair of wings on his figures and halos above their heads, which made them look like angels and I remember I smiled. How simple things like death are to the very young, how easily they seem to be able to accept things at that age.

# Chapter Two
# The Black Dog Barks

Fortunately, I had plenty of space at home, so Leanne and the children could stay for as long as they wanted, and Grace's school was understanding. They told Leanne to take whatever time they needed. Harry joined us that weekend and made us go out and do things with the children. We went to the cinema and watched the latest Disney film. I can't remember which one it was, but I do remember that the children enjoyed it, and afterwards we ordered a takeaway. It was meant to be mundane and normal, aimed to distract us from the tragic events of the previous week, and keep the children amused. It worked. When Harry left to return home on Sunday evening our spirits had been lifted.

When someone dies there is a multitude of tasks to be done, people to notify, paperwork to be completed, things to arrange. When someone is killed there is even more.

Each task, taken in isolation, was relatively simple, but there seemed so many of them and, as two people had died, there was twice as much to do. There were death certificates to be organised, probate to be applied for, banks and building societies to notify, funerals to be organised, mum's estate to be wound up and closed, her house to clear then sell. I was the sole executor and beneficiary of her estate.

There had to be an inquest, but the bodies were released so we could go ahead and arrange the funerals. The inquest itself seemed a bit of a waste of time. It concluded that my wife and my mother were killed by the dangerous driving of a third party. We already knew that but, I suppose, it was needed so the insurance could be resolved.

We held a double funeral. Mum had been the widow of the late vicar, my father, who had died in 2012, and Janet had lived in the village all her life. She had attended local schools and she still had lots of friends there, so the funeral was attended by most of the village and the current vicar presided over a beautiful ceremony.

Jonathan flew in from Australia and Larry drove over from Cambridgeshire. Leanne, Harry and the grandchildren were there, of course, and Larry's daughter, my niece Lilley, came with her wife, Kylie. Lilley was a Research Fellow in Veterinary Science at Edinburgh University. They came down for a couple of days and stayed in a pub in Abingdon.

Six weeks had passed since the fatal crash and, when the funerals were over, everyone returned home and resumed their normal lives.

Everyone, that is, except me. I had no normal life to resume and it was then, when it was all over, that I became aware of the emptiness inside of me.

Up until then I had been surrounded by my family. Leanne and the children had been there the whole time, helping me sort out Janet's and mum's affairs. There had been so much to do, so much paperwork. It hadn't really sunk in yet that I would never see my wife or my mother again. It had all seemed a bit surreal, almost as though they had just gone away on holiday together and at any moment they would walk through the door with their suitcases and smiles as though nothing had happened.

But they didn't. They really were gone.

The inquest, the paperwork, and everything associated with a death seemed to culminate in the funeral and then it was all over. Suddenly, there was no one around anymore. Suddenly there was no one to talk to, no one to distract me from my grief.

That was when my life began to fall apart and spiral out of control.

I wasn't even aware it was happening. Of course, I was sad, but I was a man, and I was strong. Wasn't I? I couldn't come to terms with, or even express, my feeling of loss. I couldn't, I didn't understand them myself. The longer time went on the more I began to think I would never recover from the empty sadness I felt.

One morning, a few weeks after the funeral, I was mooching about the house in my pyjamas, dressing gown, and tatty old slippers when I found Ted. Ted was Janet's favourite Teddy Bear and I picked him up and clutched him against my chest. I had given Ted to Janet as a joke not long after we started going out together back in 1983.

"Every night before you go to sleep," I told her when I gave him to her, "you give Ted a good cuddle and think of me. That way you'll always have sweet dreams."

It must have worked because a few months later she moved in with me and two years after that we were married, which was when I discovered that I had been adopted.

13

I held Ted close and I could smell Janet. I closed my eyes and inhaled, and for a brief moment she was with me again. She stood before me with her arms draped over my shoulders as she often did, her head tilted slightly to one side, and smiled. For the first time in decades I cried.

It started slowly. Tiny tears welled up in the corners of my eyes. Then they filled up and before I knew it, rivulets of salty tears were pouring down my cheeks and, involuntarily, I let out a loud sob. Next thing I knew I was wailing like a baby.

How I despised myself for it. How I despised my weakness, for weakness it surely was and yet I couldn't control myself. I hated myself for it. Men don't cry, I kept telling myself as I tried to pull myself together. I was shaking with grief and I couldn't stop myself.

I was seized by a feeling of utter despair. It was as though I was falling into the deep dark pit of loneliness.

After that it seemed as though anything would set me off. I felt deeply ashamed. I wasn't given to crying, it's not what men do. Crying is for girls.

I would speak to Leanne two or three times a week, but I couldn't tell her how I was really feeling.

"I'm fine," I'd assure her, "busy doing things."

Every second Sunday I would drive to Milton Keynes for Sunday lunch and spend the day with her and Harry and the grandchildren. Each time I drove home the loneliness came creeping back, smothering me like a blanket. Suffocating me and filling my head full of dark thoughts. I began to dread opening the front door and walking into my cold and empty house. My mind would be spinning as I sped down the motorway. How easy it would be for me to swerve across the central reservation, onto the opposite carriageway and into the path of an oncoming lorry; just like Janet had done.

Except she hadn't done that. Not on purpose, and such thoughts made me angry with myself for thinking them. Still, I looked at those oncoming lorries with a kind of longing, fighting back the urge to turn the steering wheel.

I made a new will.

Now Janet was no longer with me – I still struggled to admit to myself that she was dead – I felt it was sensible to ensure that my affairs were in order. Just in case, I told myself, anything should happen to me.

Just in case......

*

One night I had a dream. Janet lay down on the bed beside me. She was smiling; just the way I remembered. I loved her smile and the way her grey-blue eyes sparkled when she did so.

"How are you feeling?" she asked me.

"Like shit," I replied, "I miss you like you'll never know."

"But I do know," she assured me, "because that's just how much I miss you. You know I do."

"I know," I replied.

She leaned over then and kissed me. I smelled her hair as it fell across my face. She smells of Ted, I thought. I felt her arms around me and the tickle of her eyelashes on my neck each time she blinked.

"Wouldn't it be nice," she suggested, snuggling up to me, "to just go to sleep and never wake up?"

I kissed the top of her head. Even in death she was thinking of me and I loved her even more. I listened to her shallow breathing and I pulled her close.

"Go to sleep," she said.

When I woke up the following morning, I was cuddling Ted.

I didn't want to get out of bed that morning, so I lay there with Ted and we stared at the ceiling together. We watched as a shaft of sunlight shone through a chink in the curtains and lazily made its way from the bottom of my bed to the wall above my head. It took all day. After that it disappeared as the sun went down outside and darkness fell.

The next day I phoned Leanne to tell her I wouldn't be coming over that Sunday. I knew she'd be out before I called, and I left her a voicemail.

That evening, while I was staring into space, I heard the phone ringing in the hall. I closed my eyes and willed it to stop. Eventually, it did.

She couldn't call me on my mobile as the battery had run down.

I lost all track of time.

A few days later, after the phone had stopped ringing like it had done every night, I suddenly, and for no reason at all, felt angry. Not cross. Not frustrated. But really, bloody angry.

I felt like I'd been abandoned.

How dare Janet and my mother go off and leave me alone. Damn them, what were they thinking? Why couldn't they have sat in the traffic jam on the A34 with everyone else, instead of being clever and taking a route where there was no jam?

I knew my anger was unreasonable. I knew it was stupid and pointless, but I couldn't control myself.

Over and over in my mind I thought again; what if?

Then, for no reason, I was angry with God.

"My mum was a vicar's wife," I yelled, "she didn't deserve to die like that. Where were you? Is that how you look after your own?"

On the coffee table in front of me stood a vase. A few weeks ago, when Leanne was last here, she had filled the vase with some flowers. Janet's favourite. Now, the water had evaporated, and the flowers had died. Their grey, withered stems drooped lifelessly over the rim of the vase.

I picked it up and, with all my strength, hurled it across the room. It hit the wall opposite with a dull thud, denting the plaster and strewing the dead flowers over the floor and mantlepiece. The vase itself, which was made from thick lead crystal, bounced unharmed across the carpet, none the worse for being thrown across the room in a blind rage.

I sat and stared at the empty vase. It was silent; it didn't judge me; it just lay there and did nothing.

Nothing seemed right. Surely, five months after the funeral I should have been coming to terms with my loss, picking myself up and getting on with my life. As summer gradually came to its end I began to think.

I thought about the futility of life. The futility of everything. What was the point in a flower that only bloomed for a few days and then died? What was the point of an insect that died of old age on the same day it was born?

What was the point of life itself?

I wasn't sleeping at night and yet I struggled to get out of bed in the morning. I felt tired and listless. Often, I would have to force myself to get up because it was the afternoon. There were days when I wondered what the point of getting up was, so I stayed in bed. I rarely shaved anymore, there was no one to look nice for.

On days when I did get up, I just wandered aimlessly about the house, feeling lost. The loneliness became overwhelming. My appetite was gone but that wasn't important, I didn't have any food in the house anyway.

One afternoon in early September I sat on my sofa and didn't get up again.

I just sat there staring at the blank wall as the light gradually faded into evening.

As darkness fell the phone started ringing in the hall.

Evening became night and soon the sun came up again.

I stared at the vase lying on the carpet. It hadn't moved since I'd thrown it there. I hadn't bothered to clear it up.

In the distance I think I heard the phone ringing again, but it seemed so far away so … irrelevant.

I felt so tired. I felt guilty about being alive, but most of all, I was enveloped by a feeling of utter despair, of complete hopelessness.

I remembered the dream I'd had and began to wonder if the dead are happier and I decided I wanted to find out.

It went dark and then I was sitting in daylight again.

I couldn't move. It was as though the sofa was clinging to me, wrapping me in its arms and holding me down, preventing me from standing, preventing me from moving.

The room started spinning and I felt the walls closing in on me, pulsing in and out, in and out, in time with the beating of my heart. In and out, in and out and, as darkness slowly enveloped me, I cried out in anguish; but no one was there to hear my pain.

# Chapter Three
# Return to Rosehip Hall

"Dad? Daddy?" Leanne's voice sounded concerned and I felt her hand against my neck.

I may have groaned, but I can't be sure. I struggled to open my eyes, but my eyelids felt heavy and my eyeballs felt as though they were on fire.

"I've called an ambulance," I heard her say. Her voice seemed to come from another room although I could feel her hand clutching mine. I could smell her perfume. It smelled sweet, of roses and lavender. I lay there thinking how strange it was that I could smell her perfume so vividly and yet her voice seemed dull and distance.

I tried to get up and felt Leanne's hands assisting me.

"Here, drink this."

She held a glass to my lips. I could smell the water. I don't think I've ever considered water having a smell before. I remember our chemistry teacher telling us that at room temperature, it was a colourless, odourless, tasteless liquid. Or was that vodka? Anyway, I could clearly smell the water as it trickled through my swollen lips and into my dry mouth. I tried to swallow and ended up choking. Leanne pulled the glass away as I gasped for air.

She tried again when I had settled and this time I drank.

I lost all track of time.

At some point I was aware of blue flashing lights reflecting around the room and of someone speaking to me. I don't remember whether I replied or not, but I do remember thinking that I was flying. I was confused. I wondered what it would be like to have wings. I may have called out, I think I tried to get up but then I felt something sharp in my arm, as if I was being bitten by a mosquito, and darkness, once again washed over me.

I moved. I felt I was lying on a cloud.

"Daddy?" I blinked and opened my eyes. The room was bright, and I saw wires and tubes snaking around me. Leanne's face above me came into focus and I felt her hand on mine as her lips gently kissed my forehead.

I started to say something, but she interrupted, "Shh, don't speak," she whispered, gently stroking my hand as if to reassure me. "You're safe now, you're in hospital."

"How?"

"Shh," she repeated. "I kept phoning you. You didn't pick up, so I drove down and found you unconscious on the sofa. They thought you might have had a stroke, but they've ruled that out. Then they thought you may have taken something, pills, but the toxicology reports were clear. Thankfully they can't find anything physically wrong."

I tried to sit up and discovered that all those wires and tubes were connected to me. There was a drip going into my arm, what looked like a clothes-peg on a wire clamped over my finger and wires stuck to my chest, presumably monitoring my heart.

Tears were running down Leanne's cheek and I felt terrible. I felt I'd let her down.

"Sorry," I said. It didn't feel like enough.

I was in the John Radcliffe Hospital in Oxford and over the next few days I saw various doctors, nurses, specialists and analysts and after a lot of talking, they diagnosed me as suffering from severe depression brought on by my bereavement and exacerbated by lack of nourishment and lack of sleep.

On the second day of my stay Larry walked onto my ward and handed me a brown paper bag containing a bunch of grapes.

"You had us worried, Jim" he said, "but the doc says you'll be fine. Just need some time. I'm staying at yours, by the way, I didn't think you'd mind." Of course I didn't mind, Larry was family and he is also my best friend. "Mind you, I had to do a bit of tidying up, you left the place in a bit of a state. What happened? Did you leave in a hurry?" He laughed and I smiled. Already, after having eaten, I was feeling better physically, it was my mental health that the doctors were concerned about. "Why didn't you call me, you silly bugger? You knew I'd be there for you, just like you were there for me when Helen died." Helen was Larry's late wife. She had died six years ago, a few weeks after being diagnosed with pancreatic cancer, and Larry had come to stay with us for several weeks afterwards.

Depression, the doctors said. I had had some sort of a breakdown.

"There are different degrees of depression and different approaches to dealing with it," the doctor explained. She was young, too young to be a doctor, I thought, but she had an air of confidence about her that said; 'I know what I'm talking about and you'd better listen'. So I did. I was out of bed and dressed by then, but I was being kept in for a few more days. I'd been transferred to a mental health ward for observation.

"It can be brought on," she continued, "by any number of factors. In your case it was almost certainly brought on by your bereavement. It may have started out as fairly mild depression but, because you were on your own and with no one to talk to, no one to support you or discuss your feeling with, it festered and became severe. People with severe depression find it almost impossible to deal with every day, normal life and, in some cases, they may suffer from psychosis, seeing things that aren't there. You said that you thought you saw your wife on a couple of occasions."

"Yes, but I was dreaming."

"Maybe. I think there may have been times during your breakdown when you were unable to distinguish between whether you were awake or asleep.

"Now, we also know that depression can run in families, but unfortunately we don't know anything about your family history. What we do know is we need to manage your long-term mental health and minimise the risk of a relapse. Now, I'm not a big fan of drugs so I'd like to avoid prescribing anti-depressants if we possibly can. Your overall mental health appears to have been generally strong, so I think we'll get you started on what we call Talking Therapy.

"In a nutshell Talking Therapy is exactly what it says on the tin. We get you to talk; about yourself, about your feelings and about your thoughts, what makes you happy, what makes you sad. Basically anything you want to talk about, really. I recommend counselling, but we also have CBT and IPT available if we decide counselling isn't working, although I'd be surprised if it didn't in your case."

"What's CBT and IPT?"

"Cognitive Behavioural Therapy and Interpersonal Therapy. CBT concentrates on your thoughts and your behaviour while IPT concentrates on your personal relationships. Counselling generally works better in cases where we are dealing with a crisis, in your case the trauma of losing your wife and your mother.

"Now, I understand that you're disappearing off to the wilds of

Cambridgeshire?"

"Yes," I confirmed. Larry had suggested that I go and stay with him for as long as necessary and Leanne had agreed. I think they'd ganged up on me, so I had no choice, but I didn't mind. I would be in a familiar place and I'd be with Larry. Leanne had made it clear that she'd be visiting regularly to check up on us; presumably she didn't trust us.

"No problem," the doctor continued, "we'll arrange to send your discharge forms to your own GP and to the one that Mr ... er ..." she consulted her notes, "Hilliard has registered you with in Ely."

"Thanks."

We shook hands. I didn't even know that was still a thing people did. A few days later I was driving through the wrought iron gates, over the cattle grid and along the drive leading to Rosehip Hall.

When we were children Downham Fen was a village built either side of the A10, the main road between Cambridge and Kings Lynn. Cars and lorries drove through it all the time, although the roads were generally quieter back then. The village boasted a shop that doubled up as a post office, a church with its own vicarage, a primary school and a pub called The Three Horseshoes. Larry and I always used to joke that only in the Fens could you find a three-legged horse.

Perched on an incline rising out of the Fens the village stood, at its highest point, fifty metres above sea level and had once been classed as an Isle settlement, a refuge for pilgrims making their way to Ely along the Cambridge road.

In the early nineteen-eighties, as the A10 became busier, they built a bypass and the village became a bit isolated. The shop and pub struggled as they no longer benefitted from the passing trade they had previously enjoyed, and the village became almost forgotten.

Rosehip Hall had been built in the southern edge of the village and sat a few hundred metres behind the houses on Main Street. Its long, winding drive was protected by a pair of heavy wrought iron gates and to the back of the house the grounds sloped gently away south into the surrounding Fen, bordered by river, road and railway.

The sun hung low in the west as I turned through the gate and listened to the familiar sound of the gravel crunching beneath the tyres of my car. The drive curved first to the left, then to the right and there, in front of me, stood the old Hall framed by the sun's golden rays.

The drive took me through a second, smaller gate, then wound around a pond with a fountain to the magnificent stone frontage.

21

Rosehip Hall imposed itself on the landscape. It was three storeys of weathered sandstone, crenelated at the top, with three brick chimney stacks rising above the tiled roof, one at either end with the third in the centre; each was topped with eight pots. Every room in the house, with the exception of the kitchens, scullery and attic rooms, had its own fireplace.

Larry's dad, my Uncle Anthony, had installed central heating in the 1960s when Larry and I were kids, with the help of several generous government grants that were available back then for home improvements.

"Good to see you made it in one piece, then," Larry said, striding across the parking area. We embraced and Larry proceeded to help me unpack my things from the car. "It's great to see you, Jim, you're already looking better. Must be the Cambridgeshire air."

We had agreed that I was going to stay at least until the new year. "That'll save Harry and Leanne from having to decide which parent to spend Christmas with," he joked. They generally took it in turns to stay with one or other of us, although since they'd had the children they tended to stay at home for Christmas day and make their visits during the week between Christmas and New Year.

There are certain smells, sounds, textures and tastes that evoke memories of special times in our lives. For me, Rosehip Hall was all about memories. Memories of my childhood and those carefree days I spent with Larry during the school holidays when we had the freedom to explore as we pleased. We had no bounds and, as far as we were concerned, we were free to explore both the house and the grounds without restriction. We took the opinion that it was far better to ask forgiveness if we were wrong than to ask permission and get refused. We played games such as cowboys and Indians; British soldiers fighting the Germans; astronauts landing on the moon and, one time, we searched through every cupboard and wardrobe in the house – and there were plenty of them – to see if we could find an entrance leading to Narnia. We never did, but we did find a secret passage leading from the Library to the Smoking Room.

Being north facing, the front of the house was permanently in shadow, except for early morning and late evening in the height of summer. This gave the house a dark and quite gothic appearance. It was now early autumn and the sun sat low in the south-west and, as I looked up at the familiar sandstone frontage a dark cloud wafted across the sky, momentarily blocking out the sun. In that instant an icy breeze blew around the corner of the house and a cold shiver ran down my spine. In the sudden gloom, the grey house looked cold and uninviting, the great windows dark and empty and, for a brief moment the house appeared sinister. As the cloud cleared and the sun once again framed the house in silver and gold, the feeling passed.

I'm recovering from depression, I reminded myself, things may seem different at times. I just need to deal with it.

Despite being a bit spooked I was glad to be back here, it had been a while. I followed Larry through the porchway and into the huge, tiled hall.

"Cottage pie for dinner," Larry said as he caught me sniffing the aroma wafting in from the kitchens, "Leanne told me we have to feed you up. I think you'll be impressed; I've become a terrific cook, you know." I lay my bags on the polished round teak table that formed the centrepiece of the hall and laughed.

"Don't worry, I'm feeling better already just by being here."

"She worries about you, Jim. You could have died," he reminded me as we wandered through to the West Wing where Larry had made a pot of tea and hot buttered muffins.

"True," I admitted, hanging my head in shame. "In all honesty I didn't feel much like living anymore."

"You've been through a major trauma and you were depressed. There were times I felt like that when Helen died, God knows I still miss her – I don't think you ever stop missing them – but you helped me get through it. You and Janet."

He started pouring the tea.

"How do you feel now?" he asked.

"Now? I feel OK, I think."

"You sure?

"I'm not about to top myself, if that's what you mean."

"Good. Do you still take sugar?"

"No. I gave it up for Lent a couple of years ago and never went back to it."

"Good for you." He passed me my cup and told me to help myself to the muffins while they were still warm. My stomach gurgled, I felt peckish after the drive and I bit into it eagerly.

"I can see you haven't lost your appetite," he commented as he bit into his own. "I've put you in your old room, is that OK?"

"Perfect," I said, "thanks."

My old room was on the first floor. It overlooked the back garden and had a door which led to the connecting bathroom. There were six bedrooms on the first floor, each had a connecting door into a shared bathroom, so it was important to lock two doors when you went for a bath or shower to save embarrassment. There were a further six bedrooms with two bathrooms on the top floor. A long corridor ran along the centre, long enough for Larry and me to be able to race along it when we were children and where we held our indoor sports days. The stairs ascended from the ground floor between the first two bedrooms at the front of the house and, at the other end of the corridor, the second staircase led up to the top floor.

I sat back on the sofa and watched dust motes dancing in the sunlight.

"The doctor gave me some instructions," I told Larry, "exercise and talk."

"That sounds simple enough. Exercise is fine and talk is easy."

"But I've got to talk about myself. My feelings, my thoughts," I protested.

"Ah, that's a tough one," he said with a smile. "Me is my favourite subject but you ..." He left it hanging. What he meant was, I am a bit reticent when it comes to talking about myself, especially talking about how I feel or what I am going through. It wasn't something I was comfortable doing, and it was probably why I had had my breakdown. Perhaps if I had talked more about myself, I wouldn't have succumbed to depression. Larry, on the other hand, had never had a problem with talking about himself to anyone. He could converse with anyone; he was easy to get on with and always popular. When we left home in the late seventies, we shared a flat in St John's Wood in London. It was thanks to Larry's gift of the gab that it became a popular place for some wild parties, and we were popular with the girls.

"At least the exercise part of my program will be easy, it says a brisk walk of at least half a mile a day."

"That'll get you to the river, at least. We can take a walk this afternoon before dinner."

"At some point," I said, "I've got to go through counselling, talk about my feelings to a complete stranger."

"Sometimes, if you do find it hard to talk, it's easier to talk about such things to a complete stranger. They don't know you and they won't

24

judge you. Me, I'll just tell you you're nuts."

"But I feel so foolish. I'm depressed, apparently, I'll get over it."

"Sure you will, I don't doubt that, but maybe this counselling will help you get over it quicker, and more permanently. Remember what Bob Hoskins used to say? 'It's good to talk.'" He did a passable impression of the late, great actor Bob Hoskins.

"That was a BT advert. They were trying to get people to spend money with them by making more telephone calls."

"And talk to each other. He was right, though, it is good to talk. Dinner is ready whenever you want it. Do you fancy a stretch of your legs before dinner, it'll start getting dark in half an hour?"

I did as it happened. The drive from Sutton Courtney had been slow, particularly on the M25 where the traffic had crawled along at a snail's pace. The journey had taken me an hour longer than it should have thanks to that. There had been talk of building a road joining Cambridge and Oxford for some years, but it had never materialised. The alternatives remained drive south on the M40 to the M25 and up the M11 or north east across country to Milton Keynes, then the A428 to Cambridge. It really was a six of one, half a dozen of the other kind of choice and totally dependent on traffic flowing well on either route.

Larry dropped the tea tray off in the scullery and we grabbed our coats.

"The wind's getting up," he said as we set off across the lawn.

The wind had a cold edge to it, and we hurried across the neatly mowed top lawn to the shelter of the wildflower meadow. Throughout summer the meadow was a cornucopia of cowslip, poppy, yarrow, knapweed, cornflower, ox-eye daisy, and many other varieties of wildflowers and, as a result, the meadow teemed with wildlife. Butterflies, dragonflies, a myriad of insects, birds, frogs, slugs and snails all made their home there and were visited by hedgehogs, badgers, grass snakes, lizards and a family of foxes. My Uncle Anthony had been a keen conservationist long before it became the craze it is today and had created the wildflower meadow from the old disused cornfield.

"Listen."

We stopped and listened to the call of a magpie, clear and loud above the noise of the wind rushing through the trees. The leaves were already turning from their multitudinous shades of green and in a few weeks time they would become a palette of vivid golds, reds and yellows as they created their carpet of colour on the woodland floor.

In the distance we heard the distinctive twitter of a reed bunting, echoed moments later by a second. A woodpecker drilled in the tree high above us and I was filled with wonder. I'd only been back at the Hall for a few hours and already it felt as though a dark shroud had been lifted from my mind and for the first time in months I actually felt like smiling.

We walked on in silence, enjoying each other's company and the sounds of the woodland as birds and animals prepared for the night ahead.

A gap in the hedge in the far corner of the meadow led to the path through the woods. A little way in a wooden bridge crossed the stream which fed into the river further down, and the path wound downhill through the trees. At the bottom of the hill it reached the River Ouse, turned left and continued along its bank for about a hundred metres before turning back into the woods and back to the house from the east. About halfway along the river path Larry's dad had built a little shelter with a bench so he could watch the wildlife around the riverbank. We sat down and looked across the river and over the wild Fen beyond as it stretched away from us as far as the eye could see. A short distance to the south west I sought out the fork in the river where the Ouse was joined by the River Cam and to where, years ago, Larry and I had canoed to observe nesting cranes.

As we sat, the sound of the birds twittering and calling to each other reached a crescendo as they prepared to roost. The sun slowly sank below the horizon and the sky, now covered with broken cloud, was bathed in a wash of purple, streaked with a dazzling array of dark blues, bright yellows, deep reds, viridian and magenta. It was like gazing at a painting and we watched the dramatic show until the sun was gone and the stunning light faded away to become various shades of grey. After the cacophony of bird song the woods had fallen silent. Even the wind had died down and the only sound was the distance thrum of traffic on the A10.

It was Larry who broke the silence.

"Cottage Pie awaits," he said, "all this fresh air has made me hungry."

# Chapter Four
# Cottage Pie

The phone in the hall was ringing as we stepped through the back door and Larry suggested I answered it while he saw to the dinner.

"Daddy?" Leanne said when I answered.

"Hi, darling, how's things?"

"Fine. I'm just checking you arrived safely."

"Yes, I'm here," I assured her, "uneventful journey. Your Uncle Larry and I have just walked down to the river and back to stretch our legs and work up and appetite for dinner."

"How are you feeling?"

"Actually, being here I already feel much better." It was true. There something about Rosehip Hall that made me feel comfortable. Whether it was because of the memories it held for me or because I was with Larry or an amalgamation of the two, I couldn't say, but the old Hall was working its magic on me.

"That's good, and how's Uncle Larry." We still referred to him as Uncle Larry even though he was now her father-in-law too.

"Oh, you know Uncle Larry, he's just fine, as he always is."

"Of course he is, but remember we always thought you were 'just fine' too."

"How're the kids?" I asked, quickly changing the subject. Leanne obviously sensed I didn't want the conversation to take that route, so she didn't pursue it and we ended up making small talk. Anyway, she'd only seen me last night when she helped me prepare for my stay so really, she was just checking that I'd arrived safely.

"I'm glad you're there," she said, "send my love to Uncle Larry."

"I'm glad too, darling, and I'll pass on your love."

"I've got to go now; Harry will be home from work soon and I've got to get the children ready for bed."

"OK, thanks for ringing."

"I love you."

"I love you too and, Leanne ... don't worry, I'll be alright. It's going

27

to take a little time but I'm over the worst now."

"Thanks Daddy, I'll try not to worry. 'Bye."

"Goodbye love."

She rang off and I replaced the receiver. It rang again almost immediately, before I'd even had a chance to turn around.

"Did you forget something, darling?" I laughed.

"Er .. is that Mr Read?" A woman's voice I didn't recognise asked.

"Oh, sorry," I said to this stranger, "I thought you were someone else."

"I guess you did."

"And yes, I am Jim Read."

"Thank you, my name's Maddy Down," she said.

"Okay," I replied, warily, wondering what sort of scam call I was about to hear.

"I'm an NHS Counsellor. I'm calling to arrange your first counselling session."

"Ah, yes, right. Er, what did you say your name was again?"

She repeated it and I grabbed the pen by the phone.

"Just let me write that down, I'm not good at remembering names. Maddy? Is that double-d-y or double-d-i-e?"

"Neither. It's M-A-D-E-A."

"Oh, right. That's an unusual spelling."

"According to my mother it's the Fen way of spelling it," she said. The tone of her voice suggested she'd explained this a thousand times, and she didn't even believe herself.

"Right."

"So, can we agree a date, then?"

"Of course, did you have a specific time and day in mind?" I was expecting an appointment in a few weeks' time, which would be typical for my own surgery back home.

"Are you available this week?"

"Actually yes, I think so. I've just arrived, this afternoon, and I'll be staying for a while. I've got nothing planned yet."

"Tomorrow morning then?"

"Tomorrow's good, what time?"

"Nine o'clock?"

"Yep, I can do that. I don't actually know where the surgery is but I …"

"No problem," she interrupted, "I'll come to you. You're at Rosehip

Hall in Downham Fen aren't you?"

"Yes."

"Good. I know where it is so I'll see you at nine o'clock tomorrow morning," and she rang off before I could reply.

"Bye," I said to the 'burr' of the phone line, wondering what she might look like. She'd come across very business-like, perhaps, even, a little bit fierce, although, if she was a counsellor then I'm sure she wasn't. I replaced the receiver for the second time, half expecting it to ring again – I was always told that things happen in threes – but it remained silent this time so I headed for the dining room to lay the table for dinner. Larry had beaten me to it, and everything was ready.

"Could you open the wine while I dish up?" he said.

I opened a bottle of Ermita de San Lorenzo Gran Selección 2011 while Larry served up the Cottage pie with a selection of additional vegetables.

"That was Leanne," I told him, "she was checking up on me."

"Are you surprised?"

"I guess not, then, when we'd finished, the phone rang again. This time it was the counsellor."

"What, from the council?"

"No, my counsellor, you know, my grief counsellor, the one I was prescribed by the doctor. She's coming here tomorrow at nine."

"Coming here?"

"That's what she said."

"I didn't know they did home visits, I thought you were meant to go to them."

"So did I. Maybe she wants to check this place out, make sure it's a suitable place for my recovery."

"Perhaps she feels that if she does the first session here, with you in familiar surroundings, then you'll be more relaxed and more likely to talk."

"Maybe." I wasn't sure.

Cottage Pie has always been a favourite of mine, and this one was delicious. The wine complemented it with its rich, spicy, aromatic flavour. (Just so you know, and in case you're wondering, neither Larry nor I are wine buffs, or wine snobs, I just read that flavour description off the back label of the bottle.)

Larry followed up the main course by serving homemade blackberry and apple pie and custard. Another of my favourites.

"I grew the vegetables and the fruit myself," Larry informed me with glee, lifting his wine glass to his lips and taking a sip, "in the kitchen garden."

"Have you renovated it then?"

"Not all of it by a long chalk. I've managed to sort out a couple of beds this year, but there's a massive amount still to do."

"Maybe I can help you while I'm here, as part of my therapy."

"Our little project?"

"Sounds like a plan."

The kitchen garden was situated to the west of the back lawn, quite close to the house and surrounded on all sides by a high brick wall. It was half an acre and had been built in the mid nineteenth century, when kitchen gardens were all the rage among upper-middle class Victorian society. Since the last world war the garden had fallen into neglect. Larry's dad's love of conservation didn't stretch to a love of vegetables, and for several years now Larry had been talking about restoring it to its former glory. Now, at last, it seemed he had finally made a start and I looked forward to helping him get it done.

After dinner we retired to the Smoking Room to finish the wine and relax in each other's company. It was decades since anyone had actually smoked in the Smoking Room, but it was still known by that name. In times gone by the gentlemen of the house would retire there after dinner to enjoy cigars and port or brandy, while the ladies would gather in the Withdrawing Room, or Drawing Room for short, where they would chatter whilst embroidering or sewing. Thankfully society has changed and this practice was out of date long before Larry or I were born. Nowadays the Smoking Room was where you went if you wanted to talk, play games, read, or listen to music, and the Drawing Room was where the television was.

We talked for quite a while about nothing in particular – you probably know the sort of conversation I mean, when two people who know each other so well talk and afterwards you can't remember what you discussed even though it held your attention at the time.

It was getting late when we finished the bottle, so we cleared up and headed for bed.

"Goodnight Jim," Larry said as he headed left at the top of the stairs to the master bedroom opposite, "it really is good to have you here and to have some company again."

"G'night Larry," I replied, turning right and heading off down to the corridor to my room, "thanks for having me, it's great to be back here. See you in the morning."

"Yeah."

I unpacked my things and got myself ready for bed. The room was large with a king-size four poster bed up against the wall opposite the windows. Along the far wall was a walk-in wardrobe in which I hung my shirts, jackets, a suit and some pairs of trousers. Against the opposite wall, by the door to the adjoining bathroom, was a dresser with drawers for underwear and a mirror for vanity. Between the two ceiling high windows stood a large bureau desk on which was sat a large leather blotter with pen, pencils, paper, Sellotape, and various other office essentials. I put the box containing the remainder of my mother's papers on the floor beside it, knowing that I would have to go through it all at some point, although it was a task I had been putting off since the funeral. All the important stuff was done. I was just left with this one box to sort through, which consisted of mum's personal affairs, letters, diaries and such.

I slipped between the sheets and snuggled myself in, there's nothing quite like the feel of sliding down between fresh clean sheets, and I laid my head on the pillow. Normally I would read before I went to sleep, it was part of my going to sleep ritual, but this evening I lay there in the dark and watched the crescent moon as it slowly rose in the southern night sky. Tinged orange and pink and surrounded by stars, it rose higher and higher until it hung there, just a silver slither in the night sky. My eyelids felt heavy and I let them flicker as a wave of sleep washed over me and, for the first time in many months, I just slept. I didn't dream that first night back at Rosehip Hall, and in the morning when I awoke, I felt quite refreshed.

# Chapter Five
# Madea Down

"The purpose of this first session is so I can assess where you are on, what we call, the tasks of grief."

Madea was, as she had seemed on the phone last night, business-like and to the point, with little time, it seemed, for small talk. She had arrived on time, although we didn't hear her coming. Last night Larry had suggested that we use the Morning Room, which was in the east wing and enjoyed the morning sunshine. He was going to be working in the Library, which was in the middle of the house at the front, so we wouldn't be disturbed if he made any noise.

I guessed Madea was somewhere around her late thirties, medium height, slim build and quite pretty. She was formally dressed in a light brown skirt and matching jacket over a pale-yellow blouse that had frills around the collar. Her slender shoulders were covered by a cascade of coral-black hair and she looked up at me through dark eyes that were topped by crescent shaped eyebrows. Her smile was warm and friendly but when I shook the hand she offered me I was startled by how cold it was, almost as though she'd just been clutching a bag of frozen peas. I led her into the Morning Room, which was cosy and warm, and offered her a hot drink. She refused, saying that if she had a tea of coffee with each of her clients, she'd spend more time in the loo than doing any actual counselling. When she spoke her voice was soft, with a distinctive fen accent.

"Tasks of grief?" I asked as I sat down on the sofa opposite.

"It's just professional nomenclature," she explained, "tasks; phases; stages; they're all the same meaning in this context. Basically, it's our way of categorising the different stages in the grief process. In its simplest form we can describe it in four stages; acceptance; experience; adjustment; relocation."

The look on my face must have mirrored the confusion in my head because she smiled in that way that says 'let me explain it to you in simpler terms'.

"Acceptance is just that, accepting that the object of your grief, in your case that your wife, Janet, is not coming back." I noticed that she didn't look at any notes to remember my wife's name and I was impressed that she had done her homework, "Experience is working through the pain of your loss, and it's important that you do work through it because avoiding it can have a long term detrimental effect on you, your health and your loved ones. Adjustment is about adjusting yourself, both mentally and emotionally, to life without your wife and relocation is helping you to relocate her emotionally to enable you to move on with your life. By that we do not mean for you to forget her, but simply that her memory takes a different emotional space in your life."

Her eyes looked into mine and I felt she was looking right through them and into my very soul. I looked down and picked up my coffee cup.

"So," she said, "I've told you what I want to get out of these sessions, so why don't you start by telling me what you hope to get out of them."

"Well," I was hesitant. While I was happy to listen to her telling me about myself, I was reluctant to talk myself, and talking about myself wasn't something I was good at. "I've just been through the worst six months of my life and, in truth, I've been in a pretty dark place."

"How did that make you feel? Being in that dark place?"

"Scared, I suppose."

"Go on."

I sat and thought about for a few moments. Her voice, the way she spoke, the way she sat looking at me as though I was the most important person in her life, seemed to be making me want to open up to her.

"I felt... sad and lonely, but I wanted to be left alone and then, when I was left alone, you know, after the funeral, I felt resentful and angry. I felt I had been abandoned. People cried at the funeral but were smiling at the reception afterwards as though they were crying over a couple of children's toys that had been missed for a few moments and then replaced and forgotten. I felt like I was the only one who really cared, who genuinely missed them. I wanted to be alone but was angry that I had been deserted; I was lonely, but I didn't want to see anyone. That doesn't make sense, does it?"

"It makes sense to me."

"I felt as though their deaths had been a part of a bad dream, that

33

they weren't for real. Any minute now I expected them to walk through the door with bags of shopping, expecting me to help them unpack and then wanting me to make them a coffee, while they massaged their aching feet."

"Did your mother live with you?"

"No, she lived at the other end of our village. We saw her three or four times a week, though, and Janet would run her to the supermarket whenever she needed to go as she didn't drive anymore."

"But this time they didn't come back," Madea prompted me as I stared into space.

"I struggled to come to terms with that. I kept thinking that I'd seen Janet around the house; she would be standing in the kitchen; sitting in the lounge; lying on our bed. I had conversations with her."

"What would she say?"

"She wanted me to join her."

"But you knew she was dead."

"I was denying it."

"But you knew it was true."

"Yes, I did."

"What did she say to you?"

"She said she wanted to me to join her."

"But you didn't."

"No."

"Did you want to?"

"Yes."

"Did you feel like taking your own life?"

"No, not really but …" I let it hang.

"But?"

"But I didn't feel the desire to go on living."

"But you didn't want to end it?"

"I didn't want to kill myself," I told her, unable to meet her eyes, "but I didn't want to go on living either. I actually wanted to die."

We sat in silence for what seemed an age but was probably only a few seconds.

"And now? How do you feel now?"

"I miss her terribly," I said, hanging my head as tears began to blur my vision. She nodded sagely, obviously expecting me to say more.

"I – I feel like a part of me is missing, like … like I've had my arm cut off. I don't feel complete without her."

"How long were you married?"

"This year would have been our thirty-sixth wedding anniversary."

"How did you meet?"

"It was at a party in London in 1983. My cousin Larry, he owns this house, and I threw a party in the flat we shared. Janet came along with one of our mates, I think she was his girlfriend at the time, at least that's what he may have thought, and she wandered into the kitchen where I was mixing a bowl of my special punch and we just got talking. I suppose, as I wasn't trying to 'get off with her' or impress her in any way I was relaxed and found her easy to talk to and we just hit it off. We met up again the following week and went for a drink and before long we were going out together."

I was smiling at the memory and that memory marked the end of our first session. It seemed to me that no time at all had passed but we had been talking for an hour during which Madea had appeared to listen intently to everything I had to say. She had probed me for more and encouraged me to continue each time I had stopped and I realised she had cleverly manipulated me to talk openly and freely about myself and I found that I was quite happy to do so. Larry had been right, talking to a stranger was easy, but now it was over I felt drained. Even though I had not been up for long and had had a good night's sleep I felt tired. It was though she had physically taken me back to my past, to that party, and the journey back to the present had exhausted me.

"You've made a good start," she said, as she stood up and brushed her hands down her skirt to straighten it. "We've got a long journey ahead but together we'll get through it and I'll be there to guide you all the way. You should do something while you're here, something physical, some form of exercise, something that brings you joy, and you must never feel guilty about feeling joy."

"I've got a gardening project to work on."

She looked through the window overlooking the lawns and laughed. "There's a lot of garden here, it should keep you well occupied." I smiled.

"You were adopted, weren't you?"

Her question took me by surprise, I had thought the session was over.

"Yes."

"Have you ever thought about trying to find out who your real ancestors were?"

"No, not really," I replied, wondering where this was going. "Why, do you think it'll help me?"

"Sometimes, when adopted children lose their adoptive parents, they can lose their sense of belonging and sometimes, when that happens, finding out who their natural parents were , where they came from, can help fill that void. It may help you through the process."

She buttoned up the front of her coat and turned to me. "So, same time next week?"

"That's good for me," I said, and she turned and left. Just like that, no goodbye, no anything.

Larry joined me in the Hall as I closed the front door. There was no car in the drive; I guessed she must have walked or cycled.

"Has she arrived yet?"

"She's been and gone," I replied.

"Gone?"

"Yes, she left a few minutes ago."

He looked through the glass panel in the door and said, "She's gone."

"That's what I said."

"She must have sprinted," Larry replied, turning to me with a glint in his eye.

"I think she cycled," I returned, knowing that Larry was having a little dig.

"How was it?"

"Actually," I said, reflectively, "it was really good."

"Excellent. But never mind her," he said, "while you've been entertaining pretty girls, I've been reading some of our Grandad's old journals from the First World War and it makes some interesting reading." He turned and headed for the Library and I followed, my interest piqued.

"Really? Such as?"

"Read it for yourself," he said, indicating the book lying open on the polished oak reading table in the Library. I need a coffee do you want one?"

"Yes, please," I said and watched him retreat through the secret door that led to the Smoking Room and out across the corridor to the kitchen opposite. Moments later I heard the clattering of crockery as Larry started brewing a cafetiere of coffee.

I sat down, picked up Grandad Edward's old handwritten journal which was yellowed and brittle with age and started to read the faded words that had been written over one hundred years ago.

# Chapter Six
## Edward's Journal, Winter 1918

My nurse has told me that it helps to write things down. She tells me that not only will it bring order to the chaos in my battle-weary mind, but she says it will help me heal.

"A problem shared is a problem halved," she says in that rough fen accent of hers. "You write it down and I'll read it, then I'll know what you went through, understand what you feel and what your state of mind is."

"My state of mind is just fine," I tell her, "it's my bloody leg that's the problem here, can't you see?"

"No, I can't, that's why I want you to write it down."

"I doubt you can even read, anyway."

She didn't rise to the bait.

"Look," she says, keeping her voice calm, reasoning with me as though I'm a child, "you've been through hell and back, I know that, and you've lost a lot, I know that too, but you're young and you're healthy and I'm here to help you get your life back."

"You can't get me my leg back though, can you?"

"No, I can't, but I can help you live your life without it. Let your leg define the person you will be become in a positive way. Don't let anger get the better of you, don't let it twist you and turn you bitter; don't let it make you hate the world. It's better for you if you let it be a motivator, make it the reason, the driving force for you to move on."

"How can I move on, I haven't got a leg to stand on, let alone move on with."

This is how our sessions usually go. I'm angry. For sure I'm angry and why wouldn't I be? I'm angry with my father. Angry with my country. Angry with the world. I don't know whether she's right or wrong about writing it all down, but I've got nothing better to do so here goes. I'll start at the beginning, where my misery started.

February 16th, 1918

I listened to Sergeant Norris' screams as he lay there, bleeding in the ice-covered shell hole, ten yards in front of me, and there was nothing I nor anyone could do but pity him. If any one of us moved we would be dead in seconds, filled with lead from the guns of the German snipers who were watching us from across the frozen waste of no-man's land.

Patches of freshly fallen snow lay on the ground and I can't remember a time when I felt warm or dry. I looked along the line of men, shivering from the cold, huddled together for warmth as they crouched, tired and scared against the walls of the trench, less than one hundred yards away from our enemy. Sergeant Major Harris came stumbling over them as he made his way towards me followed by an evil looking black rat that had grown fat and bloated on the corpses of men that littered the battlefields of France. There were too many bodies to clear away or bury so they were left to rot or, more likely, be eaten by the filthy black vermin that seemed to revel in our misery.

I was just eighteen when, encouraged by my father, I signed up for officer training in September 1915, by which time the war in Europe had been raging for just over a year. Six months later, in April 1916, after training that would have normally lasted for a couple of years, I passed out with the rank of First Lieutenant and was despatched to the trenches outside Ypres in Belgium to fight on the Western front. Nearly two years later and promoted to Captain, I now stood in a similar trench on the Somme, cold and weary but still alive and with a hundred and twenty men under my command. In the trenches it doesn't matter how brave or scared we are, or whether we are complacent or stupid, at any moment a stray mortar or a gas canister fired from the enemy lines can drop into our trench and send us to oblivion.

I looked through the periscope and watched another rat as it nimbly skipped across mud and landed on Norris' helmet. Norris screamed in pain and fear as the rat unhurriedly, leant over and took a bite of flesh from his face. Norris had led the charge that morning, blowing his whistle loud to stir the men into action, and at the same time alerting the enemy to our intentions. He was the first one over the top, followed by a hundred good, brave men, and he was the first to fall, shot down and left to die with no-one to rescue him. By the time they reached halfway across the barren wasteland, all one hundred men had fallen. They were heroes, each and every one of them. Heroes to be forgotten in this war to end all wars, dead before they had a chance to live their lives. The lucky ones died quickly, the rest were left to suffer a slow and lingering death. Cold and alone with no one to comfort them in their final hours.

After two years we have become immune to the screams of the injured and dying crying out for their mothers or their loved ones. Their bodies wracked with pain and fear as their life blood oozes from their wounds, dribbling down the slimy mud to mingle with the stagnant water of the puddles that litter the field. Every morning hundreds more are sent to their death. Usually, by late afternoon most of their cries have ceased and the fields once again fall into an uneasy silence.

Ten yards. Through the periscope I could see a way to reach him.

Ten yards. We had been together for two years.

Ten yards. He was my friend, I had to try.

"Sergeant Major," I shouted.

"Sah?"

"I need you to create a diversion for me. I need you to divert the Germans' attention away from here. Think you can do it?"

"Yes, Sah," he said, saluting me. He took two men and together they made their way along the trench until they were about fifty yards away.

"Corporal Jennings, as soon as Harris starts his diversion, I need you to help me up."

"What?"

"I'm going to get Norris," I told him, "be ready."

Harris balanced a helmet on the butt of a rifle and raised it slowly over the top of the line of sandbags stacked along the lip of the trench. Seconds later a hail of bullets ricocheted off it and that was all the time I needed to slip up and into the muddy bog that we had been defending for the last two years.

Keeping my head down I slithered through the freezing ice, feeling it soaking through my filthy uniform. I heard bullets whistling over my head but there was a shallow dip in the mud, and I was low enough to remain partially hidden as I slowly made my way to where Norris lay. It was only yards, but my elbows ached from the cold and the effort of crawling, and my heart pounded painfully in my chest from fear. I was engulfed by the foul stench of rotting flesh and I didn't stop to wonder what exactly it was that I was crawling through. All I knew was that surrounded by all this death lay my Sergeant; a living being, whom I was trying to rescue.

The rat that had been feasting off Norris' left ear, screeched at me as I swatted at it and it slinked angrily away to find something else on

40

which to feast. Blood seeped from a wound in Norris' left shoulder and, to my dismay, I saw that his right foot was sticking out at an unnatural angle. The ankle had shattered as it had stuck in the mud when he was thrown to the ground.

His face was pale, and it seemed as though he was sleeping when I reached him. He had lost a lot of blood and his breathing was laboured, and I guessed he had passed out from the pain.

The shooting had stopped which meant the diversion Harris had created was over and a cold, empty silence lingered expectantly in the air. I felt a tightening in my stomach; I was only ten yards from safety, but it might as well have been a mile. I had a fallen comrade who was badly injured and barely conscious and there were a hundred or so rifles waiting for me to make my move so they could dispatch us both to our maker.

The next decisions I made would determine whether we lived or died and I, anxiously, looked around the crater. Three corpses lay half sunk in the mud and covered by a thin white layer of frost. Keeping myself low, I wrestled two of them to the edge of the pit facing the enemy to act as cover. Immediately I heard a 'thwack, thwack' as a couple of bullets thudded into the cadavers, reminding me that the Germans were alert to my presence. I shook Norris awake and he cried out in pain.

"Listen, Sergeant," I said, "I'm going to try and get you back to the trench."

"They'll kill us." His breath came in gasps as he struggled for air.

"Save your breath," I told him, "We'll get back, I promise."

"Don't make promises you can't keep," he whispered, and I determined to make it back safely.

"I'm going to lay this soldier on top of you," I explained. "All you have to do is hold onto him. Just grab him under the armpits, I'll grab you the same way and that way we can both keep down and I can drag you back to safety." In truth I wasn't sure whether this was going to work but I had to try, and it was the only plan I could come up with. Maybe we'd be killed trying, but I had to be positive. "Those two bodies up there will afford us enough cover and any stray bullets will hit this chap rather than you or me. OK?"

He looked at me as if I was out of my mind and a large part of me agreed with him. It was probably suicide but if we stayed there until nightfall, he would either die from his injuries or be eaten alive by the rats, and I wasn't prepared to allow either to happen. We had to take the

41

chance.

"Ready?"

"It won't work."

"It will," I assured him again, hoping I sounded more confident than I felt, "just hold on to this." I dropped the third dead soldier on top of him and he squealed in surprise and pain. I fixed his hands under the arms of the corpse then gathered myself behind him, placed my hands under his armpits, dug my heels in and pulled.

For a moment it seemed as though he was well and truly stuck in the thick, wet mud and he screamed as I pulled harder, momentarily forgetting about the wound in his shoulder. There was a loud slurping as the mud relinquished its hold on him and I fell back heavily with both Norris and the corpse on top of me.

"Sorry," I said as he gasped in pain.

For a moment I was stuck beneath both of them; the mud was too slippery for me to free myself and I was struggling to get a foothold. Finally, my kicking and struggling found purchase and I was sliding slowly back towards the trench dragging Norris along with me. He held onto the dead soldier and I could feel the gentle thuds of bullets as they ripped harmlessly into the dead flesh.

I made painfully slow progress. I was slipping and sliding through the waterlogged mud, occasionally getting stuck. A few times I felt panic rising but each time I managed to get control of myself, repeating over and over that I was nearly there, nearly safe and that Norris was going to live because of me.

Eventually I felt hands grab me from behind as I reached the trench and my men pulled me and Norris in.

Harris had organised two stretchers, one for me and one for Norris, assuming that I was going to be injured or killed in the rescue, but only one was needed and I watched Norris being taken away to the field hospital that was behind the coppice beyond the third line of trenches.

Once the stretcher team had carried Norris away Harris turned to me, stood to attention and saluted.

"With respect, Captain Hilliard, Sah," he said, "that was abso-fucking-lutely stupid. I may go as far as to say it was probably the one of the stupidest actions I have seen in this war, but may I be the first to congratulate you on your bravery. I only hope it pays off and Sergeant Norris lives to thank you himself," and with that he smiled and shook my hand.

"Thank you, Sergeant Major. It wasn't bravery, I was shit scared out there, but I couldn't just stand by and let one of my Sergeants die if there was any chance to save him. It's what any Captain would have done. And besides, he is my friend."

"With respect, sah, it isn't what any Captain would have done; many would have left him there to die. Some might have thought about putting him out of his misery with a bullet from their own gun, and no one would have blamed them for doing so. War is an ugly business and calls for ugly actions."

"Well, damn this bloody war then," I said and tried to light a cigarette, but my hand was shaking too much to hold the lighter still so Sergeant Major Harris lit one for me and stuck it in my mouth. "Thanks," I said, inhaling the smoke deep into my lungs and feeling the nicotine surge through my veins, calming me as it did so.

February 23rd, 1918

It was the first day of our rest period, a whole week away from the front line and away from the stench of death, the pounding of guns, and the screams of the dying. We were camped behind a row of trees not far behind the third line of trenches. On the other side of the road from our encampment was the field hospital, and I visited Norris most days. They had removed his leg from just below the knee and he had a fever. During the times when he was awake his fever made him delirious and he made little sense, and after a while he would lapse back into a restless, haunted sleep.

I received post today. There was an envelope for me containing several letters from home. Written after Christmas they were from my mother, my two younger brothers and my fifteen-year-old sister, Constance. My dear sister was a pretty, empty-headed, romantic teenager. I read her letter first because hers were always full of inconsequential nonsense which transported me away for a few moments from the madness of war, and this one didn't disappoint.

*January 9th, 1918*

*Dear Eddie,*

*Thank you for the Christmas present you left for me and the card you sent. We really missed you on Christmas day. I've kept your presents for when you next come home.*

*It must be jolly rotten to miss Christmas like that, and I hope you*

43

celebrated it where you are, although I've got no idea where you are, and no one will tell us, so I hope this letter reaches you safe and sound. You will tell me if you don't receive it, won't you? I can always write another one.

Are you still in that same ghastly place you told us about when you were home in the autumn? We're still at The Hall, but then I suspect you know that. I don't know why I even told you that really, you must think me a real dimwit! If you are back in that horrid trench place then I hope it's not too uncomfortable; the papers say that we're making lots of good progress and the war will be over soon, and they should know. Daddy doesn't like me reading the papers, I think he must think that girl's brains will explode if they read anything other than romantic novels, so I have to sneak into his study when he goes out and read it then.

Mummy has all the women in the village sewing scarves and knitting balaclavas because the papers report that it's snowing out there and our boys are cold, and it'll be good for your morale to receive such lovely gifts from all of us back home. Is it really cold out there? I don't even know if you get snow in Europe like we do.

There's lots of snow here too and it's jolly cold outside. In fact, it's so thick that it reached the top of my boots when I walked out yesterday.

Mummy told me that you're coming home on leave in April so I'm going to organise my birthday party (I'm going to be sixteen soon, you know) for when you come home, so you'd better make sure you don't get shot or anything silly like that or I'll never talk to you again.

Bill and Ed are still being horrible to me. Yesterday they found a grass snake and hid it in my bed and daddy told me off for making such a fuss and disturbing him when he was trying to get some peace in his study. It's just not fair.

Do you miss us? I miss you, you're never horrid to me.

See you at Easter,

Your ever-loving sister,

Constance.

I smiled. A silly letter from a silly little girl whom I loved dearly. She was the youngest of the four of us and was often the object of the many practical jokes played by our middle two brothers, William and Edwin, known affectionately as Bill and Ed.

My brother Bill's letter was next, and it was altogether shorter and more formal.

*January 9th, 1918*

*Dear Eddie,*

*Thank you for you for your last letter, it was good to hear about your promotion to Captain.*

*Father told me the other week that, as I will be eighteen in a few months' time, I should be applying to join up, so I applied for Officer Training and was accepted. My six months' training will start at the end of May, just after my birthday, so I will probably be coming out to fight in December, when my training is complete.*

*I'm jolly excited, can't wait to get out there and join the fighting, I just hope the war lasts until December. I have applied to join your Regiment when I've finished training, wouldn't that be fun?*

*Regards,*
*Bill (William)*

Edwin's was next.

*January 9th, 1918*

*Dear Eddie,*

*Good to hear from you at Christmas, congratulations on your fantastic promotion.*

*It's not fair that Bill gets to join up and I can't. Father says I can't join up until I'm eighteen which is over a year away yet. I think sixteen is old enough to come and fight and I'm thinking of enrolling anyway, I can always lie about my age but Father says I have to wait so I can apply for officer training like you and Bill did.*

*Bill agrees with him and said that I'll soon be eighteen but once he's gone I'll be left with only Constance and she's such a silly girl.*

*Anyway, keep the war going until I'm old enough to join you,*
*Yours sincerely,*
*Edwin*

My brothers' letters disappointed me. How could they be looking forward to going to war? Did they not listen to what I told them when I was last home on leave? What did they hear when I told them what we were going through? I wanted to shake some sense into them and tell them how stupid they were to want to join up. If they could breathe the stench of rotting corpses, feel the cold of the icy, stagnant water lining the bottom of the trenches, mixed with congealed blood and stale urine, hear the whimpers of fear or see the staring, vacant eyes of young men who were so frightened they could only crouch in a corner, shaking and muttering to themselves, they might change their minds about wanting to be a part of it. For most of these men this was the first time they'd been away from home and many of them would never return.

And my father, what was he thinking? He seemed hell bent on sending his sons to war when he owns and runs an engineering manufacturing company involved in making weapons for the war effort. We could have joined the company and avoided going to war since weapons manufacturing was a reserved occupation, but I think father wanted to prove to the powers that be just how patriotic he was. He could have saved his sons, but his own aggrandizement came first.

I remember how proud I was when I first joined up, because I knew nothing of the stark reality of what life in the trenches would be like. I thought I was being patriotic and that there was glamour in war. But there is no glamour. There is only death, pointless, bloody death and the politicians and Generals who sit in their ivory towers, safe from the daily suffering in the trenches, will never understand what we're going through. They will never know how the sound of gunfire and death screams eventually take root in your head so that you end up hearing them even when there's silence. They will never know how the bangs and cries fill your dreams so that your dreams become nightmares. They'll never know what it's like to be too scared to go to sleep but too tired to stay awake, or how your nightmares eventually start to haunt you when you're awake. They'll never understand how the slightest noise startles you and you end up living in a state of permanent fear, jumping at shadows. That's the glory of war that I see day in, day out.

Snow started falling as I folded their letters and stowed them in the pocket of my greatcoat. Finally, I opened the last one, the letter from my mother. Her main news was about my father, the father who had never once written to me himself and yet who had expected me to come out here and fight for my country. Her news about father left me cold. My patriotic father who was prepared to sacrifice his sons, or at least that's my opinion of him, and who had never himself lifted a gun in anger, had received a knighthood in the King's New Year's Honours for services to the war effort. He had inherited the family business, an engineering company that manufactured and maintained river pumping stations, the type used in the draining of the fens and which were now sold to all parts of the Empire. In 1915, the year I joined the army, he had started manufacturing heavy duty guns for the artillery and was making a fortune. While his eldest son was daily being subjected to the horrors of what those big guns inflicted, he was profiting from our misery and being rewarded with a knighthood.

How ironic life can be sometimes.

February 26th, 1918

We've been back here for two days now and I think I've finally dried out. I notice Private Crawley was limping when I held inspection this morning and made him remove his boot for a foot inspection.

I recoiled from the foul whiff of his feet and was dismayed to observe rotting flesh as he prised off his right boot and peeled his damp, threadbare sock down. His foot was all blistered and blotchy, and when he lifted his leg so that I could see the sole of his foot I saw patches of skin were peeling off. He had the dreaded Trench Foot[1] and I sent him to report to the Medical Orderly immediately. I hoped we caught it early enough.

March 2nd, 1918

I fell in my men this afternoon to inform them that Sergeant Norris had died that morning, and we held a minute's silence in his memory. Oh, the futility of war. It seems I did waste my time trying to save his life after all, but I wasn't to know that at the time. I would damn well do the same again if I felt there was a chance of saving a life. Does that make me a hero, or does it make me a fool? Is there even a difference?

It was also time for us to return to the front line after our rest period, so I marched them on, along the forest path and down the chalk-lined slope leading to the miles and miles of trenches that wended their way from the Belgian coast, through the fields of Flanders and down through north west France to the Somme.

Instantly the nauseating stink of blood, piss, shit and rotting flesh

---

[1] Trench Foot, or immersion foot syndrome, is a serious condition resulting from the foot being wet and cold for too long. The condition first became known during World War One, when soldiers developed it from standing in cold, wet trenches. If diagnosed early enough it could be treated by rest and massage; severe cases often resulted in amputation.

greeted us. It was like an unwanted gift from a maiden aunt; you dislike it intensely, but you can't get rid of it and I don't think I'll ever forget that smell for as long as I live.

We stumbled past weary soldiers, crouched down in the mud either side of the trench, either grabbing some much-needed sleep, or reading letters, writing to loved ones or playing cards. Some just stared into space with that thousand-yard stare common to men who have heard too many explosions and seen too many corpses. Some of them would shake uncontrollably, unable to take much more, and occasionally one would suddenly leap up and start screaming for no apparent reason. Sometimes, if their comrades weren't quick enough to grab them and hold them back, they would jump out of the trench and run mindlessly into no-man's land where they'd be ruthlessly mown down by German rifles.

We reached our position in the front-line trench and I fell the men out. Most of them sat down in the mud or leaned against the trench wall and lit cigarettes.

One of the new men, Private Morgan, in the war for the first time, set about catching rats with a blanket. I watched on curiously as he swiftly caught half a dozen of the foul vermin and stuffed them into a discarded barrel that had been littering the trench, sealing the lid on it when he was done.

"What're you doing, soldier?" I asked, walking over to him.

"It's something you learn in the countryside, Captain," he replied. "When we have a rat infestation, we catch a handful of rats and leave them in a barrel or something similar for two weeks without any food. Eventually there'll be one rat left in the barrel, King Rat." His eyes looked at me excitedly when he said King Rat. "King Rat will be a huge, vicious bugger as he will have killed and eaten all the other rats in the barrel, and he'll be hungry. Here's the thing though, not only will he be hungry, but he's now a cannibal, craving the flesh of other rats so when we set him free, he'll turn on them and leave us alone."

"Good God," I exclaimed, "that sounds horrendous."

"Just a way of restoring the balance of nature, Sir. Rats should eat other rats, not us."

I thought I'd seen everything out here, but I was wrong, this was a new one to me.


March 12th, 1918

The shelling started at dawn and the first missile exploded about twenty feet in front of us in no-man's land, showering us with icy mud, bits of bone and flesh from the bodies that were lying frozen in the mud, and shrapnel. There had been a heavy frost overnight and we were shivering from cold.

First, we would hear the roar of the guns that were lined up behind the enemy lines, then the high-pitched whistling of the shells as they flew overhead, and finally the ear-shattering noise of the explosion as they detonated on impact.

Our guns replied and, instead of birdsong (which we hadn't heard for two years) we were greeted to a cacophony of explosions accompanied by the screams of the wounded and the shouts of those trying to rescue them.

A shell landed in our trench, fifty yards from where we crouched, knocking us down and covering us with debris. Choking smoke billowed over us, filled with dust and dirt, blinding us and filling our mouths and noses so we couldn't breathe.

Coughing violently, I ran towards the impact site to assist any survivors, with Sergeant Jennings by my side. Part of the trench wall had collapsed, burying everyone beneath it with mud, boulders, sandbags and planks of wood. Jennings helped me to clear away the rubble and uncover our fallen comrades.

"Steady, Sergeant," I called on seeing a man's left-hand poking through the mud. "Help me here."

Being as careful as we could so as not to cause any further collapse, we removed a wooden stake that had pinned the man down and uncovered the rest of his body. His eyes flickered open and I took hold of his hand to help him to his feet. I pulled and was suddenly stumbling back. I lost my footing and crashed back against the trench wall still holding the soldier's hand in mine. It had come away in my hand, severed from the wrist, which was now pumping blood in spurts that arced about two feet through the air, spattering over Sergeant Jennings and splashing into the puddles. Jennings let out a cry of horror as I fell back still clutching the armless hand and in disgust, I threw it away from me as if it was a poisonous snake, then turned and was violently sick. By the time we had got him to a stretcher the soldier was dead. The poor bastard had pumped his blood all over the trench and bled to death.

The shelling stopped just as suddenly as it had started and, for a moment, silence fell.

Immediately, I had the men fall in, fix their bayonets and stand to arms, because heavy shelling was always followed by an enemy charge.

A thin mist clung to the ground, swirling into the craters and cloaking the dead that were lying there. Across the fields I heard the faint blows of the enemy's whistles signalling the order to charge.

"Wait until you can see them clearly," I ordered, "and make every shot count. When they're close enough, take aim and fire at will. Stand ready, men and let the day be ours."

They came out of the mist like spectres. Starting as faint shadows, pale grey under the mist, they loomed darker and grew in stature as they advanced, closing the gap between us with each hurried step. Shots rang out and men fell. The charge was as futile and as pointless as every charge had been every day of the war, whether it was us leading it or them. The only thing it achieved was the needless death of brave soldiers from both sides. I have come to the conclusion that there are no winners in war, only losers. Those who lose their lives and those who lose their loved ones.

There must have been two hundred enemy soldiers coming towards us, but they had nearly one hundred yards to cover. One hundred yards of slippery, half frozen mud covered with water filled craters, dead bodies and endless rolls of razor-sharp barbed wire. While the mist gave them a little shelter, we could see them well enough at fifty yards, and we picked them off one by one. No one stood a chance. I've never understood why anyone would give such an order, knowing that it would only result in the slaughter of good, decent men. Within fifteen minutes every enemy soldier who had charged us that morning lay dead or dying. The one German soldier who made it into our trench was felled with a single bayonet thrust before he was able to create any havoc.

"Good move, soldier," I called across as some of the men threw the enemy corpse back into no-man's land, stripped of any valuables he had about him, which were few.

After that it was quiet, so I stood the men down and we waited in silence for breakfast.

March 17th, 1918

"It's time to release King Rat," Private Morgan informed us this morning after we had completed our daily ablutions and trench tidy.

He told us to stand behind him. "You really do not want to stand in the path of an angry and vicious rat that hasn't eaten for a few days," Morgan said. "He's likely to be a bit grumpy."

Several rats were scavenging along the floor of the trench a few yards away and Morgan turned the barrel towards them before releasing the lid.

What leapt out of the barrel astonished us all. Grumpy was not the word I'd have used. Seething would have been a more appropriate description. The rat, having killed and eaten his mates had grown to the size of a large cat; his eyes had turned red, having seen no light for two weeks and his dark fur was zig-zagged with scars and matted with dried blood, both his own and those of his victims. He erupted from the barrel in a rage of high-pitched squeals and flying fur and tore into the nearest rat. The rat didn't know what hit it as its throat was ripped out by savage teeth and King Rat started noisily devouring it before it had even died.

We looked on in horror and disgust.

"Oh, fuck," Private Osborne muttered, "that's just disgusting."

Private Morrison threw up his breakfast and other rats jumped into his pile of vomit and gorged themselves hungrily.

March 20th, 1918

Since we released King Rat the general rat population in our trench has decreased significantly and in only a few days, King Rat has grown to the size of a small dog. He's a nasty, vicious creature but, while he has plenty of rats to eat, he's leaving us alone.

March 21st, 1918

I was woken this morning by a deafening barrage of explosions and immediately rallied my troops. It was 4.40am, still dark and bitterly cold.

"They're starting early this morning," Jennings said, blowing on his cold hands.

"Those bastards are up to something," I replied nervously, peering through the periscope across to the enemy lines.

"What can you see, Captain?"

"Not a thing, it's too dark."

I was worried. The daily onslaught didn't usually start this early. Normally, like us, the Germans would still be resting at this time.

As it happens, I was right to be worried. It was the start of a major German offensive right along the trench complex. Enemy shells rained down on us relentlessly. Some were aimed at the front-line trenches in which we were stationed, wreaking havoc and death upon our soldiers as they were startled from sleep. Others hit our rear lines where our artillery was lined up ready for their own dawn chorus. But the Germans' had started early. They had taken us by surprise and our guns were unable to reply. In fact, many of them were destroyed before they could fire a single shell back.

In addition to their heavy guns, we were being pounded by wave upon wave of mortar fire, including grenades, smoke canisters, and mustard and chlorine gas.

It was the most tremendous cannonade I have ever heard and all along the lines I could see a wide curve of red leaping flames bursting forth from as far as the Third Army in the north, to the Fifth Army in the south. There was no respite to the intensity of their bombardment, the like of which I have never experienced in the two years of being there.

Dawn broke to reveal a blanket of thick fog covering the ground. Mixed with the smoke from the shells and the gas from the canister grenades, visibility was reduced to as little as ten yards in places, with virtually no breeze to disperse it. This meant that we wouldn't see the enemy advancing until they were virtually on top of us. Many of the men realised that about the same time as I did and one or two of them started to panic.

The bombardment continued for five hours, and it seemed like eternity. The constant roaring of shells and the booming explosions seemed to segue into one loud, pulsing wall of deafening sound. It pounded right through us, making us feel sick, and its intensity made our ears bleed.

At 9.40am, the guns finally went silent. My head was throbbing from the prolonged bombardment and the silence was eerie. Almost more frightening than the explosions. The anticipation of what was to come grew like a cancer in the pit of my stomach, twisting like a knot, gripping my guts and turning them inside out with fear. A cheer went up amongst the newer recruits who were unused to the routine. Veterans like me knew it only heralded the next phase of attack.

"Stand to, men," I ordered, "and fix bayonets." I listened as the order was repeated along the line.

"Now, be ready men," I shouted, "and keep your eyes peeled. They'll be on their way," and we all stood and waited in silence, ready for the next onslaught. After the relentless tirade of the last five hours the silence was unnerving.

A few minutes later they came, charging at us out of the fog, screaming their battle cry and making our blood run cold. We despatched the first wave with a hail of bullets from our trusty Lee-Enfield rifles but there were more behind them.

The soldier next to me fell as a bullet hit him in the back and I spun around to see German soldiers attacking us from behind. Under the cover of the fog they had broken through our lines and we were being attacked from both sides.

Without a second thought I shot the enemy soldier who had killed my man and shouted a warning to the rest of my men. Some turned to face the enemy from behind, the rest remained facing the enemy attacking from the front. We were surrounded, and in seconds they were piling into the trench and we were fighting hand to hand with bayonets, rifles, rocks and anything we could get our hands on. Fighting for our lives.

Men on both sides were falling and those who were alive fought to stay alive. I thought about King Rat and how he had overcome all the other rats to emerge the victor and I felt a new power surge through my veins.

"Remember King Rat," I shouted to my men, "let him bring us victory."

I punched, kicked, stabbed and swiped at everything in my path, gradually moving my men back towards the joining trench so we could retreat and join the rest of my battalion. Less than half of my men were left alive as I retreated them. We fell back to the reserve battalions, and the wounded were taken away for treatment. Those of us who were uninjured were rapidly reassigned to other battalions as there were now fewer than sixty of us left.

As darkness fell their artillery opened fire once again. They seemed to know exactly where we were, and their shells devastated our forlorn and battle-weary troops. Either that or they were incredibly lucky. In no time at all the bombardment was as heavy and as intense as it had been that morning.

We were in disarray and we retreated chaotically across the fields and through the forest, ready to dig another line of trenches so we could hold them back during tomorrow's offensive.

I was exhausted as I dug through the hard earth. My ears hurt from the deafening roar of the explosions and I was covered in mud and blood.

It was a moonless night, and in the darkness, we could hear the whistle as another shell flew overhead to explode just yards from where we were digging. We cowered as debris from the explosion rained over us.

Another came over.

And another.

I didn't even feel the last explosion. I just felt a scorching heat and a shockwave hit me with the force of a heavyweight boxer. The breath was knocked from my body and I was thrown back by its force. I gasped for air and the heat seared my throat. With my limbs flailing madly, I flew across the clearing, blinded by the intense light of the explosion. Something hard thudded against my right leg and I felt my feet rising above my head as I somersaulted through the air.

Time stood still. I felt suspended in mid-air, upside down, turning, moving so slowly. Surrounded by lumps of mud, boulders, chunks of wood, shrapnel and body parts. I watched as the helmeted head of Private Osborne thumped into my stomach causing me to double up in pain. I landed heavily on my shoulders on the unyielding mud and I skidded out of control, spinning across the field.

I remember thinking that if I was going to die then let it be quick.

I remember thinking that something wasn't quite right with my body.

And then it all went black and I remembered no more.

# Chapter Seven
# The Three Horseshoes

"Wow," I said as I put down Edward's journal and squeezed the bridge of my nose between the thumb and middle finger of my left hand and rubbed it. My eyes ached from reading the handwritten account which was beginning to fade with time.

"It makes interesting reading, doesn't it?" Larry called from the Smoking Room. He'd left the secret door ajar, presumably to enable him to keep an eye on me and ensure I didn't do anything stupid.

I stood up, stretched and wandered through to join him.

"The poor bastard. Imagine having to live through all that for so long, no wonder he never wanted to talk about it."

"I'm not surprised so many war veterans suffered from shell shock, it must have been hell out there."

"And shell shock wasn't recognised as a condition back then either, nowadays it's even got its own name."

"Yeah, PTSD."

Having read the account I think we understood what he must have suffered in the trenches much better than we did when we were kids. I also think that if we had read his journal when we were teenagers, we may just have looked upon it as a damn good war story rather than the rather brutal and personal experiences of our grandfather. Well, Larry's grandfather at least.

A sudden emptiness twisted inside me. Larry's grandfather, not mine. He had been a true hero and suddenly I had a longing to know whether my real grandfather was such a hero too. For the first in my life I felt a desperate desire to know who I really was, and a wave of melancholy pricked me like a knife through the heart.

"What's the matter?"

My face must have reflected the thoughts swirling around in my head. I could hear the concern in Larry's voice.

"Oh, nothing," I said, but Larry was having none of that.

"Come on, Jim, talk to me. Remember what the doctor and your Ms

Down said, you have to talk. Don't bottle things up."

I looked at him. Through the years, as we had grown up together, there was scarcely an important moment that we hadn't shared. Perhaps we were guilty of having shared more with each other than we had with our own wives. I let out a loud sigh.

"Madea was right, you know, when she said that adopted children can lose their sense of belonging when they lose their adopted parents. Just now, when we were talking about Grandad, I felt this strong sense that he wasn't my Grandad. That I don't know who my real Grandad was. I don't even know who my real parents are; where I come from; where they come from; who I am."

"That's it?"

"Yeah, that's it. I don't know who I really am. What did my real parent do? Why did they give me up for adoption? Are they still alive? Did they have any other children? I might have other brothers and sisters for all I know."

"And you really want to know?"

"Wouldn't you?"

He sat back on the sofa and looked up at the ceiling for a moment. I knew his opinion on the parents who gave me up for adoption were similar to mine.

"Yes," he said, eventually, slowly nodding his head, "yes, I suppose I would."

"And so do I and yet, until now, I've never had the slightest inclination to do so."

"And now you need to know."

"Yes, now I need to know, but I can't help feeling that, now that mum's dead, the last chance to find out who they were is lost to me."

"You've still got Aunt Clara's personal stuff to go through, maybe you'll find something in there. If nothing else, she'll surely at least have kept your adoption papers and those will give us a start if you decide we want to research the public records. That sort of thing is much easier now than it used to be, what with so much being on the internet and public records being made public. Those ancestry programs on telly have a lot to answer for."

I wasn't sure whether I was quite ready to go through mum's private stuff yet. It was all there in that box up in my bedroom, but to read it seemed odd to me. They were private and personal. Things she had deemed important enough to want to keep. Letters, diaries, journals and such. The thought of reading them came across to me as a bit voyeuristic. They were my mother's private papers and I wasn't entirely comfortable with the prospect of reading them. Perhaps I was being silly. After all, she was dead and buried, but that's how I felt, and I can't change the way I feel.

"Give me time," I said.

"Take all the time you want, there's no rush. Why don't you discuss it with Madea next time she's here, maybe she can help you deal with it, and remember, Jim, if you need my help with it, or anything else, for that matter. I'm here for you, remember."

"Thanks. I will," I said, and I meant it. I knew Larry was looking out for me, he always had, and it made me feel better.

"Now," he said, standing up and rubbing his hands together enthusiastically, "let's pop down to the Three Horseshoes for a spot of lunch and, as it looks like it's going to be a fine afternoon, we can do a spot of work in the Kitchen Garden when we get back. A bit of fresh air and exercise before dinner will do us a world of good and build us up a decent appetite."

Ten minutes later we set off along the winding drive. Although the sun was shining there was a definite autumnal feel to the air. A flock of geese flew over in their distinctive V-formation, honking noisily to each other as they arrived in the fens for winter. As children I remember being taken to the RSPB Centre at nearby Welney during autumn and winter to watch thousands of geese and swans arrive from Canada and Russia. I learned early on to distinguish between the various types that came here.

The breeze produced little eddies of wind that picked up piles of leaves and carried them through the air to deposit them randomly across the lawn. We fastened our coats against autumn's chill fingers.

The Three Horseshoes stood on the opposite side of the road, about fifty metres walk from the gates to the Hall. It was a longer walk from the gates to the Hall than it was from the gates to the pub.

Built in Tudor times the pub was one of the few remaining thatched buildings in the village. It had an iron weathervane at one end of the roof and a straw peacock adorning the other. The front door gave entrance to the pub about two thirds along its front, opening into a small hallway which had two doors and a bar. The bar acted as a small off licence, selling sweets, crisps, bottles of wine, beer and soft drinks and loaves of bread to people not wanting to stay. The door on the left led into the dining area, which was previously the lounge bar and the opposite door lead into the public bar, and it was through this door we entered. At the bar I ordered a couple of pints of beer and we sat at a table by the window near the warm fire and read through the menu.

When Janet was alive, we would often come here to eat when we visited Larry. The beer was always good, and the food was always fresh and plentiful. There was none of that pretentious cuisine there where the portions cost a weekly wage and were barely substantial enough feed a sparrow.

"I'm going for the fish pie," I said, making my mind up as soon as I saw it on the menu. Fish Pie is one of those dishes that I really like but is too much of a faff to cook at home, especially for one.

"Ah, yes, that's usually good, I think I'll join you."

I went to the bar and ordered, and the landlady handed me a wooden spoon with a number burnt onto it. I pointedly looked around the bar and shrugged, we were the only people there.

"I'm expecting a rush," the landlady said with a grin.

"Really?"

"No. A few of regulars will be in in a minute, old Colin, Jack Farmer and Bill Turner, and maybe a couple of ramblers if we're lucky."

"Crikey, are those three still alive?" I exclaimed, "I remember them being old when I was a lad."

She laughed, "I think those three have always been old. Mind you, Colin is well into his nineties now and the other two aren't far behind. They were born and bred in this village and there's not many that can boast that these days. They worked on the farm, back in the days when farms employed labourers and now, they spend their days wandering about the fen, reminiscing about times gone by, or coming in here and getting pissed. They've each got their own mug and woe-betide anyone who sits at their table to the left of the fireplace."

"Do you get busy here then?"

"Thursday evening to Sunday lunch time we're usually fully booked in the restaurant, Friday and Saturday nights are usually quite busy in here."

Even though the pub was off the beaten track it had earned a reputation for its good food and beer and, since real ale and craft ale was enjoying a resurgence in popularity, it was deemed a pub worthy of visiting for a night out.

"It'll be about twenty-five minutes, love, it's freshly cooked," she said as she rang my food order through the till.

"No problem," I replied, "plenty of time for another beer then." I rejoined Larry with two sets of cutlery that had been lovingly wrapped in a paper napkin and took a long sip of my beer. It tasted perfect.

Across the room, on the wall by the bar, hung a small television showing some lunchtime antiques programme with the volume off and the subtitles on. The landlady was watching it when she wasn't busy serving.

A few minutes later the door opened and in walked Colin, Jack and Bill and, as they stamped across the room, the landlady was already pulling their pints. They ignored her and sat down, grumbling noisily about everything from the weather to the state of the world until the landlady delivered their pints and they were silent as they drank.

"Christ," I whispered to Larry as they settled into their conversation, "I don't think they've changed a bit."

"I'll bet they've seen a few comings and goings in this village over the years."

We listened to them complaining about cars speeding through the village and how painful their piles were.

"Certainly more 'Last of the Summer Wine' than 'Fun Boy Three'." Larry said with a smile.

Our food arrived and Larry ordered another round and treated the three old boys to a round as well, which they acknowledged with various grunts of thanks. A group of ramblers, dressed in wax jackets and walking boots with their trousers tucked into thick woollen socks, came in all hale and hearty, greeting all of us as though we were long lost friends. They sat down on the table next to ours and, seemingly at the tops of their voices, talked about their walk through our local wildlife reserve.

We ate our food, drank our beer and left.

# Chapter Eight
## Turning The Sod

The Kitchen Garden seemed smaller than I remembered, but then I was remembering it through the eyes of a child who had used it for playing games and I was no longer that child.

Surrounded by a ten-foot-high brick wall, the garden was divided into four quarters. Two bisecting gravel paths converged on the centre where stood an old, now disused fish pond topped by a stone statue of Bacchus, the Roman God of agriculture, wine and fertility; although I suspect he was frowning rather than smiling at the moment at the state of this, once beautiful, Kitchen Garden. A large wooden framed greenhouse had been built along the centre of the north wall where it enjoyed the full light of the sun throughout the day whenever it was shining.

Larry had partially cleared one of the rectangular borders and an abundance of autumn and winter vegetables were growing in the fertile black fenland soil. Half a dozen fruit trees grew against the walls and pears and apples hung from their branches or lay in heaps on the ground below them.

As autumn was taking over most of the summer growth had died back, which would make the job of clearing it much easier.

"As you can see, there's still quite a bit to do," Larry said. We stood in the arched entrance and surveyed the disarray of brambles and weeds that were growing there. "It's a bit of a mess still."

I laughed. "A bit of a mess is an understatement," I said. "This is a major project."

"I was thinking of getting someone in to clear it properly, but I reckon we could have it cleared and tidy by Christmas if we spend a couple of days a week on it. We plant all year round for the seasonal veg and I reckon we could become almost self-sufficient in vegetables within a couple of years."

"It's a great idea, and nothing tastes better than home grown fruit and veg. Janet loved her vegetable patch at home and always used to get excited when she pulled the first carrot of the season or dug up her first potato.

Janet.

A lump came to my throat. I hadn't thought about Janet since my session with Madea. It suddenly felt as though talking to Madea had made me forget her for a moment, and though I knew I shouldn't, I felt terribly guilty. I couldn't help it.

I took a deep breath and swallowed my pain as Larry walked me around the garden. In the corner by the greenhouse a couple of tomato plants stood in tubs, weighed down with their juicy, red fruit.

"I've got broccoli, carrots, cauliflower, parsnips and sprouts growing in the bed down there, so we've got plenty to eat this autumn and winter. Plus, I blanched and froze several kilos of peas and runner beans over summer.

"You're taking this seriously then?"

"I tell you Jim, I've really gotten into it. It's brilliant. Not only does the veg taste better than anything you can buy at the supermarket, but I've lost half a stone in weight and I'm feeling fitter than I've felt for a long time. I've even started watching Gardeners' World on telly."

"So, what's the plan, moving forward?"

"Well, to start with we need to clear and burn. Then we can dig the ashes back in along with some decent compost. We're even self-sufficient in that department too. Down in the south-east corner over there is our own compost heap. That corner is in shade for most of the day so we might as well use it for something useful."

As I looked over to the compost heap I could also see, along the edge of the far border, a line of blackberry bushes laden with fruit. Larry had already picked a bucket full which was sitting in the scullery waiting to be turned into something delicious like a crumble or a smoothie, and there was plenty more to be picked.

"So, this area is pretty much under control," I said, as we walked around the beds Larry had already cleared. "And what's this?"

I was pointing to a row of elongated crinkly green leaves growing in one of the cultivated beds.

"Turnips," he replied. "I'm fond of a good stew this time of year, so I've grown plenty of suitable root vegetables like turnips, parsnips and swedes. They all add flavour, along with the carrots."

Despite having eaten a big lunch my mouth was watering with all this talk of food and I found I was looking forward to getting on with the work.

There was a spare pair of wellington boots in the greenhouse, along with a variety of gardening gloves. We were soon working hard, clearing twigs; pulling dead roots; cutting old growth and unwanted bramble and then digging the soil over and removing the rest.

Fen soil is black in colour and generally very fertile owing to the wetness of the land. Eighty percent of native vegetables sold in our supermarkets are grown in the fens, particularly the root vegetables Larry had mentioned.

Larry had clearly been doing his homework. On the table in the greenhouse was a chart listing all the various fruit and vegetables we were going to grow, when and where to plant them and when they would be ready for eating. He had even planted seed trays in the greenhouse.

"Good grief," I exclaimed, looking at what he had done, "you'll make someone a wonderful wife one of these days." He grinned on hearing the expression we used to use when we were teenagers.

"I do my best."

A robin, resplendent in his red breast, landed on my fork and chattered to me as I rested from my toil. He hopped across the freshly turned earth and pulled up a small worm that was trying to make its way back underground, and I watched as it slithered down his throat. He chirruped with satisfaction.

All around the garden I was surrounded by a variety of sweet birdsong. Blackbirds and thrushes were hopping through the bushes, picking at berries or eating grubs. Towards the centre of the garden near the fishpond, a family of chaffinches was feeding from a feeder filled with sunflower hearts that Larry had topped up moments earlier.

"Don't tell me," I said pointing to the feeders, "you grow the sunflowers that supply those too."

"No, I buy those from Wilko in Ely. I reckon I spend more on their food than I do on myself. Mind you, I don't put anything out for them in summer as the wildflower gardens keep them fed well enough."

The robin flew up and settled on the handle of my fork.

"You're a brave little rascal," I said, holding my hand out and inviting him on. He looked at my outstretched hand, cocked his head to one side, let out a prolonged twitter and flew off to sit on a nearby bramble.

"If you had some seed in your hand, he might have taken it. He's very tame."

I picked up the fork and carried on with my work. It wasn't arduous. The soil was soft, and the old, dead roots came out easily enough. We made good progress. Soon enough we had cleared a sizeable area and a pile of dead vegetation had built up in the corner that we could burn later.

As I worked, I whistled, and Larry joined in. Soon we had whistled several David Bowie tunes, a few Eric Clapton numbers and tried our hand, or rather lips, at a couple of Pink Floyd tracks but failed since they were a bit more complex. When we had failed a few more attempts, Larry traipsed off to the greenhouse to get some matches for the bonfire.

The sun was low in the western sky and long shadows stretched across the garden. I leant on my fork and surveyed our progress.

As I stood there, I felt the hair on the back of my next suddenly bristle up, sending a cold shiver down my spine. The birds in the garden stopped their singing and all I could hear was the sound of the breeze blowing through leafless branches and bushes.

I had an intense feeling I was being watched. It wasn't Larry, as I could see his figure moving about inside the greenhouse. He was taking no notice of me. Yet I sensed a pair of eyes looking at me. I slowly turned around. The low sun shone straight into my eyes, temporarily blinding me. I blinked and raised my hand across my forehead to shade them.

The shadows along the south wall were dark and though I could barely even make out the outline of the reddish-brown brick wall I sensed rather than saw a figure standing beneath the branches of a large cherry tree. As my eyes adjusted to the contrasting light, I could just make out the hazy outline of a woman. She appeared to be wearing a long dark skirt and a light blouse over which she had wrapped a shawl that covered her head and shoulders, hiding her face.

A cold chill ran through my veins.

"Janet?" I said, taking a step forward. Something stopped me. A voice deep within me told me this wasn't Janet. Janet's dead, it reasoned. Dead.

My mind was flooded with memories of Janet and I threw my hands up around my head, as if to hold them there. The memories were happy ones, times of laughter and loving – of course you only ever remember happy times when you're missing someone you love.

I held a hand out to her, but she remained motionless.

She looked like Janet, but the shadow was dark and there was a haziness about her.

Besides, I knew, deep inside, that it wasn't Janet.

Who was it then? And how did she get there? There was only one entrance to the Kitchen Garden and that was in the middle of the eastern wall, which was behind me. So how could she have walked in and walked right past Larry and me without either of us seeing her?

Why was she there? What did she want?

"Taking the opportunity to have a break?" said Larry as he clapped me on my shoulder and made me jump.

I blinked, still staring across the garden but all I could see was the cherry tree, the wall and wisps of mist swirling around.

"Are you alright, Jim?"

"Er, yeah," I said, turning around and forcing a smile, "I think so."

"What is it?"

"It's alright," I said, shaking my head, "I just thought I saw a woman beneath that cherry tree over there by the wall. She was watching us. Well, watching me, I suppose."

"You?"

"I thought at first it was Janet, but I know it wasn't her, then I wondered who it could be and how she got there."

"She didn't get there, Jim, she wasn't there. She isn't there now. You were seeing things."

"Yes, I guess so. She seemed so real, but I know it wasn't. Not really."

"You're having one of those things the doctor told you you might have."

"Psychosis?"

"Yeah, that."

I began to feel a little embarrassed. I thought I was dealing with things but evidently, I wasn't. "Perhaps you're right," I said, "and yet ... oh I don't know, I must be tired, or something."

"Come on, Jim," he said putting his arm protectively around my shoulders and guiding me along the path towards the gates, "let's go and get a cup of tea."

As we walked beneath the arch, I turned and looked back. All I saw as I left the garden was the Robin hopping onto my fork, lit up by a ray of bright sunshine and, as I closed the gates, I could hear a symphony of birdsong once again.

# Chapter Nine
## Janet

"Are you awake?" Janet asked.

"Yep," I replied, "I'm having trouble sleeping."

"Me too."

I sat up in bed and yawned. In actual fact, I was still half asleep. Or was I half awake? I wasn't sure which.

Janet slipped out of bed and tiptoed to the window. A shaft of moonlight illuminated her face and the slope of her breasts which were half covered by her cotton nightdress, and I admired her slender figure and strong profile as I had done so many times before.

"It's a beautiful night," she whispered, parting the curtains to let the light flood into the room. "Come for a walk."

I threw back the covers and discovered that I was already dressed in my black suit with a white shirt, black tie and black shoes. My funeral attire.

"Come my love," she said, standing at the bedroom door dressed in her favourite yellow summer dress and open toed sandals. She gave me that beguiling smile I so adored and held her hand out to me, beckoning me to follow.

The moon cast long shadows across the damp grass. Under the light of the moon the grass appeared grey and I followed her as she glided over it. My feet felt wet and I looked down to see that I was barefoot and drops of mud had spattered up my leg and soaked the bottoms of my pyjama trousers.

I looked up and Janet was gone.

The door to the old chapel at the side of the Hall swung open as I approached. I was alone as I entered and was surprised to see beautifully white-washed walls, rather than the blackened walls I was used to, and two rows of wooden pews set out to face the altar, in front of which stood an open polished wood coffin with shiny brass handles. Inside the coffin lay Janet, still wearing her yellow summer dress and sandals, and now she clutched a small posy of peonies across her stomach. She lay still, her eyes closed and her face relaxed. So peaceful so ... at peace.

Soft music was playing from a CD player that stood on the altar, and the chapel was illuminated by a dozen or so candles that were placed around the coffin.

Of course, I thought, the yellow dress was the one Janet wore to her funeral, the one we had buried her in.

Her lips were set to make it look as though she was smiling, and they were painted with a faint trace of lipstick. I thought what a wonderful job the undertaker had done in dressing her up to look like she was sleeping rather than dead, as I ran my hand along the smooth edge of the wooden coffin in which she lay.

The flickering lights lit up the faces of mourners who had gathered to pay their respects. They converged on us from the depths of the shadows that enveloped the chapel. I scanned the crowd for familiar faces but saw none. Strangers wearing strange, old fashioned clothes, I thought. The women wore dark, calf length skirts and long over-jackets fastened at the neck. Some wore wide brimmed hats; others were wrapped in fur stoles. The men wore dark long double-breasted overcoats with Homburg or Fedora hats. All the clothes, I noticed, had seen better days; these weren't well off people, but more like locals.

I turned to gaze at Janet, longing for her to come to me, so we could return to how we were before.

I bent forward and leaned in to give her one last kiss goodbye. She seemed happy resting there, so at peace lying shrouded in the folds of the soft cream satin that lined her final resting place.

As my lips brushed against hers her eyes sprung open. I jumped back in fright. She sat up and slowly turned her head to face me. I was mesmerised. Unable to move. Unable to turn away. I wanted to run, but my feet were made of clay. The mourners had gone. I was alone. Alone with Janet. Only when I looked at her face again, it was no longer Janet. It was someone else.

"Hello, James," she said, stepping out of the coffin and gliding towards me.

She reached out to me and I scrabbled away in fear. My foot caught on the leg of the trestle on which the coffin rested, and I felt myself falling back.

The room spun around me. A blur of silver and black streaks engulfed me as I put my hand out to break my fall. The walls, floor and ceiling disappeared, and I was tumbling backwards into a black abyss.

With a jolt I was awake, lying in bed. Confused. For a moment I lay there, panting and sweating despite the chill air. Black shadows filled the room. They seemed to grow, closing in on me and I couldn't tell whether my eyes were open or closed. At last, through the cloying blackness, a silver shaft of moonlight shone through a chink in the heavy velvet curtains. My breathing steadied and I lay there in the dark reflecting on my dream ... nightmare, I suppose.

In the still silence of the night I heard the faint chimes of the grandfather clock that stood in the hall at the bottom of the stairs. One o'clock. The room was cold. I turned over and snuggled down beneath the warm duvet and closed my eyes.

I awoke and it was morning. I yawned and stretched as I sat up and slowly opened my eyes.

The dream was still vivid, every detail fresh in my mind. Was this a part of my acceptance of Janet's death? A sign that finally I was moving on, maybe? I had seen her lying in her coffin so was I now accepting that she was dead? I felt a lightness of being as I reflected on the events of my dream. I had kissed Janet's lips. Was this me saying goodbye at last? Me, finally letting go of her?

But when she had changed into someone else, it had scared me. Was this my fear of losing her? Of losing my memories of her? Perhaps this was the start of the adjustment phase that Madea had described during our session the other day. I didn't know and made a mental note to ask her at our next session.

I knew I had to write it down, I know what dreams are like. You remember them when you first wake up then, after breakfast, you've forgotten them completely. I threw off the duvet and swung my legs over the edge of the bed, and my heart missed a beat. For a second the world seemed to stand still. A pounding in my head made me feel dizzy and my vision seemed to momentarily blur.

My feet, my ankles and the bottom of my pyjama trousers were splattered in mud and covered in bits of grass.

# Chapter Ten
# Guilt

"How do you feel in yourself?" Madea asked. We were again sitting opposite one another in the Morning Room. Larry had gone into Ely first thing as he wanted to visit the market. He was also planning to go to the supermarket on the way back to get something for dinner and put petrol in his car, so I expected him back late morning. He certainly wouldn't be back before Madea left.

"Good. Mostly," I replied.

"Mostly?"

I sighed. "Last time you were here," I began, "you told me about the possibility of losing my sense of belonging. Because I was adopted?"

"I remember. And …?"

"Well, over the last few days I've begun to experience that feeling. It's never happened to me before, but I suddenly feel the urge to know who I am, to discover who my real parents were. Where they came from, who their parents were, my whole family history, in fact."

"And have you done anything about it?"

"No. Not yet."

"Why not?"

"I …" Why hadn't I done anything about it? It wasn't as though I couldn't. Larry had even offered to help. Was it fear that was holding me back? Fear of what though? Of finding out who I really was? No. Doubt perhaps?

My eyes searched Madea's face but there was nothing in her expression to help me with my answer.

"Guilt," I said, finally.

"Guilt?"

"Yes, guilt."

She just looked at me, saying nothing, her face neutral.

"I feel as though it would be a betrayal of the parents I knew and loved, who brought me up as their own, who loved me. Clara and David were my real parents in every way. Except they weren't, were they?

They weren't my biological parents, and yet, they were the only parents I knew, the only ones who ever cared for me. So why should I now want to know about my birth parents? What right have they over me? They abandoned me."

"Did they?"

"Of course they did. They gave me up for adoption, didn't they? They were the ones who didn't want me."

"Maybe it wasn't like that. Maybe something happened."

"How do you mean?"

"Maybe there were extenuating circumstances leading up to your adoption. Maybe something happened to them. Maybe they died."

We looked at each other in silence. I had truly never thought about them, so it had never occurred to me that they may have died. She continued, "Look, I know this can be difficult, and maybe you might find something you wish you hadn't but, in my experience, whatever you discover can bring enlightenment, and with enlightenment comes some kind of closure.

"You mustn't doubt your love for the two people who brought you up and loved you as their own child. For all intents and purposes they were your true parents, and nothing can, or should, take that away from you. But it is perfectly natural to be curious about your birth parents. Rather than fight it do something about it, embrace it. Find them if you can, but please, don't feel guilty about trying to do so."

We sat in silence. Outside I could see dark clouds forming in the distance. A family of Long Tailed Tits were crowded around the birdfeeder on the back lawn and I could hear the gentle, almost hypnotic ticking of the carriage clock on the mantlepiece which ticked in time with the grandfather clock that stood just outside the door at the bottom of the stairs.

"The other day," I began, hesitantly, "the other day Larry and I were working in the Kitchen Garden."

"How's that coming along?"

"Quite well, actually. We've been clearing beds and prepping them. It's been hard work and it's made me realise that I'm not as fit as I thought I was, but it's enjoyable and quite therapeutic. And the best thing is you can see the results of our work almost instantly."

"So, tell me about what happened the other day?"

"I had a feeling I was being watched."

"And were you?"

69

"No ... yes ... I'm not sure."

I recounted the episode to her.

"And your cousin didn't see anything?"

"No. I mentioned it to him, but he was adamant that he hadn't seen anything. I clearly imagined it, didn't I?"

"Why do you think that?"

"Well, the fact that Larry didn't see her, for one thing. The fact that one minute she wasn't there, then she was, and then she was gone. If she had been real, she would have had to walk past us to get from the gate. The doctor at the hospital told me that hallucinations were not uncommon in depression."

"It's a symptom, certainly."

"But she seemed so real."

"They can do. The mind is an incredible thing."

"And then there was the dream."

I recounted my dream to her. I didn't say who I thought Janet had changed into at the end of it, but I did tell her about the mud on my feet when I woke up the following morning.

"Have you ever walked in your sleep before?"

"I probably did when I was a child, but that's not unusual, is it? We grow out of it."

"It's positive," she said.

"What? What do you mean by that?"

"I can't pretend that it's easy to interpret dreams, but they are usually brought on when you're going through life changing events, particularly stress, and you have gone through a major life changing event. While it isn't my area of expertise, I believe it might be an indication of how you are dealing with Janet's death. You said her face changed into someone else, which suggests that you are now accepting she has died. You're moving her on. The fact that, in your dream, her funeral took place in the chapel could be down to you sleepwalking there. It's what you would have seen, and your mind would have imposed it into your dream. Remember, dreams aren't always logical. Did you recognise the person whom Janet changed into?"

"Is it important?"

"Possibly," she said, smiling. "If it was someone you know. I would expect it to have been someone you rely on for support. Maybe your daughter, or your cousin, Larry. Maybe even me, perhaps."

My heart skipped a beat. How could she know that?

"It ... it was you, actually," I said, after a brief pause.

"Of course."

"Why?"

"Well, you see me as someone who is helping you. Working with you to help you come to terms with Janet's death. Her changing into me in your dream means you accept that she is dead and are allowing me to help you through the 'relocation' stage. This is excellent progress."

"But why in the chapel? Her funeral took place in Sutton Courtney not here."

"Do you have memories of the chapel from your childhood?"

"Not really. It was out of bounds, of course, and the one time that Larry and I did go in we found nothing worthwhile. It was a bit of a let-down really. There was just a load of useless junk."

The clock on the mantlepiece started to chime, followed moments later by the grandfather clock. Ten o'clock already. The hour had passed so quickly.

"I think we've made really good progress today," she said, looking up and smiling. There was a warmth in her smile that lit up her face. "I think your gardening project is really helping you, both mentally and physically, which is good.

"Now, I would like you to think seriously about what we discussed at the start of today's session. Don't be afraid to research your background, it isn't a betrayal of Clara and David. You won't replace them in your heart with someone else, there's room enough in there for everyone, if they deserve it."

I helped her with her coat and let her out through the front porch. As I closed the front door behind her my mobile rang.

"Hello, Larry," I said.

"Hey Jim, how's things?"

"Yeah, good," I replied.

"Great. It's quarter past ten already, so I assume Madea's gone?"

"Yeah, she's just this minute left."

"Hey, I'm in Tesco just now, how do you fancy some nice fresh haddock for dinner?"

"Sounds good, yep, I'm up for it."

"Great. I'm at the fish counter right now and they've got some fresh in, it looks lovely. I'll get some. See you in about an hour."

I put my phone back in my pocket as I peered through the window. Two magpies were hopping over the lawn beneath the large horse chestnut tree and leaves were blowing across the drive.

Despite my initial misgivings I had found my session with Madea really useful. I'm of the old school that still sees mental health issues as a weakness, not to be discussed in polite company but rather to be kept to oneself. A taboo subject, and yet she had a way of making me feel comfortable about my feelings and of talking about them openly. It was as if she was my best friend and confidante and, as I turned away and headed to the kitchen, I found I was already looking forward to seeing her again.

On a strictly professional level, you understand.

I made myself a cup of coffee and pondered what Madea had said about researching my parents. Mum's (Clara would always be 'mum' to me) box was upstairs, waiting for me to go through it.

Did it contain any information about my birth parents?

Well, there was only one way to find out.

I finished my coffee and headed for the stairs.

# Chapter Eleven
## Clara's Letter

It was with a certain amount of trepidation that I picked the box up from the floor and placed it carefully on the bureau. It was just a tatty old cardboard box, frayed at the edges and held together with old Sellotape that had turned brown with age. It was quite heavy from all the paper it contained and yet, here I was I treating it with the same sort of reverence that a museum concierge might give to a Fabergé Egg. The box contained my mother's personal effects. I don't mean bank books and stuff like that, I'd dealt with those months ago, settled her finances, closed her accounts, cashed in her ISAs and sold her house.

No, this box contained her diaries; private letters written between her and dad when they were courting; and her University degree certificate. It was a record of her real life, her private life. There were photos of Larry and me as boys, and some of Uncle Anthony, Larry's dad. A couple were of two young men in uniform. On the back of one was written John Hilliard, Dec 1942 and the on the other was David Hilliard, Jan 1944. John and David. Our uncles. They had both had been killed in the Second World War. I could see the resemblance to Uncle Anthony in the two young men and I thought about Grandad Edward's journal that I had started reading but hadn't finished. It seems war has a habit of destroying the innocent, I thought, as I studied the photographs of John and David; two men who would never grow old, killed in their prime because of one madman's desire for power.

There were photos of mum and dad's wedding in 1953. Mum was twenty-one and dad was twenty-three when they were wed, and they were happily married for fifty-eight years until dad died in 2012. I put the photo to one side, intending to get a frame so I could put it on display.

About two thirds of the way down the pile of documents I found a thick brown A4 envelope with my name on. I pulled it out and stared at it. On the outside my mother had written, *To James Read. Warning: Only open if you want to learn about your true parents.*

I smiled at the overly dramatic comment. She had always known of my reluctance to know anything about my parents, who they were and what they did because I felt they had abandoned me. Clara had also made it clear to me that, when I was ready, then she would be happy to tell me everything I wanted to know. She had even taken the trouble to write it all down, in case the opportunity never arose. And it hadn't.

I felt a lump in my throat as I sat down at the bureau and, with shaking hands, opened the envelope and pulled out a stack of paper written in mum's fine hand. I read;

*My Darling James*

*It has always been a great regret to me that I haven't taken the opportunity to tell you about your dear mother and father, Caroline and Christopher Walters. Please forgive me for this terrible omission; it's something I should have told you when you were still a little boy but the longer I delayed telling you the more difficult it became to do so and the more you grew to hate the parents you believe had abandoned you. It's entirely my fault that I've not told you this story when I should have done so many years ago, and it's entirely my fault that you have grown to despise your parents rather than love them as you should have done. I hope you can find it in your heart to forgive me for depriving you of this information. I should have sat you down and made you listen long before you first found out you were adopted and now, regretfully, I'm dead. I know this because that's the only way you'll ever get to read this account and if I'm dead then I have died with regret and guilt, not knowing whether I've earned your forgiveness or not. I suppose God will now be my judge.*

*The truth is, your mother was my best friend and would have given you more love than I ever could if only … but I'm sure you want to know all about her first, so I'll tell you everything I know. This account starts a few years before we first met.*

*Your mother was christened Caroline Butler and was born on July 16th, 1934 to James and Gwendoline Butler, who ran a butcher's shop in Tilbury High Street, in south Essex. She was the younger of two children, her brother John being ten years older. In September 1939, with the impending outbreak of war in Europe and the threat of bombing in London, thousands of children were evacuated to the country as part of Operation Pied Piper and, as Tilbury Docks were a likely target for Hitler's bombs Caroline and John were amongst the first evacuees.*

*So, at just five years old, she was put on a train with her fifteen-year-old brother and sent to stay with Gerald and Rosemary Alderton in Sutton Courtney.*

*They were a kind couple with a seventeen-year-old son of their own, Henry, who made it his job to introduce the two children to life in the country and the beauty of nature. John and Henry became good friends during that time.*

*Rosemary regularly wrote to Gwendoline to keep her updated about her children; how they were coping at school; what they were eating; how they were sleeping and what friends they were making, to reassure her that her children were happy as well as safe.*

*Towards the end of 1939, and what was referred to as 'The Phoney War', Caroline and her brother returned home to Tilbury for Christmas and, for a while the war didn't seem to be going our way. Our soldiers were defeated in Europe and evacuated in the spring of 1940 – I was only eight years old myself and, growing up in Rosehip Hall, I was quite sheltered from all the news and was quite unaware of what was happening. I do remember my father talking about the war to my older brothers, John and David, who were teenagers then. I remember he was adamant that none of his sons would go to war and suffer what he had. He ran the family business and engineering was a reserved occupation, but both John and David insisted on signing up as soon as they were old enough. They both died for their bravery, or stupidity; I've never really understood the difference between the two. John was twenty and David nineteen when they were killed and the only reason your Uncle Anthony didn't go to war too was that it was over by the time he was old enough to go.*

*Anyway, I digress; I've always been good at that.*

*After Dunkirk, Hitler sent his Luftwaffe over to try and defeat us in the air and when, after several weeks, that failed, he instigated the Blitz which killed forty-three thousand people in London.*

*In the autumn of 1940, just a day after taking your mother and her brother back to stay with Gerald and Rosemary in Sutton Courtney, a squadron of German bombers released their load over Tilbury aiming to destroy the docks, and scored a direct hit on their little butcher's shop in the High Street, killing Gwendoline and James instantly.*

*Caroline was six and John sixteen when Hitler made them orphans. Three years later, when he was just nineteen, John, who had joined the RAF a year earlier, was shot down and killed during a bombing raid* over Holland, leaving Caroline alone.

You would think that for someone so young to lose so much she would bear a grudge against the nation that destroyed her life; many people who lost a lot less hated the Germans for years afterwards, but not Caroline. She had a big heart and a lot of love. Gerald and Rosemary loved her dearly and were allowed to adopt her after the war, otherwise she would have been sent to an orphanage.

I first met Caroline in the autumn of 1953. I had recently married David whom I met when we were both up at Oxford. I was studying English at Lady Margaret Hall and he was studying Theology at Brasenose. I think I may have told you before that we met through the Oxford University Amateur Dramatic Society and we were married soon after I graduated. David had already joined the Church and, shortly after we were married, he was appointed vicar of Sutton Courtney.

Caroline was one of our parishioners. She was nineteen by then, and we instantly became good friends. We were close in age and we seemed to have so much in common, despite our different backgrounds. I remember her happy outlook on life and wondering how could someone who had lost so much have so much love to give? She could bring a smile to anyone's face and I never once saw her sad or complain or act bitter about the way life had treated her.

Because Caroline was so young when her parents died, she didn't know anything about her family background. She thought her mother may have mentioned having a sister when she was very little, but she couldn't be sure, and all the records were lost in the blitz. She did plan on researching it one day but you know how it is when you're young. There's so much to do and finding out about a long-lost relative that you weren't even sure existed wasn't a priority and she never got around to it. And then it was too late.

Caroline was drawn to the church, she sought solace in God, and she became my best helper. She helped me organise all sorts of events such as the Church Fete, jumble sales and the Women's Group. She arranged the Church flowers, the Church Social and the Vicar's Tea party. I couldn't have asked for a better friend; she was my rock. Whenever I felt things were becoming too much for me, she was there by my side supporting me. Her energy was boundless.

I hope that by now, dearest James, you are beginning to form a good opinion of your mother. You couldn't have met a better person. Compared to her I am a mere shadow beneath her beacon of light.

*When she met Christopher Walters, your dear father, in 1954, she swept him off his feet and I don't think I've ever seen anyone so much in love as they were. They were besotted with each other.*

*Christopher was also a wonderful man and a churchgoer. He moved to the village and, within months, he was running the Church choir. He and Caroline had so much in common, it was as though they really were made for each other. In 1955 they asked David to marry them in his Church.*

*Of course, we were delighted and come the day the Church was packed. Christopher rehearsed his choir and Caroline organised her own flowers. Oh, it was such a lovely day, they were so happy. They honeymooned in Bournemouth. People didn't fly off to exotic places in those days and holidays were spent in one of our many beautiful coastal holiday resorts, travelling by train because not many of us could afford cars.*

*A few months later Caroline knocked on my door and I knew from the excitement on her face that she was going to tell me she was pregnant, and I was right.*

*I must confess, I cried when she told me. I was so happy for her but my happiness was tinged with sadness too. You see, David and I so desperately wanted to start our own family but God, in His infinite wisdom, had decided not to bless us with children. For the first time in my life I felt jealous and I was so angry with myself for allowing the green-eyed monster to raise its ugly head, but I was also strong, and I didn't allow it to consume me. Instead I rejoiced in Caroline's happiness and supported her through the early stages when she was suffering from morning sickness. Once she got over that she blossomed. As you grew inside her she became even more beautiful and she was so happy.*

*How many nights I lay awake in bed wishing it was my body that was growing that little baby instead of hers; how many tears I cried.*

*I remember the knocking at our door before dawn that morning, it was Christopher calling me to let me know Caroline was in labour. I rushed to their house to be with her. The midwife was already there, and I sat with Caroline and held her hand as her contractions wracked her body. But it soon became apparent that her labour was not going well, and we sent Christopher to get the doctor as Caroline had started bleeding, which was not a good sign.*

*The doctor and the midwife worked together for what seemed like hours and all the time I held Caroline's hand. Eventually, an ambulance was called.*

*At one point Caroline grasped my hand tightly and said, "Save my baby, please just save my baby."*

*They did save the baby but, to our distress, they couldn't stop the haemorrhaging and by the time the ambulance arrived, Caroline had died in my arms.*

*She was only twenty-three years old.*

*I was devastated looking down at her white, lifeless body lying there. How I wept for my dear friend and for her poor little boy, so helpless, who would grow up without a mother. The whole village mourned; it was a much smaller village back then and everyone knew everyone, and they all loved Caroline. When we held her funeral a few weeks later we couldn't get everyone into the Church.*

*Your mother was buried in our churchyard and the village raised the money to pay for a suitable headstone. You must go and visit it.*

*Poor Christopher. He was so in love with Caroline, and her sudden and unexpected death hit him harder than any of us. I don't think he really recovered and, shortly afterwards he accidentally set fire to his house after spending an evening drinking his way through a bottle of whiskey. Fortunately, you were staying with us that night; David and I were your Godparents and we often had you to stay so Christopher could work. Besides, looking after you made me happy. It made me feel as though I had my own little baby boy.*

*Christopher was saved from the fire, but it became clear that he was unwell. Back then there was no real understanding of mental health. It's a relatively new concept, you were either sane or insane and Christopher was declared insane and sent to the local asylum (in those days there were mental asylums in most major towns and cities).*

*We fostered you while Christopher recovered from what nowadays would be classed as severe depression and, after a few months, he was allowed home.*

*He came and stayed with us at the vicarage where he could be nursed and looked after, but he still wasn't well and one morning I got up to make breakfast and found him hanging from the stairs in the hall.*

*At the inquest the Coroner concluded that he had 'killed himself whilst the balance of his mind was disturbed' and, although no blame was ever apportioned, I've always felt guilty for not doing more to help him. How I wish I could have seen and understood the anguish he must have been going through; so terrible that it drove him to take his own life. There have even been times over the years when I wondered if I, somehow, caused their deaths; that by wishing so much that it could be me who was having the baby, that I coveted you so much that I somehow made it happen. That somehow, I had killed them.*

*I went through long periods of guilt in those early months and years and every time I gazed down at your sleeping face all I could see was your dear mother; my best friend; and I prayed for forgiveness.*

*My darling James, it pains me that I did not tell you this story when I was still alive to give you comfort. I only hope that David and I have been the best parents to you that we could have been, and I hope we gave you a happy life.*

*So, you see, you must not think badly of your true parents, Caroline and Christopher. They would have given you all the love you would ever have wanted; it's me whom you should despise for not making sure you knew this story many years ago. I hope you can find it in your heart to forgive me for my transgressions; or do I go to my grave condemned to live forever in purgatory, atoning for my sins until judgement day?*

*Whatever you decide please know this; you've always been loved.*

Tears were rolling down my cheeks as I dropped the letter onto the table of the bureau, and I buried my face in my hands.

I hadn't been abandoned after all. I hadn't been unwanted and given up for adoption as I thought I had been. It had never occurred to me that my parents had both died and certainly not in such tragic circumstances.

An acute wave of guilt swept through me. My overwhelming thought was that it was all my fault. My mother had died to give life to me; she had died because of me and, as a result my father had taken his own life because I had taken away from him the one person he loved. Both my parents were churchgoers, I thought, but where was their God when they needed Him? Why did He have to punish them so?

Why did He have to punish me? What had I ever done?

I wondered whether there was a curse on my family. My parents both died leaving me, a baby, orphaned. My mother's parents had been killed by a German bomb when she was just six years old, leaving her an orphan too.

There was nothing in the box that I could see about any family before my grandmother Gwendoline or my grandfather James, but I think, right then, I didn't want to know any more; it was already too tragic.

All kinds of emotions swept through me as I stood up.

Anger at my adoptive mother for keeping this information from me for all these years, then anger at myself for being angry with her. It wasn't fair, I reasoned, to be angry with Clara, after all, I had made it very clear that I hadn't wanted to know. But on the other hand, she could have told me I was adopted when I was a child; I would have coped with it. Why wouldn't I?

My anger then turned to Christopher. He had hanged himself and left me an orphan. How could someone do that? How could he do that? How could he do that to me?

He was suffering with depression, I reminded myself, and when you're depressed you don't think straight. I know this. I know this from my own experience, and I realised that my anger was being fuelled by my own depression that was suddenly returning in the form of a big black cloud. Unwelcome though it was, it filled the room, flowing around me and stifling the air, constricting my throat. I was gripped with an uncontrollable panic. I was being closed in, suffocated and I gagged, desperately trying to draw breath. It felt like I was being trapped inside a shrinking box that was deliberately sucking the oxygen out of the room.

My breath came in short, sharp pants as I gasped for air. The walls pulsated as they closed in on me. A cold sweat broke out all over my body as the room began to sway. I lost my balance and fell to the floor.

In my panic I scrambled to my feet and fled the room, banging against the door and stumbling.

And bumped into Larry on the landing.

"Steady on, old chap," he said, grabbing me by my shoulders. I guess he saw the look of terror in my eyes because he held me tight, stroking his hand down my back and whispering soothing words in my ear.

The panic that had gripped me so suddenly, gradually subsided and the darkness slowly lifted from my mind.

"It's alright," he said, "it's alright."

As I relaxed Larry let me go and took a step back. He looked into my eyes and said, "I only came up to tell you your fish is cooked."

# Chapter Twelve
## Forever Autumn

"How have you really been?" Leanne asked, hooking her arm through mine as we strolled together along the woodland path, away from the Hall and towards the river. She and Harry were down for the weekend with the children and, although we were having a fun time I knew Leanne wanted to talk to me on my own. When Harry had announced that he and Larry were taking the children to a soft-play area in nearby Witchford, I knew what was coming. "And be honest with me."

"Better," I replied, turning to her with a smile. "Honest. Being here, at the Hall, being with Larry, it all helps. At home I was alone with my memories and I was in pain. I still miss your mother, I miss her so much and there are times when I can feel myself slipping back into the void, and if I was alone I know I would. But Larry's here for me. He helps."

"I'm glad."

I didn't mention the episode I'd had after reading mum's letter. Larry had taken me downstairs and we'd had lunch and we'd talked about everything other than what had just happened. Larry never pushed me into things and, after lunch, as we set out to do some more digging in the kitchen garden, I told him about Clara's letter and what she'd written, who I was and why I was adopted. I worked hard that afternoon and it made me feel better.

Leanne and I walked along in comfortable silence, listening to the light breeze blowing through the naked branches overhead and rustling the leaves piled up on the ground around us. Ahead, a squirrel was sat upright on the path eating an acorn. When he saw us approaching, he dropped his snack and bounded for the nearest tree, staying as far away from us as possible whilst remaining as close to his discarded snack as he dared. All around us the damp, musty smells of autumn lingered; of rotting leaves and wet mud.

In years gone by autumn had always seemed to me to be a season of hope. The way the leaves created a myriad of beautiful colours as they danced sensuously on the wayward breezes; watching the long, scarlet sunsets through the steam of your breath in the cold crisp evening air; the droplets of dew revealing a hundred thousand strands of spider's web woven through the branches of rose bushes and hawthorn and low mists that hugged the ground like a blanket of cotton wool. All these sights and sensations had always seemed to offer me a glimpse of things to come, of something beautiful. Now, without Janet by my side, they became portents of my loneliness and seemed as cold and final as death itself.

For a moment I stood and wondered whether I would feel cold like autumn forever. I smiled to myself. Forever autumn, just like the song. In that moment I felt the words speak to me in a way they never had before.

Earlier I had shown Leanne what we had accomplished in the kitchen garden. She was impressed. We had made some good progress over the last few weeks. One of the beds was not only cleared but all planted up with spring vegetables. The whole place was looking tidier than it had for many years. We had pruned the fruit trees and cut back the bramble. There was still plenty more to do and, I think we both looked forward to the couple of hours we spent there most days, when it wasn't raining too hard.

"I found a letter from your Grandmother in her private box."

"What, that tatty old grey cardboard box that she used to keep in her cupboard under the stairs?"

"Yes, that one."

"What did it say?"

"It was an account of my real mum and dad,"

We approached the river at the turn of the path.

"Really?"

We sat down in Uncle Anthony's shelter overlooking the river and I recounted mum's letter in as much detail as I could. When I finished, she sat in silence for a few minutes. Finally, she took a deep breath and said, "Wow, what a tragic story."

A flash of blue from an overhanging branch caught my eye and we watched a kingfisher dart into the river and return to the branch with a minnow clasped in its beak.

"Now you know a bit more about your family," she said, as we sat and watched the bird finish its snack then launch itself into the water for seconds, "are you going to pursue it?"

"I don't know," I replied. "Not yet anyway. I know something about my parents and my grandparents, that's usually as much as most people know about their ancestors. Besides, look at what we've got. My mother: died in childbirth; my father: hanged himself whilst suffering from severe depression; my Uncle: killed in action in the second world war; my grandparents: killed by a German bomb in the blitz. It makes pretty miserable reading."

"Lots of people lost family during the war. What about Granny's two brothers, John and David? They were killed in the war too."

"Grandfather Edward lost his leg in the trenches and great grandfather William was murdered, here at the Hall, not long after world war one."

"Whatever you find out about your real great grandparents," she laughed, "it can't really be worse than what happened to him, can it?"

"No," I replied, smiling back, "I guess it can't."

We stood up and started walking along the river. The wind was getting up again and there was a bitter feel to it as it cut right through us. Leanne held onto me for warmth and I felt comforted by her presence. She was so like her mother that it felt like I was walking with her again.

"Didn't you tell me you read some of Edward's diary?"

"I did. I started reading it," I replied, "but I never finished it. I read about his time in the trenches in 1918, which was, by all accounts, rather brutal, but that's as far as I got with it."

"Why did you stop?"

"No reason really. I just got distracted by other things, like the gardening, my counselling, mum's letter."

Which was true, up to a point. Larry was keeping me busy to prevent me from relapsing into depression, I suppose, and Clara's letter had ended up being more important. After all, it was about me and the family I knew nothing about.

I made a mental note to dig out the diary and read the rest of it, for curiosity as much as anything else.

After all, it was a rather interesting read.

# Chapter Thirteen
## Edward's Journal – Spring 1918

On Sunday afternoon after Leanne, Harry and the grandchildren had departed, it started to rain, so I announced that I was going to retire to the library to read more of Edward's diary.

"That's fine by me," Larry said as we walked back into the Hall, "I shall settle down in the smoking room with a nice cup of tea and read the paper."

Larry must be one of the few people I know who still had a Sunday paper delivered. Sometimes we would watch the paper boy, weighed down by the myriad of supplements, sections and advertising material, struggling up the drive. Larry always gave him a generous bonus at Christmas for all his hard work. There was so much to the Sunday paper these days and it generally kept us in reading material for the whole week. Most of the time we even managed to finish the crossword by Tuesday or Wednesday.

A warm fire burned in the grate as I settled myself in the library, picked up the journal and resumed where I had previously left off.

April 1st, 1918

The sound of distant groans disturbed the silence. My body ached, and parts of it felt numb. The groaning grew louder, less distant, and, through a haze of pain I gradually became aware of a bright light shining through my flickering eyelids. I was lying on my back and I assumed I was where I had fallen after the explosion. As my mind struggled with the intense pain all I wanted to do was to slide back into unconsciousness. How I wished whoever was making the groaning noises would stop.

"Captain Hilliard?"

I felt a hand on my arm, and I tried to turn my head and open my eyes, but both simple actions seemed difficult. Tt was at that moment I realised the groaning I could hear was mine.

The white light caused me to blink as I finally managed to force my eyes open. After a few moments to focus I could make out dark shapes moving in front of me and I heard my name said once again.

The dark shapes began to take form and the face of an angel smiled at me.

"Am I in heaven?" I croaked.

Her laugh was like the jingle of tiny bells, "No, not this time."

At last my eyes became accustomed to the light and I could see the lady standing beside me. She wore a grey cape with scarlet facings over a grey dress with white cuffs above which were two scarlet bands about an inch wide. To the lapel of her cape was pinned a circular badge with the letter R in the centre, and a white muslin cap covered her dark curls which framed her round face. Her dark eyes and full red lips smiled down at me.

"Wh-who are you?"

"I'm nurse Andrews," she replied, taking hold of my wrist.

"Where …?"

"Shh," she said, "I'm trying to take your pulse."

Having completed that task, she slid a thermometer into my mouth.

"Make sure it's beneath your tongue," she instructed, "and make sure you don't bite it. Mercury doesn't taste very nice."

I stared up at her while I was waiting for her to remove the thermometer. She wasn't what most men would class as pretty, although that may have been something to do with her uniform and the angle at which I was seeing her, but I did find her quite attractive. Her accent suggested good breeding but not from a family of class. A governess maybe, or a schoolteacher.

"Where am I?" I asked as soon as the thermometer was out of my mouth, "What date is it? Where are you from? What happened to my men?"

"Whoa, slow down," she replied with a laugh, "one thing at a time. You are in a field hospital just outside Amiens, about five miles behind our lines. You were brought here from the casualty clearing station at the front line the day after the explosion. Today is April 1st. I am a nurse with Queen Alexandra's Imperial Military Nursing Service and I'm sorry, but I have no idea what became of your men. Now, how do you feel right now?"

"In pain, a lot of pain. And I seem to have no feeling in parts of my body."

While I had been lying there with the thermometer in my mouth, I had been mentally checking on various parts of my body. I had been making slight movements to check everything was still working. Everything hurt but it all seemed to move when instructed to, although my legs were numb.

"I'll get the doctor."

"I suppose what you'll do is patch me up and send me back to the front. Isn't that what you do?"

"Not this time, Captain," another voice said. I looked to my left and saw a man of about thirty, in a long white coat, holding a clipboard and studying what was written on it. Thick stubble on his chin and dark rings beneath his eyes suggested he'd hardly slept in days; he looked washed out.

"I'm Doctor Taylor." We shook hands and he said, "The war's over for you, I'm afraid."

I think I probably laughed. That wasn't how it worked. You got injured, they patched you up, they sent you back. I'd seen plenty of men who thought they were going home returned to the trenches sporting filthy, bloodstained bandages. We didn't have the luxury of being able to return men home.

"Really?" I replied, and he must have seen the scepticism in my eyes.

"Really, truly. You are lucky to be alive, Captain," he said, taking a seat beside my bed, "you took a near direct hit from a German shell and you've been badly injured. We've been waiting to stabilise you before bringing you round so that we can prepare you for the trip home."

A vision flashed through my mind; of darkness, an explosion, of me flying through the air, a scorching heat, the breath being knocked from my body on impact. I opened my eyes, and the realisation of what had happened hit me.

"I've been burnt, haven't I?" I said, "How bad is it?"

"Your burns are serious enough, but they'll heal. They'll leave scars, but they'll heal," he said, avoiding my eye, "but there's more, I'm afraid. You lost your right leg in the explosion."

At first I didn't think I'd heard him right, I was sure he'd said I'd lost my right leg, but a moment ago I'd been moving it. I told him so.

"I'm afraid it's true," he continued, "and it's not unusual to feel a limb that isn't there. Sometimes the nerves in your body still feel it. We call it phantom limb syndrome."

"So, I've really lost my right leg?"

"Just above the knee. Sorry."

I closed my eyes and with my mind I checked my body once again. I realised with a start that I could feel no pain from below my right knee. Just a numbness.

"My right leg?" I felt that if I kept saying right leg it might magically be there again.

"Yes, Captain." He must have gone through this same conversation with hundreds of soldiers during his time in the field hospital.

"You cut off my leg?" I was now going through the indignant stage. How dare they cut off my leg without me knowing about it?

"No Captain, we didn't, it was blown off by the Germans. We did manage to save the rest of you though."

"Yeah, what's left of me. I think I'd rather have died out there than be mutilated like this. What use am I with only one leg?" I was raising my voice, becoming hysterical. "No use at all. I'll be sent back to England to be paraded and pitied; I'll be …hey."

I felt a slight sharp pain in my right arm, like a mosquito bite, and turned my head. The nurse was injecting me with something, and I felt a cold sensation spreading up my arm and flowing into my body.

"He's getting distressed," I heard a voice saying from a nearby cloud.

"Morphine …" another whispered from a faraway hill.

The pain slowly subsided and I felt myself floating away, high above the bed on a mattress of soft flowers and cotton wool. I felt an overwhelming sense of peace and tranquillity as I drifted away into a hazy darkness and I remember thinking that it was April Fool's day today and that it was I who must be the fool.

April 7th, 1918

I don't remember anything much about the last week. It must be the morphine they keep injecting into me, but they've either run out or stopped giving it to me because this morning I was woken by a deafening noise.

I am lying in some sort of cot in a makeshift hospital. Presumably I'm still just outside Amiens as I'm not aware of being moved during my periods of unconsciousness. It's dark and it's cold.

Blinding flashes of light lit up the room in fluorescent silver grey, creating silhouettes of my surroundings. A stupendous clap of thunder ripped through the air. The sound of the rain, hammering down on the canvass roof above was loud enough to drown out most of the screams of my fellow patients. Probably my own too.

The flashes. The bangs. The screams. How relentlessly they all surged through my head. Echoing. As they reached their crescendo, I was transported, once again, to my trench with a barrage of German shells, exploding about me. I tried to marshal my men to safety but when I tried to follow them I found I was strapped down, unable to move.

I was gripped by an uncontrollable fear. Cold sweat broke out all over my body and my overriding thought was of running away. I wanted, no needed, to run away. Wanting to run made me feel like a coward and I heard my father's voice telling me to act like a man. All I wanted to do was run. Get away. I couldn't. I couldn't run. I couldn't escape the bombardment in my head and as I thrashed about in my cot, I finally heard my screams above the noise of the pounding rain, and I was sickened by them.

Another series of lightning flashes lit up the room, accompanied by further deafening claps of thunder.

I was no longer in control of my emotions; I was overwhelmed by the need to escape from the battle raging in my head. I felt as though, at any moment, my head would explode, and in the ensuing darkness, I wished it would and so put me out of my misery.

Strong hands gripped my arms as I tried to leap from the bed.

Voices from far away called to me, but they were so distant, and I couldn't make out what they were saying. I tried calling to them, letting them know where I was.

Cold numbness once again seeped through my right arm and into my body and, once again, I settled comfortably into the arms of darkness.

April 14th, 1918

I've been awake for a few days now and nurse Andrews (I must find out what her Christian name is) told me that they've tried lowering my dose of morphine as they want to get me fit enough to manage the Channel crossing so that they can send me home. She also told me that they didn't want me to start becoming dependant on it.

This morning, while I was lying there staring into space, I began to wonder whether they sold shoes singly as I no longer need a complete pair. Would I have to buy both and then look for someone who only needed the same size right foot? That way we could share the cost.

Sergeant Jennings came to see me later and I shared this question with him. For some reason he found it amusing.

Then he told me that Harris, Morrison, Crawley and Osborne were all dead, along with ninety-seven more of my men. Ten more were alive but seriously injured, having lost an arm, a leg, or both, or all. The remainder had been, for the most part, patched up and were to be granted home leave before returning to the front in a few weeks' time.

We talked some more about inconsequential things until the nurse came along and sent him away, telling him I needed to rest. He shook my hand. "It was an honour to serve with you, sir," he said, then stood to attention and saluted. I smiled and returned the salute as best I could. "You too, Mike," I replied. It was the first time I had used his Christian name and I think I saw a tear in his eye as he turned and marched away.

It was when he had gone that the information really sank in. One hundred of my men had lost their lives. One hundred men with whom I'd shared mud and cigarettes, bullets and jokes. One hundred men who would never return home. I wept.

I wept for the men with whom I'd stood, shoulder to shoulder, who had become friends.

I wept for the wives and girlfriends they'd left behind.

I wept for their mothers and fathers and reflected that no parent should ever have to bury their children.

I wept for their children, those lucky enough to have had them, who were left orphaned by the madness taking place in a muddy field in a corner of Belgium.

I wept for the futility of war and wondered what it hoped to achieve.

April 17th, 1918

Amelia. That was nurse Andrews' Christian name, Amelia. Anyway, Amelia told me this morning that she was going to change my dressing. It wasn't the first time she had done this, but all the other times I had been unconscious, so this was a first for me and I was both eager and scared at the prospect.

First, she took my temperature and measured my pulse.

"All normal," she informed me with a smile. "Your fever's gone, and your heartbeat has slowed to a more normal rate. A few more days and we'll be putting you on that boat back to England."

"Thanks."

"Oh, don't be thanking me," she said, "all I've done is serve you food, wash your face and wipe your arse."

"And change my dressing."

"That too. Now, lie back while I do it again."

"No, I'm going to sit up and watch." I shuffled myself into an upright position so I could see what she was doing.

"Fair enough, it's your leg."

"Well, strictly speaking that's not true, is it? My leg is lying somewhere out there in a stinking puddle of mud, rotting away and feeding the rats."

I was trying for a bit of levity, but it came out a bit darker than I had anticipated and Amelia screwed up her nose in disgust. In truth I was devastated at having lost my leg. I was also suffering from bad dreams. I was tired, my nerves felt frayed, I was scared, and I was uncertain.

There had been no repeat of last week's massive storm, but it was turning out to be another very wet month. It's funny but when I was in the trenches and it rained, I hardly even noticed it. We were perpetually wet and cold; we shivered the whole time and yet we just got on with it. Lying in my hospital bed with nothing else to do I was acutely aware of the rain, of the noise it made on the roof above my head, of the noise it made on the leaves of the bushes outside, and of the noise of it splashing in the puddles.

The makeshift ward I was on was crammed with wounded soldiers of all ranks. I became used to the pervading stench of death mixed with rotting flesh, blood, piss and shit. Not even the copious buckets of bleach they used, or the fact that we were almost outside, could disguise it.

There was a high turnover of patients as so many soldiers who came in died from their injuries. Only three of us had been there for any length of time. We called the tent 'The Terminal', because for most men that's exactly what it was; terminal. Very few got out alive.

No one had expected me to survive when I was brought in, but I had managed to prove them wrong.

Despite the squalor of our surroundings the bandage around my leg was remarkably clean, at least on the outside. Amelia carefully unwound it, then peeled back the lint sock that covered my stump.

Nearly a month had passed since the explosion that had ended my war and the stump was still red and inflamed. The doctors had cleaned it and sewn the flaps of flesh over the end to cover the splintered bone. A thick yellow pus oozed from between the joins and Amelia drew in a sharp breath.

90

"A little infection still," she said, pouring something over it.

"Owww!" I said, recoiling with pain, "what's that?"

"Relax, it's just a mild saline solution," she told me. "Now, hold still and stop acting like a baby."

"Saline? You're pouring salt into my wounds? Why don't you use an antiseptic?"

"Doctor Taylor studied under a Doctor Fleming who says that antiseptic on wounds like yours causes tissue damage. He says wounds respond better to being cleaned with saline solution, allowing the body's own mechanisms to heal them, so that's what you get and by the look of your leg it seems he is right. Apart from a slight residual infection, this is healing up nicely."

"It looks a mess to me."

"Oh, this is neat, believe me," she assured me, "there are a lot that are much worse than this."

"That's not reassuring," I replied, lying back with a smile.

"Doctor Taylor is an excellent surgeon working under dreadful conditions. He's one of the best, so you're lucky."

"It seems I can't stop being lucky."

"Yes, well, your luck might just be holding. By the look of this I think he might allow you to travel in a few days."

Almost as if on cue Doctor Taylor appeared and gave me a big smile.

"Nurse Andrews looking after you?" he asked.

"Well, she changed my dressing," I replied, "but she refused to jump into bed with me."

I noticed Amelia blush and I laughed at her discomfort.

"I'm only joking," I said with a smile. "Actually, we were just talking about you," I told him, sitting up again.

"Nothing nice, I trust?" He quipped. "Now let's have a look at this, shall we."

I winced as he squeezed my stump.

"Hurt?"

"Like buggery," I replied.

"That's good, that means you have feeling there."

"Oh," I said. "Good."

He sat down, produced a packet of cigarettes from the pocket of his white coat and offered me one.

I inhaled deeply, drawing the soothing smoke into my lungs, allowing it to remain there momentarily before exhaling it.

"So, how's it really doing?" I asked.

"Actually, pretty good, I'd say. You're quite lucky, you know."

"So I keep being told," I replied. "Now define lucky."

"Well," he hesitated, "I meant you're lucky to be alive after that explosion. Most of your division didn't make it. I've never seen such a barrage in all the time I've been out here, it was quite a show. The Germans breached our lines in several places and pushed us back nearly half a mile before we were able to stop them. Their offensive continued but it's stalled now and we're managing to hold them back."

"All those dead for half a mile stretch of saturated mud in the middle of nowhere. What's the fucking point?"

"It's just where it happened, I suppose. It's where we managed to stop their advance in 1915, and it's been stuck there or thereabouts ever since. Ten yards gained here, ten yards lost there; it's what war is all about. Anyway, they'll be exhausted by now. Then, I guess, it'll be our turn. Only this time it will be without you because I reckon in a few days' time you'll be fit enough to get on that boat to England."

"Where will I go then?"

"Well, there are hospitals all over the place. I don't really know where they'll send you but I'll make a note and see if they can get you somewhere near home if possible. Where do you live?"

"Near Ely, in Cambridgeshire. Cambridge, Downham Market, Huntingdon are all close."

"Ely? The little town with the big cathedral?"

"Actually, it's a city, not a town."

"Really?"

"Yes, and it has the distinction of being the smallest city in Britain."

"I didn't know that. I have been there, though. I studied medicine at Cambridge, and we rowed there one weekend."

He wrote something on my notes and excused himself.

"Right," Amelia said, returning as Doctor Taylor moved to see to his next patient, "let's get this dressed again. First, some Vaseline."

"Vaseline? What for?"

"It'll stop the skin around the wound from drying out. We need to keep it supple and hydrated otherwise it will crack and cause you problems. Also, it's really good on wounds as it seals them and protects them from dirt and germs."

She was being gentle as she rubbed it over the end of my leg, but I still winced.

92

"Sorry."

"It's sore."

"Sure it is, but remember this; it's better today than it was yesterday and it's worse today than it'll be tomorrow."

"Thanks. I'll try and bear it in mind."

Five minutes later and my ugly stump was dressed and wrapped in a fresh bandage.

In the distance the faint sounds of explosions reminded me of the battles being fought several miles away and I closed my eyes to pray for the lives of those poor, brave men.

April 20th, 1918

I received a letter from Constance today.

*March 30th, 1918*

*Dear Eddie,*

*Jolly bad luck on you to get shot up like that, mummy tells me that you lost a leg. That's a bit rotten but she says they'll give you one of those pathetic legs when you get back, so you'll still be able to walk.*

*I had to have my sixteenth birthday party without you, which made me a bit sad, but I couldn't wait until you were well enough because I don't know when that'll be and I might be seventeen by then and mummy said we had to have it before Bill goes off in May so only one brother misses it. Sorry, maybe we can celebrate it when you get home as well, that way I'll get two parties.*

*I got a puppy dog from mummy and daddy. I don't think daddy likes her all that much; she barks a lot and the other day she did a poo in the hall and daddy was really cross. I wanted to have a sausage dog but daddy said I couldn't have one of those because sausage dogs are German and we don't like the Germans anymore, so I got a Yorkshire terrier instead and I've called her Bunty. Bunty adores going for runs in the grounds and when I take her for walks she wees at least a hundred times. Bill says she does that to mark her territory but I'm worried that there might be something wrong with her, after all, I don't go around weeing all over the grounds when I go for a walk. I think I'll take her to the vet and get her looked at.*

*I also got some new dresses which are all the fashion. I look really pretty in them and I've asked daddy if I can go to the summer ball in Ely this year. He said he'll see, which means no, so I'll have to ask mummy*

93

*to try and persuade him.*

*I love the set of watercolour paints you sent me, thank you so much. I'm going to paint a pretty picture for you which you can have when you get home.*

*I miss you so much. Bill is all serious now he's about to go off and be a soldier and Ed is all sulky and mopes about all day because he is too young to go yet.*

*I hope you're not annoying all those pretty nurses who are trying to make you better,*

*Lots and lots of love,*

*Constance xxx*

Her letters were always charming to read. Constance, being the only girl and my youngest sibling, was self-centred and vain in the most delightful way. She was also a bit empty-headed, which comes from having a father who doesn't believe women should be allowed do anything except sew, drink tea and gossip, all of which Constance did with remarkable aplomb. She was always happy, always enthusiastic and I loved her dearly. My two brothers were a bit pompous and were much more like our father than I was.

I had to stop for a moment after reading her first paragraph because I was laughing at her mistaken use of pathetic rather than prosthetic, although, on reflection, maybe it wasn't so stupid after all. Pathetic was probably more appropriate. A false limb for all those poor, pathetic sods returning from war no longer in one piece.

Amelia was right though I was one of the lucky ones. I may be leaving a part of my body behind in those foul trenches but there were many thousands who were leaving their minds behinds and there were no prosthetic minds to replace them. What a sad state they were in.

April 22nd, 1918

I'm leaving here today. Just after breakfast this morning a couple of orderlies came to collect me. Before they came Amelia changed my dressing. One last time she said, then gave me a hug and kissed me.

"I'm going to miss you," she said. "Now, you mind how you go and make sure you're nice to those nurses at whatever hospital they send you to."

"I'm going to miss you too," I admitted. "I've kind of grown accustomed to having you around." In truth I'd grown quite fond of her and I would miss her cheery smile and her tender touch when she changed my dressing. "Thank you. You know, for everything."

I was stretchered into the back of the Red Cross army van with one other stretcher and four walking wounded and we were bounced across the fields of Belgium to the nearest railway station. Most of the ambulance journey was through muddy fields, pock-marked with craters and strewn with debris from the multitude of bombs that had exploded there over the last few years, changing the landscape forever. All around us were burnt out buildings and barns, dead trees reduced to branchless trunks, stubs of fence posts, blackened by fire and smoke and splintered husks of farm vehicles that all painted an apocalyptic landscape and made progress difficult as the ambulance zig-zagged to avoid these useless obstacles.

From our position in the back of the van, with no windows except those at the front, it was a bit disorienting for the two of us strapped onto stretchers and we relied on commentaries from our companions for route details.

Eventually we made it to a proper road, or at least what was left of it, and our progress improved slightly, although not by much as there were just as many bomb craters on the road as in the fields.

By mid-morning we were being unloaded and put on a hospital train bound for the coast then onwards to blighty.

"Captain Hilliard?" I turned to see an officer with a clipboard. "Major Turner, Captain."

"Major," I said and tried to salute.

"Don't bother saluting, Captain," he said in a rather bored voice, "your war is nearly over. I hope your journey here was reasonably uneventful."

"A bit bouncy and we probably drove twice the distance to avoid the potholes, but generally it was acceptable, sir."

He looked down a list on his clipboard. "You're scheduled for a boat home tomorrow, The Onward, so we'd best make sure we get you on the right train."

I looked around. "There's a lot of people, sir."

"Yes, it's a logistical nightmare, Captain, but we seem to be managing. So far."

It turned out that I wasn't on the train bound for the coast, after all, but in a hospital clearing station where it was decided whether I was fit enough to return to the front or whether my injuries were bad enough for

95

me to be sent home. It came as no surprise to learn that I was going home. I'm not sure that I could have managed the trenches with one leg missing.

"Thank you, Major," I said.

"Don't thank me, son," he replied, turning to me with a scowl, "you can thank Kaiser Wilhelm. If it was down to me, we'd slap a false leg on you and send you back to the trenches." As he walked away I'm sure I heard him mutter "damn malingerers, anything to get sent home," under his breath. I'd heard people like him existed, people who'd never been to the front or experienced the hardship we experienced but who thought they knew how to run the war. People like him were the reason we were there.

I decided I didn't much like Major Turner.

By mid-afternoon, amid the bustle of the station, I was finally stretchered into a carriage with a dozen others like me and the train pulled away, groaning under the weight of the many carriages it was pulling.

We were heading for the coast and home.

My overriding memory of Dunkirk was of chaos. Absolute chaos, and I'm surprised anyone actually got to where they were meant to go. Trains arrived and departed in billowing, choking clouds of smoke and steam and the pungent smell of sulphur permeated the atmosphere. Soldiers ran back and forth across the docks, shouting orders, marshalling men and directing ambulances and horses from one place to the next.

Occasionally a German plane would fly over, and everyone would panic and run around aimlessly like rabbits running from a fox as they desperately searched for cover as, invariably it would drop a bomb or strafe the dock with bullets. Late in the afternoon we watched a dogfight between a Fokker Triplane and a Sopwith Camel which seemed to last for hours. Each plane dodged and dived, trying to better the other until, eventually, the Camel performed an intricate double loop and opened fire on the Triplane. A massive cheer erupted as smoke started pouring out of the Fokker's engine and it retreated with the Camel in close pursuit. Seconds later we heard a loud explosion as the Fokker crashed and an even louder cheer went up across the dock.

Boats of all shapes and sizes were lined up on the dockside and I watched as men were loaded up and as each boat departed, bound for Folkestone or Dover. Each boat arrived with fresh troops who were quickly disembarked to be sent off to the front to be replaced by the wounded. I wondered how they must have felt, being greeted by waves of maimed and crippled soldiers, with filthy, blood-stained bandages hanging like rags from various parts of their bodies, or lying on stretchers with limbs missing, suffering from burns, half blind or just mad, lining up on the dock, wailing and crying. In some cases, this would be their first view of the reality of war, and it must have put the fear of God into them, wondering if that would be them in a few months' time.

There seemed to be thousands of us waiting to go home. Some, like me, veterans with a few years' experience, nerves frayed to their limit; some, who had only been there for a few months, barely old enough to shave, but all of us bearing life changing scars that would remain with us forever, as a reminder of everything that's wrong with the world.

Darkness fell and what little warmth there was turned to bitter cold, and still the operation continued unabated. New troops arrived, were sorted and sent to their regiments by train and the trains arrived with fresh wounded for the return journey.

There was a lot of shouting and noise and despite the apparent chaos, things got done and people got sorted. Everyone, it seemed, knew what they were doing.

April 23rd, 1918

"What day is it?" I asked as the two orderlies picked up my stretcher and carried me to dockside. The sun was just rising in the east, stretching its blood-red fingers across the grey sky. I was shivering with cold.

"Tuesday, of course," one of them replied, "what day did you think it was?"

"It's the day you go home," said the other with a smile, "for a well-earned rest," and he leaned forward to pat me on the leg that I didn't have. "Bloody hell, sorry mate."

I laughed, as much at his discomfort as anything else, and offered him a cigarette. He declined, saying that he needed his hands to carry me, but could he have it when he'd got me to where he was meant to get me?

They weaved their way through the melee of men rushing about, busying themselves to prepare for the morning rush and deposited me by a marking post manned by a young sergeant.

"You're on the n-n-nine f-f-fifteen sailing, s-s-sir," he said, ticking my name off on his list. Poor sod, I thought, as if he hadn't got a difficult enough job without having a speech impediment.

Over the next hour or so more soldiers arrived, some on stretchers, some on crutches, some walking, all accompanied by medical orderlies and all left in the charge of the stammering sergeant and his clipboard.

"How long have you been out here, sergeant?" I asked when things had settled. He gave me the startled look of a rabbit caught in a torchlight, I could see the fear in his eyes; fear of human contact and I wondered whether he stammered because he was shy or whether he was shy because he stammered. Whatever the case I felt sorry for him and inwardly cursed the officer who had thought it right to put him in a role where he couldn't avoid talking to people.

"I-I-I arrived l-l-last week, s-s-sir," he replied eventually.

A couple of soldiers who were lined up behind me started loudly making fun of him and for a moment I thought he was going to cry.

"Stop that, soldiers," I shouted.

"Who are you to order us about?" one of the soldiers demanded, striding over to me in a threatening manner.

"Stand to attention when you address an officer," I snapped, sitting up so he could see my rank, "you're still a soldier."

Immediately he sprang to attention; an insubordination charge was the last thing he needed just as he was going home.

"Yes, Sah. Sorry, Sah."

"And you can both apologise to the sergeant."

"Yes, Sah," and he turned to the lad. "Sorry, sergeant."

"Captain Hilliard?"

I turned as a shadow of a man fell over me, blocking out the early sun still low on the horizon.

"Yes?"

"Private Morgan, Sir."

I sat up, pleased to hear a familiar voice and I held out my hand to him. As he struggled to get around the stretcher I could see that he was unable to take it as he had lost his right arm and his left was clutching a crutch.

"Sorry," I said, withdrawing my hand. He had bandages wrapped around his head and dried blood stained his filthy cheeks. If he hadn't told me who he was I wouldn't have recognised him. "Looks like you got it pretty badly, soldier."

He shrugged, "I'm alive, which is more than I can say for some of the poor sods back there."

"Sit down. How bad?"

"Lost me arm and me right eye, Sir, and shrapnel in me leg. I don't think I'm going to be catching rats again."

"Cigarette?" He sat down beside me and together we smoked in silence, watching the hundreds of soldiers as they disembarked from the boats. The acrid taste of the smoke lingering over the dock mingled with the taste of the cigarette, making it taste bitter. I coughed and spat out a lump of black phlegm.

At last our time arrived and we were instructed to board in an orderly fashion. The SS Onward stood, magnificent in the morning sun, and the two soldiers I had admonished earlier carried me up the ramp and the crew instructed them to take me to the lounge with the other officers. Morgan hobbled up the ramp beside me and was directed to the front deck. He turned and bid me goodbye and I wondered if I'd ever see him again.

I was left by a large window so I could watch our progress across the channel.

The sergeant had told me that the ship, which was owned by the South Eastern and Chatham Railway Company, would be taking us to Folkestone where we would be transferred to a train for London. Everything seemed well organised, although he couldn't tell me where I was bound after London, and I sensed there was an underlying mild panic in all those trying to make things happen. That said, and fair due to the sergeant and his men, the ship was loaded and sailed on time and soon I was watching the waves of the English Channel lashing the ship as it cut through the water.

About ninety minutes into the journey, when we were well over halfway across and we could see the cliffs of England rising out of the sea, a wave of panic spread through the ship. A German U-Boat had been spotted. It was following us and, since those bloody Germans showed no respect for medical ships we were clearly in their sights.

Had it come to this that, having survived all we'd been through, we were to meet our end just as we were about to reach safety? It seemed that fate had one last card to play and a strange silence fell over the ship as, collectively, we held our breath. It was as though if we stayed silent the U-Boat wouldn't notice our presence and pass us by. Ridiculous, I know, but we always look for hope in the face of adversity.

My eyes scanned the horizon for a glimpse of our would-be

executioner. The sea was threatening and as dark as death. The ship began to turn, trying to face the enemy in an attempt to give it a smaller target and as we turned I momentarily glimpsed the tell-tale sign of a periscope poking up through the choppy waters some distance ahead. Others saw it at the same time as me and it seemed as though everyone was suddenly crowded around my stretcher to get sight of it.

We were turning as fast as the strong currents allowed, but were we turning fast enough? A long light-green plume just below the sea's surface erupted from the U-Boat, followed immediately by a second and together they made their way ominously towards us. The U-Boat had fired its torpedoes and the countdown to our destruction had begun. We watched in helpless indigence as the two tubes of death wended their way towards The Onward.

A strange sense of peace from deep within welled up inside of me. I had escaped death on many occasions over the last few years and the last escape had signalled the end of my participation in the war but now, it seemed, my luck was finally about to run out.

The ship groaned, straining under the increased power of the engines as they tried to turn us around and we watched the ocean bubble and swell where the U-Boat surfaced to enable the German sailors watch our demise. The Onward was a railway transport ship, it had no means of defence and we were easy prey to the cowardly action of the German U-Boat.

I heard cheers from the upper deck, and I looked out through the porthole in time to see the first torpedo sailing harmlessly past about fifteen feet away leaving a pale green wake behind it. Judging from the sounds from the officers on the other side, the same had happened to the second torpedo.

Thanks to the ship's Captain's quick thinking and skill at sea, the torpedoes, having been aimed fore and aft, had both passed by us and we were now facing the U-Boat and sailing parallel to the English coast. I was now looking out to sea towards the French coast.

"What's happening now?" I shouted as more cheers erupted from the other side of the lounge.

"The Dover Patrol has arrived," someone shouted back.

"With two beautiful ships," said another.

"A sight for sore eyes, they are, to be sure."

Our ship was now turning back towards the English coast and, as it did, I could once again see the German U-Boat. It was still on the surface but, by the look of it, rapidly trying to submerge to avoid the imminent attack.

As the sea around it appeared to boil a volley of shells, fired from the two Dover Patrol ships, began exploding around it. The U-Boat was rapidly disappearing below the water's surface and I could just about see the flat top of its deck protruding when one of our shells hit the top of its conning tower.

For a moment the U-Boat was lost to sight in the ensuing explosion but, as the smoke began to disperse, we could see it was damaged and, although it was not destroyed, there was a large fire and it was now trying to rapidly re-surface.

Already I could see German sailors pouring out from the forward hatches and running along the deck.

Another barrage of shells rained down and it suffered another direct hit. This time the exposed submarine was hit just below its tower and an almighty explosion erupted from the sea, throwing the running men across the water and I knew the image of those burning bodies as they flew through the air would haunt me forever. I screwed up my eyes to try and shut out the horror of it all.

Around me men were cheering, but I felt sick. I knew, of course, that the U-Boat fully intended to destroy us, despite us being a hospital ship, but I was sick of seeing death and destruction and I was sick of hearing the sound of guns and explosions. I held my hands over my ears, pressing as hard as I could to try and shut out the noise of celebrating and, for a while, all I could hear was the sounds of my inner screaming. I had to get out. I had to run from this living nightmare. I didn't want to see another dead body. I'd had enough. I screamed out loud and I thrashed about on my stretcher, crying and shouting and for a moment I wished the torpedoes hadn't missed their target. I wished they had struck us, that they had blown The Onward to oblivion.

How I wished for the blessed relief that only death offered, and I looked around frantically for his welcoming arms. He was nowhere to be seen. Not in this room, at least. I could only see men dancing with joy at being spared his clutches and I hated them for their joy. I cried out to them to stop. I tried to tell them that there's been too much death, but they couldn't hear me, they were oblivious to my presence.

Two orderlies grabbed me and held me down and I struggled like a madman, possessed by demons.

"Fuck off," I screamed as I tried to free myself from their grasp, "fuck right off," but it was hopeless. I felt trapped and I gnashed my teeth and roared at them like some wild beast, and I just couldn't stop. I couldn't control my anger. I couldn't control myself. A sharp prick in my arm and, gradually, my panic subsided. A blessed blackness washed over me and bore me away into the arms of Morpheus.

I sat back, stretched my arms out and yawned, staring at the forlorn words written on the pages in front me. A twinge in the small of my back made me wince and I stood up and leant forward to ease the pain.

"Do you want a cup of tea?" Larry called from the other room where he was reading the sport supplement.

"Sounds like a good idea," I replied, standing in the open secret door that connected the library to the smoking room. Larry looked up from his supplement and gave me that smile that always accompanied one of his quips.

"Well, while you're making yours can you make me one?" and he held out his empty mug to me.

"You old sod, you," I laughed, taking it and going to the kitchen opposite.

As I waited for the kettle to boil, which seemed to take an age, I reflected on Edward's diary and tried to imagine the sheer horror and turmoil he and his generation had experienced.

I then wondered how people of today would cope with a war on that scale, and I worried. I couldn't imagine the selfish society of today ever working together to support and help one another. I remembered back to a few years ago when tanker drivers went on strike and everyone panic bought fuel even though we were told, quite categorically, that if we didn't stockpile there was enough to go round and allow everyone a fair share. And it seemed to me that, the more we have advanced the less smart we had become, to a point where we had evolved to a level of stupidity, brought about by our own selfishness and greed, that had surely laid the foundation of our future destruction.

I poured the tea.

# Chapter Fourteen
## The Chapel

I must confess to finding Edward's journal both exhausting and exhilarating. As an avid reader, I love books, their feel, their smell, but I had never read anything quite like this. Maybe because it was a true account, but then I've read true accounts before, most likely it was because I knew the author. Afterall, I had grown up with him around, sitting in his wheelchair or hobbling along on his false leg and yet, in all the time I knew him - he died when I was ten - he had never once spoken of his experiences in the First World War or about the murder of his father. Come to think of it, we knew virtually nothing about him or his family apart from what was written in his journal, which was turning out to be quite a revelation. What, for instance, had happened to his brothers and sister? Neither Larry nor I could remember anyone ever talking about them. It was as though they had never existed. And what of his mother? It was almost as if, by committing it to paper he had expunged it from his mind and set it free. I knew he had been awarded medals, but I never really knew what his role had been.

As much as I found it interesting, and as much as I wanted to continue, I felt I needed a break. I couldn't read anymore for now, so I decided to go for a walk before it got dark and carry on reading in the morning.

"Wait up," said Larry, putting down the sporting supplement, "I think I'll join you; I could do with some fresh air myself. That is, unless you'd rather be alone."

"No, come on, join me. You're always welcome, but we'd best hurry up, it'll be dark soon.

The light was already fading as we set off across the back lawn to walk through the wildflower meadow opposite the kitchen garden. The rain had stopped but it was still wet underfoot, and the bottom of my trousers were soaked by the time we reached the bridge that crossed the stream and took the path into the wood. Water dripped off the overhanging branches of the trees and bushes that lined the path and the dampness in the air had a bitter chill to it.

"I wouldn't be surprised if we got a frost soon," Larry said, pushing his hands deep into his coat pockets. We stood on the little wooden bridge and watched the stream flowing lazily beneath us. "Do you remember playing 'Pooh Sticks' here when we were kids?"

"Amongst other things, yes." I laughed at the memory; they were halcyon days for us. Occasionally as kids we played sensible games like Monopoly or Cluedo, but more often we were climbing trees, fishing or pretending to be soldiers or cowboys and charging around in the woods, shouting, laughing and having fun.

We walked on in silence, momentarily lost in the games of our childhood.

A robin flew onto a low branch and trilled angrily at us. The wood was always full of wildlife, some obvious and some less so. As boys we would often go out after dark and observe some of the more secretive animals that lived there. We discovered a badger set a short distance from the path near a small clearing. The badgers were still there, some fifty years on. Or at least, their descendants were.

Sometimes we would hear the barking of foxes or the screeching of owls, and we knew deer visited from time to time. There was always something to see or hear, and wildlife had always been encouraged, certainly for as long as we could remember.

"Do you know we've got bats living in the old icehouse?" Larry said, as we walked past the mound under which it lay.

"Really? That's brilliant."

"A small colony of long-eared bats," he said. "I found them a while ago. I was checking on the icehouse one afternoon and I looked up and there they were. A dozen little faces staring at me. I got out so as not to disturb them and informed the Bat Conservation Trust. I check on them occasionally and I'm pleased to say I had baby bats this year."

"I'm sure you'll make a wonderful father."

I've always loved bats. Often on a warm summer evening we would sit out in the garden and watch them flying around, sweeping across the lawn as they harvested the many insects that swarmed above the grass.

"I do love this place," I said, looking around, lost in the memories.

"I know you do," he replied, "and you know what?"

"What?"

"You can live here with me. If you want to, that is."

"I'm here now."

"No, I mean permanently."

"What?"

"Look at this place, Jim, it's massive and I live here by myself. It gets lonely, and now you're on your own, you'll get lonely too. Think about it. It makes sense. We can be lonely together. And besides, you're family. Who's going to inherit this place when I'm gone? Harry and Leanne. My son and your daughter. Anyway, if you're living here with me it means that they'll never have to make a choice of who they should visit, they can visit both of us at the same time. Kill two birds with one stone. We hardly ever see Lillie and Kylie anyway, and Jonathan lives the other side of the world."

I said nothing, just carried on walking. It made sense, of course it did. Larry was my best friend as well as my cousin. We had both spent a lot of time growing up here, living here during school holidays when our parents were at work in the family business.

"Give it some thought, Jim, I'm quite serious. In any case, stay as long as you like. No pressure."

Of course there was no pressure, we weren't like that. Offers like this were often only stated once and never repeated; just left open.

We took a right turn shortly after passing the icehouse and walked into a clearing known as Pilgrim's Rest. The central feature of the clearing was a huge beech tree, whose lower branches were so long they rested on the surrounding grass, creating a merry-go-round-like structure. The tree was like an old friend.

"Remember when you fell out of that?" Larry said, nudging me in the side in that way he did when he wanted to draw my attention to something.

"I remember you pushing me out of it, if that's what you mean" I retorted.

"It wasn't a push," he protested, "not really."

"What would you call it then?"

"Well, more a sort of … nudge, I suppose."

"A nudge?" I laughed, "you pushed me."

He pushed me. I remember it well. We were about nine or ten at the time and it was during the summer holiday and we were down from boarding school. I remember it being a hot summer that year; the Beatles had released their Sergeant Pepper album and the world was preaching flower power and free love and we were too young to enjoy either. Larry and I were outside playing, and I had challenged Larry to a tree climbing

105

contest. Who could climb the highest quickest. We both ran up the lower branches and leapt into the tree like a couple of monkeys. We were good at climbing back then; we had no fear and the tree was an easy climb. We were about fifteen feet up and I was in the lead. Larry didn't like losing - we were both very competitive as kids - so he shoulder-barged my legs, knocking my feet off the branch on which I was standing, and I slipped and fell.

There were enough branches below us to break my fall, but I still fell out of the tree and I landed badly, breaking my arm in two places. The rest of my summer holidays was spent with my arm in a sling unable to join in any more tree climbing expeditions and I also missed the first few rugby matches at the beginning of the autumn term, which nearly cost me my place in the under-11s first fifteen.

"You're not still mad at me over that, are you?"

"Hardly, you were the one who brought it up. I'd forgotten about it."

"Fair enough."

A flock of starlings, random black dots against the greying background, began an intricate, seemingly random dance above us. Further starlings joined in and their twittering and tweeting interrupted an otherwise tranquil twilight as they swerved and careened about each other, creating intricate and beautiful patterns in the darkening sky.

The patterns they painted changed rapidly, swelling or shrinking apparently at will, elongating then retracting like elastic. They swirled, faster and faster as more birds joined the throng to perform the spectacular dance. We could hear the whooshing of their wings as they swooped and dived, never colliding, never making a wrong move. A choreographer could not have created a more beautiful sight, of hundreds of co-ordinated birds dancing to celebrate the sunset.

We stood transfixed, holding our breath so as not to disturb the pandemonium playing out above us.

On and on it went. Minutes flew by and the dance seemed to be never-ending as it weaved and wafted through the air until, finally, it reached its climax as the starlings weaved and dived and then, as suddenly as it had started, they dropped onto the branches of the beech tree that we were so fond of and the wood was plunged into an eerie silence.

"Beautiful," I whispered. I was awestruck by the spectacle.

"Wow," Larry muttered, "I do love a murmuration. Do you remember the first one we ever saw? You were staying for the autumn half term holiday …"

"Yes, and Uncle Anthony took us down to the river before dusk because he wanted us to see the short-eared owl he had discovered nesting there, which he said was unusual as they were generally more common in the north and Scotland. We didn't see the owl that evening but we did see the murmuration."

"That's right and we didn't know what it was or why they did it. Dad explained that it was to scare away predators so they could roost in peace. Roost in peace," he repeated to himself, chuckling, "that's funny."

We skirted the beech listening to the low chattering of the starlings as they settled in for the night. "Lights out in five minutes," Larry whispered, looking up at them as we passed.

"You sound like Mr Owlston," I said. Mr Owlston had been our housemaster at the Prep school we attended back in the nineteen-sixties.

"Now there's a name I haven't heard mentioned in decades."

A faint movement ahead caught my eye and I peered into the gathering gloom. Someone was standing on the path we were headed for. A woman. I was sure of it.

I stopped. For a moment I was gripped by the hands of panic as a wave of fear rose within me. In the gloom I could see her eyes shining; glaring at me, and I had the feeling this was the same woman I had seen before in the kitchen garden.

But who was she? What did she want?

I was seeing things as though through a tunnel; a tunnel leading from me to her and the world around me fell silent. Slowly, she turned away and disappeared into the encroaching shadows, and for a moment she was gone.

I set off after her. What started as a determined stride quickly became a jog, then a run as I reached the place on the path where she had stood. I looked about. She was ahead, further along the path and as I caught sight of her once more, she turned to the right and disappeared again.

How had she gone so far so fast?

I heard Larry's voice calling urgently in the distance. He sounded worried, almost frightened and I wondered what had made him so. But I couldn't stop to find out, I had to follow this strange woman who was leading me to goodness knows where.

I ran along the path leading out of Pilgrim's Rest and on through the wood. I heard footsteps running behind me and glanced back to see Larry in pursuit.

"Stop!" he yelled. "Jim, stop!" But I couldn't.

At the end of the path I turned right. I could see her ahead, a long way away. She turned left, just after the kitchen garden, and I realised she was headed for the chapel.

My breath came in pants as I ran. My heart beat heavily in my chest. As I rounded the edge of the kitchen garden wall I came to the tiny chapel. It was a dark shadow in the gloom, overhung by branches which gave it an eerie, almost haunted appearance.

I stopped short. The chapel stood in darkness, undisturbed; the woman was nowhere to be seen. Anxiously, I looked around, bewildered.

"What the hell's happening, Jim?" Larry gasped, stopping beside me and bending double to catch his breath. "What is it?"

"I saw someone," I explained. "A woman."

"The one you saw before?"

"Yes."

"Except you didn't see her before, Jim. You were seeing things. Remember."

"She went into the chapel."

"She didn't. She didn't go into the chapel. You're hallucinating, Jim, she's just a figment of your imagination. Let's go back to the house, get a drink." He gently put his arm around my shoulders to steer me away from the chapel. I shook him off.

"I didn't imagine it, Larry," I insisted, "I'm sure I didn't."

"Don't worry," he whispered gently, trying to soothe me. "Come, let's go."

"She seemed so real."

Even to my ears that sounded lame. My rational self agreed with Larry, I was seeing things. I was tired. I was excited at having seen Leanne and her family over the weekend and almost certainly affected by what I had read in Edward's journal. Clearly, I was also still suffering from the remnants of my depression. It was obvious when I stopped to think about it, I just didn't want to admit it. I was suffering from another psychotic episode.

"Come on," said Larry, "Let's put your mind at rest, let's look inside."

I nodded in agreement. I felt like I was in a strange place. A gamut of emotions swirled around in my head. Anger, fear, angst, frustration. I wanted to shout out loud, scream even, to vent my feelings. Why wasn't I getting better? Why did I have to keep on going through this crazy living nightmare?

Larry stooped down and retrieved a large iron key from under a nearby rock, unlocked the door to the chapel and pushed it open. It was dark inside and he reached in and flicked a switch.

Bright light flooded out and onto the path, momentarily dazzling us. We peered inside.

"See, empty," he said, looking around, "nothing to see but piles of junk." Everything was as we expected to find it. Stuff was piled up against the black stained walls and the altar was firmly rooted to the floor where it had stood undisturbed for centuries.

"That's odd," he said, stopping at the entrance.

"What is?"

"No. That's not possible," he said and abruptly slammed the door shut. He turned to me. "That door was locked, wasn't it?"

"What are you talking about? Of course it was locked, I saw you unlock it."

"Then how do you explain this?"

He pushed open the door and stood aside to let me see in.

"Explain what?" I asked, confused.

"The floor, look …" I looked down. The floor was covered in a thick layer of dirt and dust, just as it always was. Nothing had disturbed it, nothing was different. "What the …?"

He turned to me and in the light cast from within the chapel I could see confusion in his eyes. He looked at the floor again, then shook his head in disbelief.

"I must have imagined it," he said, eventually.

"Imagined what?"

"Did you not see it?" He seemed to be pleading with me to say yes.

"See what?"

"The footprints on the floor."

"Footprints? What? No. There were no footprints."

Then I realise what he was doing.

"Look Larry, don't."

"What?" he said with a look of surprise on his face.

"Don't wind me up like that, I don't need it right now. I really did think I'd seen the woman walk to the chapel. I'm sorry, but you don't have to pretend you're seeing things too just to make me feel better."

"What? Jim, you have to believe me. I wouldn't make fun of what you're going through, I wouldn't even humour you by pretending something that isn't. You know I'm speaking the truth when I swear to you that I thought I saw footprints on the floor just now. Wet footprints, like someone had just come in after walking through wet grass."

"Seriously?"

"Seriously."

My eyes searched his face. Knowing him as well as I did I knew when he was joshing and I knew when he was being sincere.

Right now, he was being sincere.

"In that case," I said, "whatever it is I've got, you've caught. There are no footprints, so you are imagining things as well."

"Maybe" he said philosophically, "it was just a trick of the light. Look, it's dark already."

He switched off the light and then closed and locked the door.

"What did she look like, this woman of yours?" he asked as we made our way back to the Hall.

"She's not my woman," I replied, but as we walked, I tried to picture her in my mind.

"No, of course she isn't."

I couldn't quite bring her image back but, despite that, a name did come to me. I shook my head.

No way.

# Chapter Fifteen
## Therapy

"As I said previously, focusing on someone other than Janet means you are working positively through your depression. This is good."

"It doesn't feel so good."

"It takes time."

"But you? Why you?"

"Who else do you know to focus on? Who else have you had similar contact with over the last few weeks? I am the person who is focussing your angst, helping you to deal with your grief so it stands to reason you imagined she was me. After all, you're not going to imagine it was Leanne, are you. She's your daughter."

"And what about the footprints Larry thought he saw?"

"A simple trick of the light."

"He seemed so certain."

"You seemed so certain you'd seen that woman, and then you were certain she was me."

"But that's different."

"Perhaps it was brought on by a form of mass hysteria."

"What?"

"Mass hysteria. You know, where a psychosis is shared or transferred from one party to another. It's very rare, and extremely unlikely, especially in someone of your age, but it's not unknown."

"But why the chapel?"

"What do you mean?"

"Well, it's the second time I've ended up in the chapel. Remember? I slept walked there?"

I was having difficulty with this conversation, particularly admitting that I thought the woman I had seen bore some resemblance to Madea who was, right now, sitting with me in the Morning Room, trying to get me to reason through what I had seen, or thought I had seen, the previous day. To some extent I was getting used to the symptoms of psychosis, but Larry had been quite spooked by it.

111

After we had locked up the chapel we had returned to the Hall and opened a bottle of 18-year-old The Glenlivet and proceeded to drink our way through half the bottle before staggering off to bed.

Larry had gone out to Newmarket for the morning to meet with some old business colleagues and shortly after his departure Madea called asking if she could bring our next appointment forward to this morning. I was planning to carry on reading Edward's journal but, in the light of yesterday's incident, I was quite keen to see her.

"I know it's short notice," she said, "but you'll be doing me a big favour if you can accommodate the change."

"Actually," I replied, "it's quite convenient and there is something specific I need to discuss with you."

"Right," she said, "I'll come straight away."

I hadn't slept well after my strange... I'm not sure whether to call it encounter, sighting, vision or haunting. What was it? What had I actually seen? Or thought I had seen? A ghost? She certainly wasn't real, otherwise Larry would have seen her too, but ghosts don't exist either. So Madea had come and here we were sitting, as usual, talking.

"I had thought that, by now, the psychosis would have stopped," I told her. I was shaken by the reality of the vision – let's call it that for now. It wasn't as though it had been a fleeting glimpse, seen out of the corner of my eye. This had been a full-on chase from Pilgrim's Rest to the chapel, which was some considerable distance.

"You said you had an episode after reading you mother's letter?"

"I felt a wave of depression, but no psychosis. The contents of the letter came as quite a shock."

"Did it?"

"Yes. Why wouldn't it? I had just found out my real mother had died in childbirth and my father had hanged himself."

"He was ill. He was suffering from depression."

"What goes around, comes around."

She looked at me quizzically, staring deep into my eyes. I felt as though she was searching my soul.

"He killed himself over the death of his wife, and I nearly did the same over the death of mine," I explained, "it must run in the family."

"Depression can certainly run in families," she agreed, "but today we know how to treat it. All you have to do is make sure you talk to someone. Make sure you ask for help when you are falling into your black hole."

112

"That's why you're here, isn't it?"

"Yes, that's exactly why I am here, only I'm not here twenty-four hours a day. That's where your cousin can, hopefully, help you."

"He helps, for sure."

"Good."

"But why am I still having these episodes. Isn't your therapy working?"

"It is but it takes time. I don't have a magic wand that I can just wave and make you better. On top of your depression you've had a few extra surprises. You found out what happened to your real parents and you learned who your grandparents were. You've even traced your family back to Tilbury in the 1930s. That was a bonus. The thing is you know about them now and you didn't before. Couple that with the rather grim experiences you're reading about your grandfather during World War One and it's no surprise you're having nightmares."

"So, do you think I should stop reading the journal?"

"Oh no. I think you should make a point of finishing the journal. It might give you closure."

"Closure? Of what?"

"Who knows? Of Edward's life perhaps, and the influence it may have had on yours. Maybe you'll find out more about yourself in it; I really don't know. At the moment you don't know what happened to your grandfather. And what about his wife? Do you know anything about her?"

"Not really. She died when I was three or four. The only thing I remember about her was her curly white hair and the jar of sweets she kept in the cupboard that she allowed Larry and me to open whenever we visited. I don't even remember what type of sweets they were." She laughed.

"Good memories then?"

"Yes, insofar as they go."

"So read the journal, it's helping you to move on."

"Do you really think so?"

"I do, as it happens. You're finding out things and they're distracting you from your own grief, because you're finding out that you are not alone with it; Clara lost two of her brothers in the war, Caroline lost her brother and both parents when she was very young. Knowing this is helping you, it's therapeutic."

"It doesn't feel so." Why was I being so contrary this morning?

113

"It may seem like that right now, but believe me, it is. Healing is a slow process, I can't make you better, but I can steer you on the right course to help you through the process. That's why I'm here."

Talking to Madea did make me feel better about myself. Maybe because she was a stranger and therefore detached from any personal involvement that I felt able to talk to her, or maybe it was because I felt she wasn't judging me, but rather understood me when I opened up to her. In fairness I never felt Larry judged me either, but he was too close to have the type of discussion I had with Madea. I needed her detachment.

The clock in the hall chimed the half hour, signifying the end of another session.

"Back to the normal time next week?" I asked as I helped her on with her coat.

"Yes," she replied, gathering up her bag and heading for the door.

I saw her out, closing the door behind her. A gust of wind blew in and a door slammed behind me. I jumped and turned to see which one. When I turned back to the window Larry's car was coming down the drive.

# Chapter Sixteen
## Out & About

As it happened, it was a good couple of weeks before I sat down again to read Edward's journal. I felt I needed to gather my strength, both mentally and physically, so I decided to spend some more time exercising and getting out and about.

To this end I dug out my National Trust and English Heritage handbooks. Larry and I took the car and spent our time driving all over Norfolk, Suffolk, Cambridgeshire and Bedfordshire to visit all manner of stately homes; preserved ruins; garden estates and nature reserves. We walked miles along the north Norfolk Coastal path – although when we got to Holt we did hop on the steam railway and enjoy the ride to Sheringham - and a large swathe of Peddar's Way. We'd lunch at convenient pubs along the routes, and we explored some fascinating houses. I'd forgotten what a wealth of old and ancient places we have in East Anglia.

One day we visited Grimes Graves, a Neolithic flint mine. Dug some 5,000 years ago, it was accessed by climbing down a 9-metre-long ladder. It was an interesting experience; I don't recall ever having climbed such a long ladder.

Another day we visited Oxburgh Hall, in Norfolk. The beautiful, moated residence of the Bedingfield family boasted a priest hole and Larry was keen to see it, close to. I had my reservations, but Larry insisted. It was a tiny, cramped hole with its hidden entrance at the top of the turret just outside the Lady of the house's chamber. He disappeared into the black depths and I swung my legs over the edge to follow him down. As I sat there about to ease myself in, I was gripped by sudden, irrational fear. I've suffered from claustrophobia since childhood. At times it can be so severe that I can't bear to have anything over my face for fear of not being able to get it off again. It's hard to explain but it grabbed me then and I had to rush outside in a state of panic for fresh air and open space.

Apart from that incident we enjoyed our exploring and walking through our beautiful countryside; we even spent an afternoon walking through the fields in which Constable had sat when he painted his famous masterpieces, such as The Hay Wain and Flatford Mill.

The weather turned during the first half of November and the first frost of winter casually breezed in one cold, dark morning. I opened the curtains to see ice patterns painted over my bedroom window. Storms threatened but never quite happened, although strong winds blew the remaining leaves from the trees and Larry and I wrapped ourselves up against its bitter bite. We followed the basic rule of; if it was dry, we would visit nature reserves and walk and if it was wet, we visited houses and went inside.

In Ickworth we had a laugh trying on period costumes that had been left out in the servant kitchens for children to try on. As there were no children around on the day we went we tried them on ourselves. At Felbrigg Hall we were told off by one of the volunteers in the shop who thought we were too old to be trying on helmets and preparing for a sword fight.

The day we visited the Blickling Estate it was a bitterly cold morning, but the sun was shining. Dark clouds were gathering on the distant horizon as we parked up, threatening rain later, so we opted to walk the grounds before lunch and visit the house after. We set off across the fields, walked around the lake and took the path around the far side of the house to the old village. As we crossed the road facing the house two hours later and walked up the massive drive, which was more like walking up a large, leafy avenue, we felt the first drops of rain and dived into the café for a pie and a welcome cup of coffee.

"Oh, that's interesting," I said, picking up a leaflet as we sat down, "apparently, there's an RAF war museum here."

"Really? Where?"

"Upstairs," I replied, "just above this café."

Neither Larry nor I knew that the RAF had been stationed at Blickling during the war although, as the estate was situated on the north-east coast of Norfolk, it made sense. From the information sheet I had picked up this place was a strategic base housing both medium range bombers, such as the Blenheim, and longer range ones, such as the Fortress Heavy Bomber.

The museum was fascinating. It was laid out to give an accurate insight into life there during World War Two. To make it as realistic as possible they had recreated the crew room, a place for pilots to spend

116

their leisure time between operations. Unfinished jigsaws, letter writing paraphernalia, books and magazines were strewn across tables, and an old radio set sat in the corner, where it would have played music of the era, like Glen Miller and Vera Lynn.

The room evoked an atmosphere of a bygone era, even down to the smell of corned beef and powdered eggs, and in the car as we drove home my mind turned to another era, perfectly illustrated by Edward's eloquent account, and I determined to get back to reading his journal.

# Chapter Seventeen
## Edward's Journal – Summer 1918

April 24<sup>th</sup>, 1918

I woke up on the train to London after being given something on the ship to knock me out. I was clearly out for several hours because the sun was rising when I awoke.

"Cor blimey, I thought you'd died."

I turned to see a corporal on the stretcher next to mine. He grinned and held out his hand to me. I took it and we shook.

"Fred Moss," he said. "You've made a boring companion on this ride so far." He had a well-defined cockney accent and I wondered whether to count my fingers to check they were all still there after shaking his hand. You know what these east end chaps are like; steal from you as soon as look at you. He seemed friendly enough and I reasoned that, if he had wanted to steal from me, he'd had plenty of opportunity to do so while I was lying unconscious next to him.

"Edward Hilliard," I replied, returning his smile as best I could. I was still groggy from the drugs, so I probably appeared to him as a bit dopey.

"So, what 'appened to you?"

"Lost my right leg. You?"

"'Ad me foot shot off," he replied, and he held his leg up for me to see. "A permanent reminder of the war's legacy."

"Bad luck."

"I was a footballer before I got sent to war," he told me, "played inside left for The 'Ammers. I don't suppose there's much call for one footed players, unless they're planning to create a cripples' league, and there's enough of us to make it work."

"I'm sorry."

"Nah, don't be. There's plenty much worse off than me and anyway, me dad runs a pub down Shoreditch so I can always work for 'im. Least I've got summat. Some of these poor bastards 'ave nuffin' if they can't get back to their old jobs. They're the buggers you wanna feel sorry for."

I hadn't really thought about that, but he was right. What had many of these young men got to look forward to? Disfigured and crippled, unlikely to get jobs just because they were missing an arm or a leg. I shook my head, sadly. I had a job to go back to, the family engineering firm; the one that had won my father his knighthood for supporting the war effort. In my mind I made a vow; wherever possible I would ensure that neither I nor my father would turn our backs on any of our employees returning back from war.

"Where are we headed, Fred?"

"Lundon," he told me. "Victoria station. Then we'll be shipped off to various 'ospitals around the country. Depends on what's wrong wiv you, what space they 'ave and whether you're a posh nob or not. I 'ope I gets a Lundon one so as I'm close to me family."

"I hope you do too. I live in the country, so I hope I'll be sent somewhere nearby."

As it happened, I was sent to Roehampton, a hospital just to the north of London. It specialised in men like me who had lost limbs, and it had workshops set up in its grounds to manufacture prosthetic limbs.

April 26th, 1918

Finally, here I am at Roehampton Hospital.

What an absolute palaver the last twenty-four hours have been. When we arrived at Victoria station it was absolute pandemonium; worse than the docks at Dunkirk, and we weren't even threatened by German planes flying overhead and trying to attack us every few minutes.

While at Dunkirk the atmosphere had been one of organised chaos, where everyone seemed to know what they were trying to achieve and between them they managed to achieve it. At Victoria, it was altogether a different matter. Everyone seemed to be working against one another so that there was all of the chaos and none of the organisation. I felt like I was being treated like a parcel sent in the mail that was destined to be lost; and indeed, that's exactly what happened.

When we arrived, they laid all of us who were on the stretchers out on the platform. Then an orderly with a clipboard checked our names off on his list and informed us which hospital we were headed for. Fred got his wish; he was told he was being sent to St Thomas' Hospital and I was told I was going to Roehampton, which I'd never heard of, but the orderly told me it was opened especially as a war casualty hospital in 1915 by Queen Mary.

Throughout the day men on stretchers were collected by orderlies and either put on trains to be despatched to wherever they were going or taken by ambulance to other railway stations or to local hospitals.

At one point two orderlies collected me and carried me along the platform before they realised that I wasn't their patient, so they deposited me where they were, which was a way away from where I had been and left me there. As I was about to point it out to them another train came steaming into the station and they ran off to start unloading fresh wounded and I became lost in the system.

As I lay there, abandoned and alone, I began to feel unwell. I started shivering and felt cold. I lost all track of time but sometime during the day, it was still light, some food was left for me and a lady came along and gave me a cup of tea.

"You don't look too well, luv," she said, holding her hand to my forehead. "Ooh, not surprising, you're running a temperature. Don't go away, I'll see if I can get you something." The something turned out to be a blanket and she wrapped me up, and I lay in it and shivered miserably.

I was too exhausted to make a fuss. I was ill. My head was pounding, and I ached all over. Even my bones ached. Sometime during the evening, I was fed some hot broth and I could feel its warmth seeping through my body.

In the morning I was awakened by the bustle on the platform. My leg was throbbing. It hurt like hell and I developed a maddening itch in the foot I no longer had and for a while I was driven mad by being unable to scratch it.

In my fevered state I dozed, fitfully, shivering as I fought my fever. Someone brought a bucket to enable me to relieve myself, but it was awkward and very public. What little dignity I had left I lost on that station platform.

"Captain Hilliard?"

"Eh?" I had been sleeping when I heard my name being called.

"Are you Captain Hilliard? Captain Edward Hilliard?" the medical orderly asked, walking to the end of my stretcher where my name was pinned. He wore a khaki uniform and sported a red cross armband.

"Yes."

"Oh, thank God for that, we've been looking all over for you. We thought we'd lost you, sir. You're not meant to be down here, you know, we were meant to pick you up yesterday from over there," and he pointed in the direction of where I had originally been when I was first unloaded from my train. "It's alright, Alf," he yelled down the platform, trying to be heard above the general noise and hubbub, "I've found 'im. He's moved down here."

"'Ow the 'ell did 'e do that?" came the reply from another orderly, presumably Alf, who came scurrying up the platform, appearing through the smoke like a ghost. I had a brief flashback to the trenches and of German soldiers appearing through the mist at dawn and I cried out.

"Don't worry, it's only Alf," the first orderly informed me, "'e's 'armless."

"Blimey, guv, where you bin 'iding?"

"I was originally down there," I croaked, "where you've been looking for me, but I got moved and another train arrived, and I got forgotten."

"Well, they shouldn't've moved you. 'Ow do they expect us to find you if they keep movin' you?" The tone of his voice implied that he thought it was my fault that I'd been moved and left. "You don't look too 'ealthy, either, must be the smoky platform. Ain't good for a man's 'elth, lying 'ere all day."

"Come on, Alf, we've got 'im now. Let's load 'im up and bugger orff before 'e dies, then 'e's not our problem." And with that they picked me up and walked me across the platform to a waiting army ambulance, shut me in and we drove off.

April 27th, 1918

I woke in the night, bathed in sweat and still shivering. I felt I was drowning and sat upright with a coughing fit. A nurse took my temperature and gave me a pill and some water, and I spluttered as I drank.

In the morning my stump was throbbing but, on the whole, I was feeling better, as though the worse of my fever had broken and I was on the road to getting better. The nurse took my temperature and measured my pulse.

"I do feel a bit better this morning," I told her, "but I still feel lethargic and achy."

"You were some trouble last night, I hear, but your temperature, while still high, has come right down."

"And my stump is throbbing," I told her. "It really hurts, in fact."

"I'd better take a look."

She drew back the covers and in no time at all had removed the bandages and my stump sock. As she lifted it up to inspect it it started shaking uncontrollably. "Keep still, you," she muttered.

"Sorry, I can't help it."

"Ah, no, I wasn't talking to you, I was talking to your stump," and she pursed her lips and held it tightly between her hands.

"Ow!" I protested, "that hurts."

"Sorry," she said and relaxed her grip. Instantly my stump began shaking again, as it if had a life of its own.

I find it quite interesting, in a perverse way, that my stump seemed to have developed into an entity in its own right. When I had both legs, I didn't think anything of them. They were just legs and I took them for granted. I never gave them a second thought. They had simply been a part of the whole; unremarkable in themselves and certainly not a subject to be discussed for any purpose, unless I developed a cramp or something minor. Now my leg, or rather lack of it, seemed like the most important part of my body, to be poked, prodded and rubbed by total strangers and with apparent enthusiasm. It was almost as if, rather than losing a leg, I had gained a stump, only the stump had its own life. This is something that I will have to grin and bear for the rest of my life, I suppose; a constant reminder of my part in the war that would end all wars.

Right now, it was making its presence known with a vengeance by going into spasm, presumably as a protest at being roughly handled by the nurse. It was being a nuisance, that's for sure.

The nurse excused herself and walked off without re-dressing my misbehaving stump. As soon as she put it down and turned away, it calmed down and lay quietly on the bed in front of me.

I looked around the ward. An army of nurses in starched uniforms bearing a large red cross on the front busied themselves with their patients, like ants running around for the good of the nest. The ward smelled of disinfectant and half a dozen other women dressed in beige overalls carried buckets and mops, to clean the ward. I supposed that a place like this where everyone in the hospital has lost a limb of some description, be it an arm, leg, hand or foot, cleanliness is vital to minimise the chance of infection.

I yawned and felt my bones creak as I stretched my arms above my head.

"Jumpy stump eh?"

"What?" I looked up to see my nurse returning with a doctor. He was mid-forties, wore a grey suit beneath his white hospital coat and his piercing blue eyes peered at me through a pair of round lensed spectacles.

"Good morning, Captain. I'm Doctor Edred Corner, your doctor for your stay in our wonderful hotel. Nurse here tells me you have jumpy stump syndrome." I gave him a puzzled look and he continued. "Jumpy stump is where your stump goes into major spasm and starts jerking uncontrollably when someone touches it, it's not uncommon."

"It certainly seemed to take on a life of its own this morning," I concurred.

"Well, let's have a look, shall we?"

He placed his hands on my upper thigh. I winced and drew in a rapid breath; not from pain for I felt none, but because his hands were freezing cold.

"Sorry about that," he said, grinning from ear to ear, "at least we know you've got feeling there."

"Too right I have, that's the bit the Germans didn't blow off."

He rubbed his hands together to warm them up and tried again. As he ran his hands down my thigh towards my stump it started jerking in his hands and he held it tighter.

"Does that hurt?"

"It feels like someone's driving a tank over my leg, but… it's weird, but…"

"It feels like it's your lower leg that hurts. The part that's not there?"

"Yes."

He withdrew his hands and the spasm stopped. Then, without forewarning me, he withdrew a tiny rod with a rubber wheel at one end and tapped the very end of my stump. I nearly leapt up to the ceiling.

"Ahh, fuck! Jesus!" I yelled. "Sorry, but that really hurt."

"Where?"

"My… foot."

"My dear boy, I fully expected that. It's probably what's causing your jumpy stump."

"What do you mean?"

He laughed.

"When your leg was blown off," he explained, "the nerve endings were left behind, and they've become exposed. They're confused and, unless we do something, you will suffer from phantom leg syndrome because your mind will believe that the leg is still there, and it won't heal properly. It also means that you won't be able to wear a prosthetic leg."

"So, can you do anything about it?"

"Oh yes, no problem."

"Thanks."

"It will involve surgery though."

"Oh."

"I'm afraid it's the only option. We're going to have to open the wound and carefully cauterize the nerve endings which should solve the problem."

"Should? What if it doesn't?"

"Then the problem isn't organic."

"Meaning?"

"If it isn't organic then it's likely as not neurasthenic and then it's a different ball game as I'm an orthopaedic surgeon not a psychiatrist."

"Psychiatrist? You mean if you can't fix it with surgery then it's all in my mind? That I'm mad?"

"Oh, I wouldn't go quite that far," he said, "but yes, in a nutshell, that's the long and short of it. So, let's not waste time, eh? Let's see if we can fix you or if we have to send you to the funny farm." He laughed as he started writing on my notes.

"You've got a strange sense of humour, doctor."

"Comes with the territory, old chap. Nurse White, let's prep this man for surgery, shall we? Let us do our worst."

He smiled again then he turned and left me with Nurse White.

"Don't worry," she told me, "he's one of the best surgeons in his field and has been a pioneer for amputation surgery and the use of prosthetics. He'll have you playing football in a few months' time."

"I look forward to it," I said.

As it was it was a few days before I could go to theatre as I the fever I had had turned out to be influenza and it took me a few more days to shake it off completely.

May 7th, 1918

It's been a week since Doctor Corner operated and now that the pain has subsided, my stump is feeling much better. No more annoying spasms when Nurse White dresses it and it's healing nicely, so I'm told.

Next week they're going to start on preparing my stump for prosthesis. It may be up to three months before I get one though as, according to the good doctor, my stump will shrink as it hardens and heals. Well, you learn something new every day, I suppose, but three months is going to seem like a lifetime for someone like me who has always led an active life. I'm not sure I'm ready for such enforced boredom.

I sat on my bed and read The Times this afternoon. It seems we have managed to contain the German offensive in which I sustained my injury, and we've dug in again. Another stalemate, another waste of time and men's lives.

The paper also reported that influenza has been spreading through troops returning home and they're spreading it to their friends and families. A bit of an outbreak was how they reported it. From the sounds of it, the chaps in the trenches are suffering from it too, as if they're not suffering enough. Usual symptoms for 'flu; high temperature, bit of a fever, lasts a few days. Just like I had had. A few people have died from it, but then that's nothing unusual with seasonal influenza, according to The Times.

May 18th, 1918

Today I learned to play wheelchair basketball. In the last few days I have become a bit more mobile thanks to the use of a wheelchair, and today I was taken to the gymnasium to do some exercises. Having been prone for so long, the muscles in my good leg are becoming weak so I'm going to need to exercise it daily to give it strength as, after all, it will be my sole weight bearing limb when I'm back on my feet. Well, back on my foot, anyway. So, with the aid of the parallel bars I walked my first steps in several weeks and they were the most difficult steps I have ever made.

At the far end of the room some of the chaps in wheelchairs were playing basketball. The noise of the ball bouncing on the wooden floor, and the laughter of men obviously having fun was a joy to behold. There's little enough laughter in this place. We're all a bit wrapped up in our own self-pity; from those newly admitted getting used to their injuries, to those longer term patients undergoing the trials and tribulations of learning to walk on an artificial leg without falling over or using a wooden arm to lift a tea-cup without breaking it. The regime we lived in seemed brutal at times, and men were paraded on the wards in various states of déshabillé whilst trying on their prosthetics.

I asked Nurse White, whose name I finally discovered is Edith, if I could join in and she said that provided I completed my exercises in accordance with Doctor Corner's instructions, she would allow me five minutes.

I have to say that after completing the exercises I was almost beaten. My arms ached from taking my weight and my good leg ached from being used for the first time in weeks. Nurse Edith persuaded me to join in when I had decided not to, and I'm glad she did. Although I ached from the bars, the few minutes I spent with the basketball players was tremendous fun. It seemed the main aim of the game was levity rather than competition and the play was accompanied by much laughter and hilarity, and soon my sides ached as well as my arms and legs. I was tired from my exertions by the time Edith returned me to the ward and I fell asleep for an hour and nearly missed lunch.

"Right," she said, as she pushed me back to the ward, "your days of peaceful contemplation are now over and there is a timetable we're going to be following from here on in."

"And that is?"

"Nine to eleven daily you will be in the gymnasium; parallel bars and walking exercises, followed by half an hour break before one hour of intense massage to start strengthening and hardening your stump. After lunch you will attending classes."

"Classes?"

"Yes, classes. Every afternoon you're going to learn a craft or a trade of some sort. It's to keep you from getting bored as you become more active as well as teaching you useful things for when you get out and return to civilian life."

"I'm an engineer," I replied tartly, "I hardly need to learn a craft."

"Well, it'll stop you getting bored, anyway," she replied, as I transferred to the chair by my bed, "and as a senior officer we expect you to set an example to the others."

Well, that certainly put me in my place.

I had a cup of tea and a biscuit before she returned twenty minutes later.

"Your massage and stump care session will start in a few minutes so let's get you to the clinic."

No one had prepared me for what I was about to endure. I was looking forward to a soothing massage but what I got was an hour of pure hell administered by what I can only describe as a Rottweiler with lipstick.

At first, she seemed quite pleasant. She helped me onto the treatment couch and unwound my bandage. So far, so good.

I lay back on the couch, relaxed and closed my eyes ready to enjoy an hour of feminine ministrations, so when she grabbed my leg and roughly squeezed it in between her strong hands I nearly hit the roof.

"Stop your moaning," she said, "you're not the first person to have lost a leg, you know, and you won't be the last. My job isn't to pamper you it's to make little Stanley here strong and hardy as quickly as possible so he'll take your weight and we can fix you up and get you out."

"Stanley?" I wasn't too keen on her bedside manner.

"Stanley Stump," she said. "To make it easier for you to deal with my work I like to give your stump a name; yours is called Stanley," and she started rubbing it vigorously. It was excruciating and, I'm ashamed to say, I soon had tears running down my face. I was already struggling to cope with the pain, and we were barely a few minutes in. This was going to last for an hour. To take my mind off the relentless torture she was inflicting on me I spent my time devising ways to make her suffer if the boot was on the other foot.

I think I may have passed out because suddenly she was slapping the end of my stump, hard, with the flat of her hands. The end of my leg went numb until she stopped and resumed the massage. On and on it went, alternating between massaging and slapping. Never soft or gentle but rough and as hard as it could possibly be.

"Cruel to be kind," she said, smiling as she slapped, "I don't apologise, I do my job and get you prepared."

I had no answer, but I had the distinct feeling she was deriving pleasure from my discomfort.

Have you ever noticed how when you experience pleasure, time flies past in the wink of an eye but when you are undergoing severe pain and trauma it seems to slow to the pace of a snail crossing a road? That's what I was experiencing right now. The passing of time seemed to have slowed almost to a stop, and I swear I must have passed out a dozen times at the hands of this sadist in a skirt.

I think at those moments, I understood the meaning of eternity.

Finally, she stopped, but she hadn't finished. Just as I relaxed, sighing with relief that it was all over, she pulled a sponge from a bucket, liberally soaked it in some purple liquid and splashed it over my stump.

"Jesus Christ on a bicycle," I yelled, "what the fuck is that you're washing me with?"

"Methylated spirit," she replied. "Hold still."

"Christ, I got better treatment in the hospital at Amiens," I told her, anger finally overcoming my politeness, "they only used saline."

"Saline is good for cleaning wounds," she told me, "yours is not only clean, it's healing and, as it heals we need to harden it up, otherwise you'll never be able to wear your false leg."

"And you use methylated spirit?"

"You'd better get used to it."

"I'm not sure I'll ever get used to it," I replied, "but I don't seem to have any choice in the matter."

"You have a choice. Endure my treatment and you'll walk out of here in a few months' time, or don't and you'll spend the rest of your life mouldering in a wheelchair. Look, Captain, I make no apology for putting you through this. I know it's painful but it's for your own good and I can't make it less so. Wearing a prosthetic leg will put enormous amount of strain on your stump, and in order to keep it healthy we must harden it. All I can say is that as your stump hardens the pain will become less. This place is not so much a hospital as a human repair factory, and we're trying to fix you. Who knows," she smiled, "one day you may even thank me, but probably not today."

I felt sick but I kept quiet. She was probably right, and maybe I had misjudged her. She was just doing her job, but she couldn't know what we were going through, our physical scars were obvious, our mental ones less so.


May 22nd, 1918

A man from Critchley of Liverpool, purveyors of fine prosthetics, measured me up for my new leg this morning.

After a few days of undergoing intense physiotherapy I am now quite adept at using the parallel bars and playing wheelchair basketball. Mind you, I ache. Oh, my goodness how I ache. My good leg aches from not being used for so long and my muscles are screaming at me to give them a rest. The physiotherapy sessions on my stump have continued unabated and, although the pain she puts me through is second to none, the treatment seems to be working. Each time she works on me the pain becomes a bit less as she promised me it would. Or maybe I'm just getting used to it.

In the grounds of the hospital, and I can see it from the windows by my bed, is what looks like a huge refugee camp. In actual fact it contains the workshops of several companies that make false limbs and one of those workshops belongs to Critchley of Liverpool.

"Fitting the leg will be a process," Mr Thomas, their specialist fitter, told me. "Your prosthetic leg will be made using metal rods that replicate the bones in your lower leg and give it strength, surrounded by carefully crafted wood to make it, as best we can, a match for your good leg. The leg will be attached to the leather glove which is designed to fit snugly around the stump of your leg. Strong springs connect the knee and ankle joints allowing them to flex just like a real limb. It's so realistic that no one will ever know you have a false leg."

"Really?" I replied with a certain amount of scepticism. As a salesman he had an easy patter, but he hardly had to do a hard sell on me, after all, it was His Majesty's Government that was paying for it, not me, so I would take whatever was given to me and be grateful for the privilege.

"Of course," he continued, ignoring my tone, "we'll work with you over the next few months."

"Months?"

"Well, we have quite a lot of limbs to make," he said, looking pointedly around the ward, "but that's not the problem as we have quite an army of craftsmen down there. No, the reason it takes so long is that over time, as your stump hardens, it also shrinks – I'm sure they've told you this – so we can't give you the finished article until your leg is good and ready. Until then we'll be teaching you to walk using something simple, like this." He held up a wooden peg leg attached to a leather pouch.

My face must have given away my thoughts because he quickly added, "No, no, don't worry, this is only to help you get started and used to wearing a prosthetic. It's nothing like your real false leg will look like."

I smiled at the oxymoron.

May 28th, 1918

God bless my little sister, Constance. I do love the pretty little thing but sometimes I wish someone would give her some brains. This morning I received post from my mother and my sister – not once have I received any communication from my father – and Constance had sent me a book.

*"Dear Ed,"* she had written, *"I've just read a wonderful swashbuckling adventure story set on a desert island on the high seas*

*and, knowing how you like adventure stories and, to take your mind off all the horrid things they're doing to you, I decided to send it to you now I've finished reading it."*

So, to take my mind off my injuries my dear little sister had sent me her copy of Treasure Island by Robert Louis Stevenson and, while I grant it's a great adventure, I wasn't really in the mood to read a book where one of the main characters is a one legged pirate who goes by the name of Long John Silver.

May 29th, 1918

Today, eleven days since my first physiotherapy session to harden my stump, I did my first impression of Long John Silver.

Nurse Edith wheeled me to the gymnasium where I was left with the esteemed Mr Thomas of Critchley of Liverpool.

Thomas, to give him his due, knows his job. His attention to my comfort was a credit to him and his company.

"First and foremost Captain, a healed stump is a happy stump and a happy stump is what we want. And once he's a happy stump we need to keep him that way by maintaining a strict regime of cleanliness and exercise." By we, he meant me, of course. "If we don't look after him then he'll develop sores and if they become infected you could end up losing more of your leg, or even your life, so we cannot emphasise too much how much care you need to give him." That he referred to my stump as a 'he' did not go unnoticed; it seems that stumps were anthropomorphically personified throughout the hospital.

"You must keep him dry," he continued. "If he's wet the leather glove will rub and cause friction burns and sores, so you should use plenty of talcum powder, especially in hot weather, and make sure you change your stump sock regularly. At least once a day, more in summer, to lessen the risk of infection."

Despite talking without seeming to take a breath he explained in meticulous detail how the prosthetic was strapped on, and he demonstrated the process to me using the peg leg he'd brought with him, allowing me to do it for myself so I could get used to it.

Once it was on and was tight and secure, Thomas, and his assistant Johnston, held my arms and helped me upright. I stood with all my weight on my left leg and held the peg leg slightly off the floor.

"Now, gently let the false leg touch the floor," he said. Gingerly, I lowered it. "That's excellent, Captain," and I could hear the excited encouragement in his voice as he stood facing me. "Now, gradually put some weight on it... not too much... that's it. Now, how does that feel?"

Johnston was still holding onto me to help me balance and it was painful, despite all the physiotherapy I'd had, but I needed to do this.

I gritted my teeth and screwed up my face against the pain and, little by little, shifted my weight onto it. Once or twice I had to shift the weight back to my left and start again, so it was a slow process, but the pair of them demonstrated the patience of Job, and progress was made.

Finally, I stood there, weight evenly distributed - well perhaps slightly biased to my left leg – and Johnston let go of my arm to let me stand unaided for the first time in two months. Despite the pain I felt elated. I experienced the kind of joy and excitement an infant might display when standing for the first time without the aid of a sofa or table.

I realised, as I stood grinning like a church gargoyle, that I didn't know what to do next and I remembered Thomas telling me at our first meeting that I was going to have to learn to walk again as if for the first time.

May 30th, 1918

My nightmares have taken a new turn. They've never left me since the explosion that ended my war; relentless in their constancy, haunting in their nature and terrifying in their content.

I was standing in the trench with my men, just before dawn. An uneasy silence hung in the air like an unspoken lie and, in the dawn's early light the orders came. We were to launch our attack at 07hr00. I looked at my watch, its luminous dial glowed in the gloom and I could sense the restless anticipation of the men around me.

One minute to go.

All along the trench men readied themselves. Many would not survive the attack instigated by those orders that came from some faceless General who sat in a comfortable office several miles behind the lines, unaware of the reality of the conditions in which we lived.

Slowly the second hand crept past the six.

Twenty-five second to go - I pulled my revolver from its holster.

Twenty seconds to go - I fumbled for my service whistle. My hand was shaking in fear of the horror with which I had grown familiar.

Fifteen seconds - I placed the end of the whistle to my mouth. Its metal was cold to my lips.

Ten seconds - I looked along the trench and saw the Captain further along the line raise his hand to ready his men and, reluctantly, I followed suit.

Five seconds - I looked at my men. I could smell their fear.

Four seconds - along the trench men braced themselves.

Three seconds - I grasped the ladder and looked to the top of the trench.

Two seconds - I raised my foot to the first rung.

One second - I wondered if there was a God and whether he would look favourably at me when I met Him.

Zero - all along the trench the sounds of whistles echoed, and we leapt up and into no-man's land. I was halfway up the ladder, blowing mine as loudly as I could. Then, as I spat it out I shouted to my men, "Follow me lads. Let's make this a day to remember," There we were splashing through the thick brown mud, charging towards the enemy line with their bullets flying past us and their shells exploding around us as we made our suicidal charge.

I noticed that neither I, nor any of my men had legs; we were all dragging ourselves forward using our hands to pull our bodies through the sticky mud.

A bullet struck one man and he was suddenly propelled into the air on a huge metal spring, like a jack-in-the-box. He was wearing a bright red and white striped shirt with a blue polka-dot bow tie and white gloves, and he had a huge bright red smile painted across his face.

The same was happening to the rest of my men, and soon the field was full of men bouncing around in the air on giant springs like some ghastly clowns. Then I was the only one left, scrabbling through the mire that was trying to suck me down and drag me into its depths.

I threw myself to the ground to avoid the bullets only to bounce straight back upright again. Looking down I saw that my lower body was now encased in a hemi-spherical yellow plastic base which kept righting me every time I fell, like a roly-poly toy with its equilibrium in its bottom, leaving me exposed to the rain of death being inflicted by the Germans from the safety of their trenches.

A hail of bullets pummelled into my right leg, a leg I didn't have a moment ago. An explosion threw me high into the air and, as I screamed, I woke with a start.

I was sweating. My heart was pounding in my chest and I felt a shooting pain in my stump. My throat felt constricted as I tried to draw breath, but I couldn't. I couldn't breathe. I coughed, rasped, desperately clawing for air. A nurse came running to my side and helped me sit up. She pushed my head between my knees and rubbed my back.

My eyes felt as though they were going to burst from their sockets, and I desperately fought for breath. I could feel a pounding in my head and a blood red wave of dizziness blurred my vision.

The nurse pushed a mask over my nose and mouth. I fought against it, but she was stronger. I was beginning to lose my battle for air. Black spots floated before my eyes. As I began to lose consciousness a waft of oxygen filled the mask and I gasped.

Finally, I managed to draw breath; only a little at first, then a bigger one.

Slowly, after what seemed an age, I began to calm down. My breath still came in gasps, but I was breathing. Eventually, the nurse removed the mask from my face and my breathing slowed to normal.

"Thanks," I whispered. She handed me a glass of water and I took a small sip.

"Nightmare?"

"Yes."

The sun was rising over the horizon and the dawn chorus flowed through the open window above me. Men were still sleeping, some snoring, some whimpering. One cried out in his sleep. A couple, at the far end of the ward, were sitting up, smoking.

The nightmare lingered. My stump went into cramp and I rubbed it in an attempt to stretch the muscles.

June 2nd, 1918

It's been just over three weeks since I took my first tentative steps using Thomas' peg leg, and I have become quite adept at hobbling along on it. I no longer need the support of the parallel bars and I've even walked outside, through the grounds of Roehampton.

To feel the warmth of the sun on my face, smell the sweet scent of flowers growing in the borders and beds and hear the buzzing of bees was so uplifting. To think I've never appreciated these simple things before. Three years stuck in a trench enveloped by the stench of death, putrid flesh, stagnant water and damp, soggy mud, followed by all those clinical hospital smells and, more recently, the methylated spirits in which my stump is marinated, tends to dull the senses to the beauty of which I've been deprived for so long and which now surrounds me.

July 5th, 1918

I had my first proper fitting for my new prosthetic leg today. Thomas and Johnston spent the morning with me making sure it was exactly the right height to enable me to stand properly upright and to attention without listing like a sinking ship. Also, the height of the knee needs to be the same as the height of my left knee, otherwise I would walk with too much of a limp, which could create problems with curvature of the spine over time and mean I wouldn't be able to walk in a straight line as easily as I should.

Who would have thought that an artificial limb could be so complicated?

Doctor Corner visited me this afternoon – I've never felt so important, receiving all these distinguished visitors dedicated to my wellbeing – and gave me some good news. Once Thomas and Johnston are happy that I'm managing with my new leg and everyone is satisfied that it is fit for purpose, they want to discharge me. Set me free. Release me back into the wild. Send me home.

Oh, how good those words sound; going home at last. It does seem like I've been here for an eternity and, if I'm not careful, I could be in danger of becoming institutionalised, so this really is wonderful news.

Now don't get me wrong, the staff here have been fantastic, and I am eternally grateful to them for their care and assistance in getting me mobile once again. Nurse Edith, who has looked after me and wheeled me about to various clinics, Messrs Thomas and Johnston from Critchley of Liverpool, who have worked so diligently to make me a new leg and teach me to walk and even the physiotherapist who, despite her less than tender ministrations, or should that be *because* of her less than tender ministrations, has prepared my stump for its new role as one half of a new partnership between flesh and leather.

But I'm not gone yet.


July 6th, 1918

There's a lot of talk on the ward and around the hospital about a 'flu epidemic, but there's been nothing reported in the newspapers about it. There was a mention of it a couple of months ago but that was back in May and it's now July. Apparently, it's been spreading so fast because of all the troop movement across Europe. No one seems to know much about it or where it started but there are plenty of rumours flying about. According to some Spanish newspapers about half of the troops, from

134

both sides, fighting on the western front are infected with it. When I returned from the front back in April I was suffering from it. It wasn't serious, just a seasonal 'flu as I remember, but I suppose it's able to spread so quickly because all the soldiers are in close proximity to one another. They're calling it Spanish Flu for some reason, and it seems to be quite contagious.

Thomas and Johnston came along this afternoon for another fitting. I'm quite excited about the prospect of my new leg, although I'd still rather have my real one. I suppose my excitement is because once I've got it and I'm competent at walking with it, I get to go home, so I'm working hard to be a good patient.

I was able to walk up and down the ward today and the leg flexes and stretches just like a real one. It seems strange that when something happens naturally, like the bending of a knee, we tend to take for granted. We accept it, we never question how or why it happens. But when that leg is replaced by an artificial one and you have to learn how it works in order to walk with it, it highlights our fragility. But I'm getting used to it and the way it works, the way it bends and straightens, and I am quite comfortable with walking on it now, although I don't think I'll ever grace a rugger field again.

July 10th, 1918

A few adjustments have been made to my false leg as, apparently, my stump shrunk slightly at the beginning of the month. Thomas is pleased that it now appears to have stopped shrinking, meaning that these adjustments should be the final ones they need to make.

Thomas spent a few hours explaining in detail what every part of the prosthetic is, what it does and how it works. He showed me how to maintain it and what parts I need to give special attention to, such as the springs that enable the joint flexibility while at the same time ensuring the limb supports me. He stressed again the importance of ensuring my stump is healthy, keeping it dry and changing the sock regularly, particularly in the heat of summer, and he impressed on me the importance of using plenty of talcum powder.

I've been walking on my new leg every day and each day I walk for a bit longer. Everyday I get better with it and I'm beginning to get quite used it now. I do have an obvious limp, which I guess I'll never get rid of, which means I'll be stared at every time I'm out and about, something I really don't wish to endure, but I won't be able to avoid. The burn scars

I can cover, although the ones on my neck and cheek will always show, but they're not too bad.

Still, I'm luckier than many. Those whose burns have disfigured them beyond all recognition. Those whose eyelids, lips or noses were burnt away, who will have to wear masks and live with the realisation that people will cross the street to avoid them when they approach, and children will run away from them screaming. I'm not sure how I could live with that if it was me and I wonder how many won't. I wonder how many will be so badly affected that they'd rather end their lives than continue to be shunned and feared by the society they fought to save.

I thought of my own situation. Compared to those men I am relatively whole and, although I am generally strong in my mind, I do suffer from some seriously bad days, when my mood is dark and I'm full of self-pity and self-loathing. There are times when I've felt the enormous weight of guilt. Guilt that I'm alive when so many of my men are lying dead somewhere in a foreign field; buried without a grave; remembered by the few but forgotten by many. Sometimes that guilt becomes so unbearable that I want to end my life and join my men, but then I'm too scared to do it. What does that say about me?

I know I should feel grateful that I'm alive, grateful that I have a future when so many have none; and often I do, but occasionally, for no reason at all, I feel the opposite and I just want to shout and scream and cry out in my anger and frustration.

And then there's the nightmare. At times I am too afraid to go to sleep for fear of the night terrors. At times the nightmares are so vivid that I'm no longer sure whether I'm asleep or awake. One thing is for sure though, in every dream and every nightmare I have I wake up just as I'm about to die some horrible death. Sometimes I see a bullet, careering through the air in slow motion, making its way towards my chest, my heart, and however urgent my movement, I am unable to get out of its way. Then, just as the tip of the bullet presses against the pocket of my tunic, before it rips through my clothes and tears into my flesh, I wake up with a start, shouting in panic, crying out in fear.

Will these dreams ever abate or am I doomed to be haunted by them for all eternity?

July 23rd, 1918

That's it! I'm free!

This morning Doctor Corner and Mr Thomas visited me together and agreed that they are happy with my progress and that I can go home tomorrow.

I got Nurse Edith to send a telegram home so someone will be there to meet me at Ely station. Then I spent the afternoon packing my things and going around the hospital saying goodbye to the staff and inmates whose company I have had the pleasure of enjoying over the past few months.

I must say it seems as though I've been here for a lifetime and lived several more since I first left home in 1915 to join my regiment and on to the trenches. Just four months ago I was fighting on the front lines and a few days later I was fighting for my life in a field hospital just outside Amiens in Belgium. A lot has happened since then and I remember what my physiotherapist said to me when we first met. As much as I disliked her description of this place, she was absolutely right; Roehampton was nothing more than a human repair factory, and I am a perfect example of their work. I arrived here on a stretcher, seriously wounded and sick from fever and tomorrow I shall walk out, unaided, with my head held high.

July 24th, 1918

Accompanied by Nurse Edith and carrying my suitcase in one hand and my new walking stick in the other, dressed in a new suit, shirt and tie, courtesy of the British Government, I walked along the ward to the rapturous applause we afforded every patient walking out to return to civvy street after their stay in Roehampton.

I was no longer a soldier. Along with my discharge from hospital I have been discharged from the army with a letter of thanks from His Majesty, King George V, and a new suit to travel home in. I had already received my military discharge papers and, as an officer, I had had to resign my commission in accordance with military protocol. No problem with that, of course. Even if I'd wanted to go back and fight I couldn't on account of me being one limb short of a full set.

A taxi was waiting outside the hospital to drive me to Kings Cross Station, from where I would catch my train home. All paid for, of course.

# Chapter Eighteen
## Dream Time

And that was it. I had come to the end of the journal.

I turned to the next page to find it blank. In frustration I flicked through the book to find the rest of the pages similarly blank. For reasons known only to him, Grandad had finished writing the account of his life during the First World War upon his discharge from hospital. Presumably his return home had left him too busy to resume writing, or he had lost the desire or motivation to continue. Either way, having read it thus far, I wanted to know more.

"I can't believe he stopped writing when he did," I told Larry, who was sitting doing the crossword in the smoking room. He looked up at me from the settee where he sat with his feet resting on the coffee table as I wandered through from the library. A warm fire burned brightly, creating flickering shadows across the walls and filling the room with the acrid smell of woodsmoke.

The dark winter afternoon outside was rapidly changing into a cold evening, making the smoking room feel even more cosy. Thick clouds covered an otherwise bright gibbous moon and a bitter wind howled around the old Hall, whistling noisily through the architraves and balustrades that adorned the walls and windows outside. The flames leapt high in the grate as the wind, blowing across the tops of the stacks, created a sudden updraft.

"Finds the spirit through nets, anagram, 11 letters," Larry said, as I sat down on the settee opposite. His cheeks glowed red from the heat of the fire and he appeared flushed.

"No idea," I replied, frustrated that he obviously hadn't listened to what I had said. "I was talking about Grandad's journal. He left it unfinished."

"Infuriating, eh?" He swung his legs off the table and sat up. "You know, I'd love to know what happened next, but I couldn't find anything more. I scoured the library cupboards where he kept his things."

"So? What?" I said, opening my arms in a quizzical shrug.

"What do you mean, so, what?"

"So, that's it's then? No more journal?"

"Nope. No more journal. I've looked in the cupboards, I've looked in the drawers, I've looked everywhere he might have left personal papers, but I found nothing."

"Pity."

"Yes. And I'm stuck on this dratted crossword. There's only one clue to complete."

"Read it to me again."

"Finds the spirit through nets, anagram, 11 letters."

"Have you got any letters?"

He held the paper up and counted. "The third letter is an 'o', tenth letter's an 'e'."

"That's it?"

"Yes."

"Doesn't help much, does it?"

"No, not really."

He threw the paper on the table, stood up and stretched his arms above his head with a loud groan.

"Brandy?"

"Thanks. Yes please." I watched him walk stiffly across the room.

"My leg's gone to sleep," he complained.

"Imagine having it blown off," I said cupping my hands around the bowl of the glass to warm it through, "and having to go through what Grandad went through."

"His whole war experience was remarkable. I can't even begin to imagine the stress and trauma he went through. They all went through. And they did it because they were told to do it."

I felt the brandy send its warming fingers through my body, content at being warmed from the inside by the drink and from the outside by the fire. I was in a reflective mood. I pondered on the last few months I had spent staying at Rosehip Hall, and how healing Larry's companionship had been. I thought about what might have become of me had Leanne not been concerned about my wellbeing back in summer and had let me remain at home on my own.

I considered the strange episodes I had experienced; the woman I had seen who didn't exist and yet who resembled my grief counsellor, and the vivid dreams I had suffered. I was thankful for the support I had had from those who cared about me, from Larry, Leanne and, yes, Madea. I reflected that, finally, I felt positive for the future and I was no longer allowing past events to dominate and control my life.

In short, I was moving on.

Larry, comfortable on his settee surrounded by soft cushions, sat staring across the room. I watched with some amusement as his eyes slowly glazed over, his eyelids drooped, and his head lolled slowly to one side as he fell asleep.

The wind had died down outside and the crackling of the wood burning in the hearth was the only sound that disturbed the silence. That and Larry's gentle snores. I crossed to the fireplace and threw more logs on the fire before it burned out.

"That'll probably do for now, Bennet," said a voice behind me I didn't recognise.

"What!" I exclaimed, standing up and spinning around.

"You can probably lock up and retire for the night," said the man sitting in the old leather armchair that hadn't been there a moment ago. He was young, probably around twenty or twenty-one years old, dressed in a dark double-breasted suit, with a white shirt, collar and dark, sober, tie.

"Who are you?" I stuttered, taken aback somewhat by this bizarre occurrence.

"Yes, sir," another voice I didn't recognise answered, ignoring me completely. A movement on the other side of the mantelpiece caught my eye and I saw a short, balding man straightening up from placing more logs on the fire. "What about Miss Violet, sir? Do you need someone to escort her home or will she be staying?"

Bennet was dressed in grey pinstripe trousers with a dark jacket and matching tie. I guessed he must have been the butler, or some such employee of the house.

"I had Beth make up the spare room for her earlier."

"What...? Who...?" I repeated, but they didn't appear to hear me or, indeed, be aware of my presence. The room, although it was the same, was different, and not just because two complete strangers were conversing in it, in apparent ignorance of my presence.

I shook my head to try and clear it. Surely, I was asleep. Surely, I was just dreaming. Perhaps if I pinched myself I would wake up, but it didn't work. The dream was as vivid as if it was really happening, only I knew it wasn't. The room smelled of cigarette smoke and I could feel a cold draught blowing in from beneath the door to the corridor. I shivered. I don't think I've ever had dreams before in which I could smell things.

And where was Larry? I looked around but he was nowhere in sight. The way the room was furnished was different. A dark oak table stood behind two armchairs, and the walls were adorned with a thick, presumably expensive, brown and dark orange patterned paper. The polished parquet flooring was covered by thick pile oriental rugs and heavy drapes were drawn across the windows to shut out the dark, uninviting night. In one of the armchairs this interloper sat, smoking a cigarette and brandishing a large brandy as if he owned the place.

"Very good, sir, goodnight." Bennet replied and quietly left the room.

I was confused. I was so sure I hadn't fallen asleep, but it was the only explanation.

But at what point had I fallen asleep? Presumably before I got up to throw the logs on the fire.

But if that was the case then why did I now feel the warmth from it? It was dying down when I got up from the settee.

The room looked as it might have looked a hundred years ago. It was, without a doubt, same room; the doors, windows and fireplace were all in the right place. It's just the furnishings were so different, so... old fashioned.

The man in the armchair emptied his glass, put it down on the occasional table between the two chairs and, with an obvious effort, struggled to stand up. At first, I thought it was because he was drunk, but I realised as soon as he started limping across to the drinks table, that he had a bad leg. Then it dawned on me. The décor of the room, the clothes he was wearing, the limp. I was dreaming of Grandad Edward.

The door through which Bennet had recently departed opened again and in walked a pretty young lady dressed in a cream, calf-length silk dress, tied at the waist with a wide ribbon. Her short, dark, curly hair framed her pale face and her make-up was tastefully applied to highlight her ruby-red lips and her long eyelashes. She smiled as she saw Edward across the room as she closed the door behind her.

"Violet," he said, acting as though he had been caught in the middle of some misdemeanour.

Violet walked daintily, but determinedly, across to him and gently removed the decanter from his grasp, replaced the stopper and put it back on the table.

"I think you've had enough, Edward," she said, "you know what they said about too much drink." Her voice had a slight country accent, she was clearly a local girl.

In response, Edward grabbed her waist and pulled her around, so she stood facing him. She let out a little squeal of delight and they laughed. She was a few inches shorter and she tilted her head up to face him, smiled and fluttered her eyelashes coquettishly. I thought how beautiful she was.

"I do love you, you know," he said.

"I know, my love," she smiled, "and you know I love you. Now, put me down before anyone comes in and sees us."

"Let them come. Let them see us," he said, "I've nothing to be ashamed of."

"No, Edward."

"Why not?"

"You know why not. I'm only nineteen."

"So?"

"You know my father would never give his consent to us becoming engaged. We'll have to wait until I'm twenty-one and we no longer need his permission."

"Why does your father dislike our family so much? Your mother has worked here for over ten years when he's been mostly unemployed. If it wasn't for us, you all would have starved."

"And that's part of his problem. He resents that mummy has been able to hold down a regular job when he can't, and he resents that your family has, apparently, been our benefactor."

"We all know why. He drinks too much. He spends too much of his time in the Three Horseshoes when he should be at work and when he gets drunk, he gets violent. One of these days he's going to kill someone in one of his drunken rages and then they'll take him away and hang him."

"I sometime wish he would, then he won't be a danger to us anymore."

"What do you mean?"

"When he gets drunk, he gets aggressive. He's always getting into fights at the pub, and most of the village is scared of him. Then he comes home and takes it out on us. That's why Gwen left. He came home one night and beat her up. Mummy locked me in my room, so I couldn't go and try to save her. In the morning mummy had bruises all over her face and Gwen was gone. She ran away to London." She sobbed, "Poor Gwen, she ran away to escape father only to get killed by Spanish Flu.

142

That's so unfair."

Edward wrapped her tenderly in his arms.

"The bastard," he whispered.

She looked up at him again and this time their lips met in a brief, chaste kiss.

"He doesn't like it that I'm here either," she said.

"You're here as my nurse."

"And that means that two of us are employed by the Hilliards, and he isn't. He also hates that you're a war hero."

"Good God, why? I'm not a hero," Edward protested. "I lost a leg fighting for my country. I did what was expected of me and I did what I was ordered to do. I came home, which is more than many other poor bastards managed. He has no idea what it was like out there, he has no right to be jealous."

"You were awarded the Military Cross. Did you write that in your journal?"

"No."

"You should, you know."

"I've finished the journal."

"Why?"

"I don't need it anymore."

"But you should…"

"You told me I should write it to make me feel better after the deaths of my mother, Constance and my brothers. I've written as much as I can."

"How far did you get?"

"Up to the day when I left hospital to come home."

"And has it helped?"

"It's helped. But I couldn't bring myself to write about after my return home."

"Why not?"

"I don't know. I still can't face their deaths."

"Maybe later on?"

"Maybe. Depends."

"On what?"

"On when we get married."

"I've already told you. We have to wait until I'm twenty-one."

"That's two years way."

"No, it's sooner than that. I'll be twenty next month, remember?"

"So, we could get married in January 1920?"

"Yes. Well no."

"Yes? No? Which is it? Are you so intent on teasing me?" he laughed.

"We need to have a reasonable period of engagement first, otherwise people might wonder why we're rushing into it."

"I don't care what people think, it's none of their business. They're just villagers with nothing better to talk about."

"Well, I do. I'm one of them, remember. So, when we no longer need my father's permission, we'll do it properly."

"But…"

"Or not at all."

"Oh."

"We don't have to have a long engagement. We could be married by the Easter."

She reached up and kissed his lips again, only this time the kiss lingered before she pulled away. "Now," she said, with her bright smile on her face, "I'm going to my bed, and you'll do well to get to yours. I'm sure your father expects to see you return to work tomorrow."

Violet disentangled herself from Edward's embrace and left the room. I watched as he refilled his glass and limped to the fireplace where he leant on the mantlepiece and surveyed the room. I was still standing by the woodpile on the other side of the fireplace and, as he looked about, his eyes momentarily fixed on mine. A look of shock passed across his face and he stepped back in surprise. When he looked again I guess I was gone to him, as he visibly relaxed, although I noticed he put his drink down and didn't touch it again.

This was strange. Normally I am part of my own dreams, for better or for worse – recently for worse – so why was I now, apparently, an observer in this one? It didn't make sense. Also, I don't normally realise that I am in a dream until I wake up, usually in some distress. But here I was, aware that I was dreaming and worrying about what was happening to me.

The door opened again and this time an older man, somewhere about fifty years old by my reckoning, walked in. He strode purposefully, almost arrogantly, across the room and poured himself a large whisky before sitting down and lighting a cigarette. Eventually he looked at Edward and acknowledged his presence. I guessed this was great grandfather William.

"Well?" he addressed Edward, gruffly.

"Well, what?" Edward replied.

"Well, are you returning to work tomorrow or not?"

"I am."

"It's been three weeks, you know."

"Nearer four, father."

"Then it's about time. You need to get hold of your life; stop letting the past control you."

"People have been telling me that since I was blown up in April and discovered I was missing a leg. Which I felt was quite important, although others may have dismissed it."

You could have cut the atmosphere with a knife. In such a short space of time I could feel the antagonism between them; there was an argument brewing. It seemed that both of them were spoiling for a fight. Even I could see that.

"And now it's December. Perhaps you need to heed that advice, boy."

"I've been in mourning, or haven't you noticed? I just got used to the loss of my leg. I came home to recuperate, only to lose my mother, my sister and my two brothers to Spanish Flu."

"It was a tragedy I grant you that. Unfortunate I know, but it wasn't your fault."

Unfortunate? I could hardly believe what I was hearing. This man, my great grandfather, had lost nearly all his family and he referred to it as unfortunate.

I reminded myself that this was just a strange dream. William's words were the words my mind was putting into his mouth.

What did that say about me?

"Not my fault?" Edward spat. "Of course it wasn't my fault, but that doesn't stop me grieving for them. I miss them. It wasn't your fault either and yet you didn't take time off work to mourn them."

"I attended their funerals."

"Very noble of you, I'm so glad you managed to squeeze them into your busy schedule."

"What did you expect?"

"Can you hear yourself? You managed to spare time to attend the funerals of your wife, your only daughter and two of your sons. I'm surprised you bothered."

William flinched at Edward's barbed remark and took a long sip of his whisky. This argument was clearly overdue.

William took a long look at his son with what looked like pity in his eyes.

"When we received a telegram earlier this year," he said softly, "informing us that you were missing in action, we all assumed you had been killed and we waited for the next telegram with fear and trepidation. I was devastated. I kept telling myself that it was all my fault. I could have saved you. I could have kept you at the factory. You were in a reserved occupation, but no, I wanted you to go to fight for your honour, fight for your country. I even encouraged you to go, maybe I forced you, and your death was to be on my hands.

"You cannot even begin to understand the relief I felt when the second telegram came informing us that you were badly injured, but you were safe. Alive. You would be coming home."

"You were relieved that I was safe and yet you simply accepted the death of the rest of your family as if it was just something that happened."

"I was upset."

"I didn't notice."

"Well, I was. I just didn't dwell on it, that's all. They died. I had no control of that. It was that bally Spanish Flu that killed them, not me."

"So, what you're saying is, the real reason you would have grieved for me was because you thought my death was your fault."

William drained his glass and I could see his hand shaking.

"You. Selfish. Old. Man." Edward hissed angrily. "You didn't grieve for me, just like you didn't grieve for mother, for Constance, for Bill, or for Eddie. You grieved for yourself. Your own self-pity. You thought my death would be on your conscience because it was you who made me go to war. It was you who sent me to suffer for three years in the trenches, and you couldn't bear the thought of having to live for the rest of your life knowing that you could have saved me. But the rest of them? Their deaths had nothing to do with you. An inconvenience maybe. Unfortunate, definitely, but not your fault. So your conscience is clear, and you can go on living your life as though they didn't exist."

"How dare you," William roared, leaping from his chair and advancing on Edward. His face was apoplectic with rage, and for a moment, I thought he might suffer a heart attack. He stood glaring angrily at Edward, his breath coming in heavy bursts, but he managed to control himself. Eventually he turned and stormed out of the room, slamming the door loudly behind him.

I listened to his heavy steps stomping along the corridor, fading into the distance as he headed for the hall. When I turned back Edward was no longer there and I was once again standing by the fireplace in the present-day smoking room, and there was Larry sitting up on the settee with the Sunday Times crossword on his lap.

"What was that bang?" he asked, looking around.

"Bang?" I said.

"Yes. It sounded like a door being slammed. Didn't you hear it?"

I looked at him, putting on an innocent look.

"I was having a strange dream," he continued, I was sitting doing the crossword when you got up to put a log on the fire."

"You weren't dreaming," I said, "here I am having put said logs on said fire."

"Yes, yes, let me finish. It was you but it wasn't you. You seemed to morph into someone else who was putting the logs on the fire. You looked like someone from the 1920s. Then a door slammed, and I woke up. Dreams can be weird, can't they?"

I stared at him, incredulously. Had he shared my dream? Well, a very small part of it, anyway. But how can two people share the same dream?

I was still standing, leaning on the mantlepiece and the fire was roaring in the grate from the logs I had thrown on it. I hadn't been sleeping standing up, of that I was sure, and yet the dream, or whatever it was, had started after I had banked up the fire.

What was happening to me? Was it a vision? A psychic incident?

I felt the blood drain from my face, and I put my hand out to steady myself.

"What's up, Jim? You look as though you've seen a ghost."

I closed my eyes, briefly, to try and clear my head, then I resumed my seat on the settee opposite Larry and related the events that had just taken place.

He listened intently, never once interrupting my story and, when I had finished, he looked at me with an excited look in his eyes.

He leapt up, brandy glass in hand, and walked around the settee.

"Do you believe in ghosts?" he said, turning to me. His face was animated, and his grey eyes showed his excitement. As he walked across the room the flames from the fire threw flickering shadows that danced a sinister salsa across his face.

"Err, no, not really."

"Think about it, Jim," he said as he shimmied around the room. "You've just been transported one hundred years back in time to December 1918 and, even though I was asleep, I experienced it too. At least a little bit. Not like you did, admittedly, but I was there and if I hadn't been asleep, who knows, I might have been right there with you. We now know what happened to the family, to Great Grandmother and Grandad's brothers and sister. We know they died from Spanish Flu. Edward didn't get it because he'd had it earlier in the year when it wasn't so dangerous. Remember, he mentioned it in his journal?"

"But it's not proof."

"What do you mean?"

"I had a… I don't really know what I had. Some sort of daydream, maybe, but that doesn't prove they died from Spanish Flu. That's just conjecture gleaned from a dream that I just had. It's a figment of my imagination."

"It's a plausible explanation. Afterall, until reading Grandad's journal we didn't even know he had any brothers or sisters. Now, thanks to your ghostly endeavours, we know what happened to them.

"We don't know that for sure," I protested.

"I'm prepared to bet that, when we research it, you're right, and that's exactly what they did die from.

"How can we research it?"

"The family was important in the community. If over half of them died from Spanish Flu, or anything else for that matter, it'll have been reported in the papers. We can look it up."

Larry was clearly excited at the possibility of ghosts and, I suppose, in different circumstance, I'd have been excited too.

I stared into the flames crackling away in the fireplace. My mind was a blur of emotions and confusion and I didn't know what to think. I don't think I actually wanted to think about it.

Finally, Larry sat down again, picked up the newspaper and started writing. I could see him frantically jotting down letters around the crossword he'd been trying to solve earlier.

"Ghosthunter. Of course."

"What?" I said started out of my reverie by his sudden cry.

"Finds the spirit through nets, anagram, eleven letters. Finds the spirit. If you find spirits what does that make you? A ghosthunter of course, and ghosthunter is an anagram of 'through nets'. There nothing like a good anagram. Excellent, that's the crossword completed."

148

# Chapter Nineteen
## A Matter of Record

I couldn't sleep. I lay on my back in the dark staring sightlessly at the ceiling. No light, not even faint, peeped through the chinks in the curtains and the only light in the room was the pale green glow from the alarm clock radio on my bedside table. I turned over noisily and huffed loudly.

Since when had my mattress become so uncomfortable?

Normally, I would lie in bed, read for a bit, and then turn out the light and sleep until morning. But not, it seemed, tonight. I suffered from dreams, of course, but they didn't stop me sleeping. The events of the evening had disturbed me, and a cornucopia of befuddled thoughts swarmed around inside my head, uninvited and unwanted, like a nest of wasps. All kinds of explanations presented themselves; from haunting to time travel; from Janet's sudden death to Spanish Flu; from psychosis to counselling; but nothing made sense. Nothing ever makes any sense in the dead of night.

Was my depression returning? Was I in the throes of a relapse?

What I was currently going through wasn't the same as before. It wasn't like my previous episode for, despite the confusion of thoughts exploding through my mind, there was an uncertain clarity to them that I'd never experienced when I was having my breakdown. This time I felt... I don't know, maybe exhilaration as well as fear.

What if I really was experiencing paranormal events; the woman in the garden and the chapel; this evening's vision. Were they all triggered by my illness? Were they just side effects? Psychotic events?

We were back to the idea of 'cause and effect'. But I thought the psychosis only occurred when depression got worse, and I knew I was getting better. For goodness sake, I felt better, I was looking forward to things.

Yes, I know I could still have incidents if my depression overwhelmed me, but I did not feel overwhelmed. I felt better than I had felt for months.

I was hot. I threw the covers off and seconds later regretted it as the cold air chilled me. I pulled them back over me. I banged my head down on the pillow several times as if it would make it more comfortable. It felt as though it was full of rocks. Banging my head failed so I sat up and fluffed it up. Even that didn't work. It just seemed to make the rocks larger. I climbed out of bed and walked around the room. I pulled back the curtains and looked out across the garden. Out there, in the darkness, there was no light, just a jumble of shapes bathed in pallid shades of grey.

Snowflakes swirled past the window, blowing on wayward breezes and I shivered in the cold air of the room. The colourless world outside was somehow reassuring. Normal.

I suppose part of me expected something else, something out of the ordinary. I'm sure I wouldn't have been surprised if something had been out there, but there was nothing. Just the lawn, edged by the bushes and trees that lead to the wildflower garden, the walls of the kitchen garden and the washed-out walls of the chapel, tucked away between the kitchen garden and the house. I relaxed, turned away and climbed back into bed.

In my brief absence the sheets had turned cold and I had to kick my legs about to create some warmth before snuggling down and closing my eyes.

For the rest of the night I dozed, woke up, slept fitfully and woke again.

I checked the clock at one-thirty; five-past-two; ten-to-three and seemingly every twenty to thirty minutes throughout the night until the welcome pale grey fingers of dawn crept through the curtains and across the floor, barely perceptible in the gloom of the winter morning.

I sat up, feeling exhausted from lack of sleep and proper rest and it was a real effort to drag my weary body out of bed and into the bathroom.

But, twenty minutes later, shower refreshed and dressed, I ventured downstairs, bracing myself to face Larry's energetic pertinacity.

Larry, always an early riser and even more so when he has the bit between his teeth, was already on his second cup of coffee and I was greeted to the smell of bacon grilling when I entered the kitchen bleary eyed and bedraggled.

"Crikey," he exclaimed, looking at me through cheery eyes. "Look at you. Bad night?"

"Yeah, you could say that."

"Last night's events upset you?"

"Yeah, a bit."

"There's coffee in the dining room, go and help yourself and I'll bring your breakfast through."

I dragged myself along the corridor and into the dining room, feeling like I'd gone fifteen rounds with Tyson Fury. Every joint and muscle ached, and my head felt thick with unresolved thoughts and worries. I peered out through the large windows. A blanket of virgin snow lay over the lawn, pristine and white and the grey clouds above threatened more.

By the time the coffee was having an effect Larry was sitting opposite me and we were tucking into bacon, sausages and fried eggs. I was feeling vaguely human at last. We rarely had more than cereal or toast for breakfast, so this was a welcome treat.

"I made a start this morning while you were still lazing about in bed," he said, pushing his empty plate away.

"On what?"

"Researching old newspapers for news on our ancestors. I found a great website that has electronic copies of all the Cambridge Daily News newspapers for 1918. I've found an article from December 27th that has William's murder on the front page. Did you know he was murdered on Christmas Eve?"

"No," I said, finishing my last mouthful of sausage, "I don't think I did. That's a bit sad though, isn't it?"

"And that would have finished an already shit year for Grandad. Losing his leg in the war, then his mum, sister and brothers to Spanish Flu, and finally his dad being murdered. No wonder he never talked about it. I'm surprised he talked about anything, ever, after such an 'annus horribilis'."

"So, what did it say?"

"Wait a sec." Larry left the room and returned moments later with his laptop. "Here, read this."

'Knight Killed By Crazed Christmas Killer.'

"I see they were into their sensational headlines even back then. So, what does it say?"

"Read it."

I took the laptop from him and started reading. 'Sir William Hilliard, who was knighted in 1917 for his services to our war effort; a war that ended last month with an allied victory, was brutally murdered by

151

unemployed local man, Seth Chambers. Chambers, who had been drinking for several hours in the Three Horseshoes in Downham Fen on Christmas Eve, embarked on his killing spree after being thrown out of the public house for aggressive behaviour towards one of the other Christmas Eve revellers.

'Sir William, who lived at Rosehip Hall, was enjoying a quiet evening with his son, war veteran and hero, Edward Hilliard MC, when Chambers barged in on them. A row followed resulting in a chase through the grounds of the Hall. At some point Chambers overcame Edward Hilliard and left him in the adjoining Chapel before setting fire to it. Then, using Sir William's own shot gun he shot Sir William.

'An unidentified villager dragged Edward out of the chapel that had become a blazing inferno. He was taken to hospital but has since been discharged.

'Chambers' wife, Elizabeth (Beth), has disappeared and it is believed that Chambers killed her too. Police are still searching for her body.

'Sir William is succeeded by Edward, who lost a leg in the trenches earlier in the year.'

"So, Grandad was awarded the Military Cross," I said, "wow, he never mentioned that."

"No, he kept it quiet. He kept a lot of things quiet."

"I don't think he liked his father all that much, to be honest, from the odd comments he made in his journal."

"And from what you said about what you saw last night."

"No, no, no," I objected, "you cannot read anything into something I dreamt."

"You think you dreamt."

"It doesn't mention any of the others in the article, does it?" I said, refusing to be drawn into this discussion.

"Implying they were, indeed, already dead. I'll look back and see if I can find anything on what happened."

"I'll clear up."

Twenty minutes later I heard Larry yell, "Eureka!" and he dashed into the kitchen with an excited look on his face.

"I've found it, Jim. Come and have a look."

I'd finished what I was doing and was just drying my hands, so I followed him back into the dining room where he'd left his laptop.

"There," he said, "read that."

I sat down and read the article, written on November 15th, 1918, just a few days after the war ended.

## HILLIARDS' HIT HARD

Spanish Flu, which is sweeping through our country like a bushfire has claimed more lives as it hits Ely and the surrounding villages with a vengeance.

And it seems as though it has no discrimination; old and young; healthy and sick; rich and poor are all equally susceptible to its evil tendrils and this is demonstrated by the deaths of the family of local entrepreneur, Sir William Hilliard. The family has reported the deaths of Sir William's wife, Lady Charlotte; their daughter, Constance (16), and sons William (18), who recently completed his officer training, and Edwin (17). Sir William and his remaining son, Edward, who was recently awarded the Military Cross for his bravery in the trenches on the Western Front, are both well.

October has been a particularly bad month for deaths in Great Britain from this virulent disease, claiming over 100,000 deaths nationwide. Several hundred of these were in Cambridgeshire.

"Four of them within a few days of each other," I said, sadly. "That's terrible."

"I suppose after four years of war no one was expecting it to end with something like this. Didn't more people die from Spanish Flu than died in the war?"

"I think so. The nearest thing we've had to that recently was the SARS outbreak a few years ago."

"Bird Flu? Yes, I remember it, but at least they contained it fairly easily."

"They can these days, the technology is there. Nothing like Spanish Flu could ever happen again."

"Thank goodness for that."

"So, in a nine-month period," I said, getting back to the subject on hand, "as well as losing his right leg, Grandad lost his whole family."

"Doesn't bear thinking about, does it?"

"Horrible." I shook my head, reflectively. What a tragic family we must have seemed back then. I can imagine people saying things like, 'look at them, they had all the money in the world, and it didn't bring them happiness,' or 'it only goes to show, money is the root of all evil.' People love to draw conclusions. I smiled at my thoughts, for here we were trying to do exactly that; draw conclusions. Only we were being a bit more analytical about it.

"Looks like that dream of yours last night was real after all," Larry said. "Looks like it was more than just a dream too."

I looked up. "Don't start that again. What you're suggesting is rubbish."

"What's your explanation then?"

"There must be something logical. Rational."

"Like what? We've just proved that what you saw was true."

"I don't know, do I? Not ghosts, though."

"How can you be so sure?"

"Come on Larry, listen to yourself. Ghosts? I mean, really?"

"Could be, why not? Don't be so quick to dismiss them."

"Do you remember that time at school we were frightened when we thought we heard the ghost of the dead porter dragging his broken leg along the corridor outside the dorm?"

"Yes."

"And it turned out to be George Young playing a joke on us. Ghosts don't exist."

"Hmmm."

I could see the doubt in Larry's eyes. He so wanted it to be ghosts. I think he's always wanted to think Rosehip Hall was haunted and, in a way, I think I probably did too.

Certainly, I couldn't think of a better explanation.

# Chapter Twenty
## Tangible Support, Tactical Encouragement

Larry had some business in Ely, and I was expecting Madea to arrive any minute for a counselling session.

I watched as the red tails lights of Larry's car disappeared along the snowy drive, leaving icy ruts in its wake where the wheels had spun and slid. The snow was soft and wet, perfect for building a snowman or for having a snowball fight. I scooped up a handful, squeezed it and hurled it at the back of the car, and in response I heard the horn blow and Larry's hand waving from his window.

As boys we had enjoyed many a snow adventure, either when we came to stay over at Christmas or at school during the Lent term. Nowadays we generally thought of it as pretty to begin with but within hours we would be wishing for it to clear as we watched the country inevitably come to a halt. I shivered as the cold penetrated through to my bones and vigorously rubbed my hands together, red from handling the wet, cold snow. I stomped my feet on the rug in the porch and changed into my slippers in the hall before going to brew a pot of coffee, in preparation for my session with Madea.

As usual, I made plenty, in case she wanted a cup, although I had never seen her eat or drink anything while she had been my counsellor.

As if on cue the doorbell rang just as I put the tray down on the table in the morning room, and I went to admit her. She was dressed in a long blue Burberry coat with a thick woollen scarf wrapped snugly around her slender neck.

We made ourselves comfortable with her sitting opposite me as she usually did, and I started to speak. She listened intently as I related, in some detail, the strange occurrence from the other night, and I wondered what she'd make of it.

"I thought I was making such good progress," I said in conclusion, "and then, out of the blue, this happens."

"First of all, remember that setbacks do happen, so please don't panic. It's something I would typically expect, and I did warn you about it when we first started."

"So, you don't think I'm heading back into my depression?"

"Grief can be an emotional rollercoaster, and it affects different people in different ways. This incident is much more likely to be what we class as a 'remnant of grief'. These can come when you least expect them to and are generally out of our control, but they rarely signal a downward spiral back into depression.

"I know it may be difficult to believe," she continued, "and it's easy to deflect all this by using well-worn clichés like 'life goes on', and all that, but we will never tell you that time heals. You react to grief in your own way. Nothing that helps you deal with it is necessarily wrong, except drugs and alcohol of course, and without a doubt, time does help, but it may not cure. It can, and often does, lessen the intensity of the pain of loss, but those feelings may never go away completely, and that is fine. What we try to work on is acceptance of this new normal and how we can embrace it, thereby reconciling you to your loss."

"But that's exactly what I thought I'd done. What I thought we'd done. I felt you'd guided me through that particular minefield," I was almost pleading, "and I really felt we'd made good progress, and now this. It felt so vivid; really real, as though I was actually there in that room. With them."

"No one denies what you saw."

"What I thought I saw."

"If you like."

"But it's implausible."

"Maybe, but not impossible."

I stopped at that and looked her in the eye. "What do you mean?"

"OK, let's step back and analyse it. You saw people who, you say, lived a hundred years ago."

"That's right."

"What makes you think it was a hundred years ago? How could you tell when it was?"

"We know my Grandad Edward came home in July 1918. That's written in his journal."

"OK."

"And we know that his father, William, was murdered on Christmas Eve of the same year, that's a matter of public record. We read it in the newspaper. We also know that his mother, Constance, William and Edwin all died of Spanish Flu just after the end of the war."

156

"Good."

"Finally, in their conversation, they mentioned that it had been four weeks since they'd died which makes it sometime in mid-December 1918. It could even have been the exact date as now, just a hundred years earlier."

"And do you think that's significant?"

"I have no idea."

"So, what do you think?"

I sat and looked out of the window. Outside it was snowing again and the new snow was settling on the old. It wasn't heavy, just steady. Fortunately, Larry had lit a fire in the morning room before he went out, so the room was cosy and warm.

I walked over and threw some logs on the fire, deliberately giving myself time to think of a suitable answer. Truth is, I didn't really know what I thought. Over the last few days, I'd thought of very little else but had drawn no conclusions and I was struggling to verbalise my thoughts.

"That I was dreaming?" I suggested eventually.

"It wasn't a trick question, James," she said, "there's no right or wrong answer here, just your thoughts."

"But I know what you're thinking."

"Really? And what might that be?"

"You think I'm being hysterical, imagining that something happened when it didn't."

"Why would I think that?"

"Well, wouldn't you? It didn't happen, did it? It couldn't happen. I mean, one hundred years ago? It even sounds ridiculous to me, and it's my experience."

"And yet, you say Larry experienced it too."

"He was dreaming."

"And is that what you think was happening to you?"

"What, that I was dreaming? Is that what you think?"

"It's not about what I think, James, it's about what you think."

I drained my cup and placed it carefully on the saucer. I began slowly, "I'd been reading Edward's journal for most of the afternoon. I suppose you could almost say I lived it; it was mesmerising."

"And you were disappointed when it ended?"

"Yes. So, perhaps I just dreamed it all up, to make up for there being nothing more to read."

"Even though everything you said you saw turned out to be true."

157

"I..., maybe I just worked it out. Lucky guess. It was obvious from what he wrote in his journal that Edward didn't have a particularly good relationship with his father and Larry and I had been discussing earlier how we had been unaware that Edward had any siblings until we read about them. Also, Edward recorded that he had flu when he arrived back in London and I remember Granny Violet, as I've told you before, from when Larry and I were young. I don't remember much about her, but I do remember her a bit. Perhaps my mind put all that together, filled in the blanks and, hey presto, by some fluke, I got it right. So it probably wasn't that difficult to come to the right conclusion."

"So, do you think it's all just a coincidence?"

"Yes... No... I don't know. It all seemed so real. Maybe..."

"Maybe?"

"Well, I was standing by the fire, drinking brandy, staring into flames..."

"So?"

"So, maybe I was hypnotised by the flames."

"Really?"

It seemed rational to me.

"I've heard flames can have that effect. Warm room, bit of alcohol, feeling a bit drowsy. Yeah, why not? All those thoughts whirring about in my head and my mind just created this incredible story. Isn't that all dreams are, just a collection of stories made up in your mind about things that happen? And yet Larry saw it too. That's the bit I can't seem to reconcile."

Now I was arguing with myself, but I suppose that was Madea's aim, to get me to work through it. However, having just convinced myself that I had a compelling argument I was now destroying it.

"You don't accept your reasoning?"

How did this woman manage to read my thoughts like that? I stared at her and frowned. She held my stare and I looked away.

"I'm confused," I admitted. "I've thought about it, tried to rationalise it, and every time I come up with a reasonable conclusion, I find I can no longer justify it. There's always something that doesn't fit right. Like now, hypnotism doesn't really work, does it? Because I couldn't have hypnotised Larry. The same argument applies to the dream theory, we can't both have had the same dream, even though Larry didn't see all of it like I did."

"What about that?"

"What do you mean?"

"Let's focus on Larry for a moment, rather than you."

"OK, but he wasn't really a part of it."

"Explain that."

"Well, he fell asleep, didn't he?"

"And stopped dreaming."

"Of course... er..." I thought back to what Larry had said to me at the time. "He said he had watched me get up to put the log on the fire, then said I seemed to be someone else."

"And then what?"

"And then he was woken by the sound of the door slamming. How strange."

I walked to the window and, for a moment, watched the snow falling outside. Everything seemed so still, so calm, so completely opposite to the turmoil in my head. Having seemingly steered me to one conclusion, it was as if she was now steering me towards another. My mind kept repeating, 'Larry stopped dreaming when he fell asleep', but how can you stop dreaming when you fall asleep? The answer was simple. When you're not dreaming, of course.

"Larry stopped seeing it because he fell asleep," I said, repeating my thoughts. "He was dozing when I got up to put the logs the fire. In that half-asleep, half-awake state. At that moment he saw the vision like I saw it. Then he fell asleep until he was woken by the door slamming."

I was aware that Madea was looking at me even though I had my back to her. My confusion was worse, not better.

"Now I really don't understand," I said, turning to face her. "If Larry saw it, albeit briefly, before he fell asleep, that means it must have been real. But that can't be true, can it?"

"What are you thinking?"

"The conclusion I'm coming to is that I must have seen ghosts."

She sat in silence. Her eyes followed me as I walked around the room, waiting for me to say something.

"But ghosts don't exist, do they?" I said, "I mean, they make great stories at Christmas but they're not real."

Madea said nothing as I tried to make sense of what I was trying to say.

"Larry wants to believe it's ghosts."

"Do you?" she said eventually. Her voice was almost a whisper.

A log on the fire spat a burning ember onto the hearth rug and I licked my fingers to pick it up and fling it back into the fire.

"No," I said, then hesitated. "I don't know. No, I don't. I'd quite like to believe they exist but, how can they? This is somehow down to my imagination."

"Maybe," she said. "Maybe it's because you are still seeking answers."

"To what?"

"To you. When we first started these sessions, you knew nothing of your background. You knew you had been adopted but beyond that you didn't know who you are. In the last few months, you've discovered who your real parents were and what became of them, and you've learnt a lot about your grandfather, Edward... your adoptive grandfather, that is. Maybe you are trying to match the two, fit them together, somehow make them join..."

"Like a jigsaw?"

"Yes, if you like."

"But, to use your analogy, they're from two separate, unrelated pictures, so they can't possibly fit together."

"But perhaps in your mind they do and, subconsciously, you are trying to find the one piece that does join them."

"But they're not joined. That piece does not exist because they have nothing to do with each other."

"Very possibly. Your mind is in a hypersensitive state at the moment, and maybe, in an attempt to make sense and move on, it has latched onto the idea that what you've learned about your family and what you've learned about your grandfather are somehow related. That's what I mean by you're looking for answers."

"Where none exist."

"You don't know that for sure."

"No, my mind has just made one and one equal three."

"Not necessarily."

"Are you suggesting that there is a link?"

"Of course there's a link," she said, and I looked up at her, quizzically. "The link is you. What I am suggesting though, is that you still need to find answers to something."

"But what?"

"That I can't tell you, but until you find them you might continue to experience these visions."

"So you don't think it's ghosts, after all?"

160

"I'm not saying it is or it isn't."

"But you don't believe in ghosts."

"I'm not saying that either. As I've said before, it's not about what I think or believe, it's about you. It's about what you thought you saw and how you interpret it. I'm just a sounding board, trying to help you navigate through the complexities of your thoughts."

"Like steering a ship through a storm."

"Precisely. There's always plenty of ways through and some are better than others. Some might seem quicker but may not be so effective. What I'm trying to do is help you find the easiest safe path."

"What do you suggest I do?"

"I suggest you do two things to begin with," she said. "First you should continue investigating your past. You might find something. Get Larry to help you. You might find something that will prove one way or another whether any link exists between what you've already found out."

"Which I doubt."

"Maybe."

"And the second?"

"Do as Violet suggested to Edward. Write it all down, make a journal of your journey. Write down everything that has happened to you since Janet and your mother were killed. Write down your thoughts; how you feel; what you see. Whatever you think will help you put your thoughts in order and make them make sense."

"Will it work?"

"It will help your recovery. It'll be a bit like a confession. Once you've written it down, it'll be as though you've released it and it'll be there, in the open, no longer having a hold on you. It will help you move on."

The clock in the hall chimed to signify that time was up.

I thanked her, once again, for her time and her support and escorted her to the hall. There, she wrapped her scarf around her neck, buttoned her coat and I opened the front door to let her out. I was greeted by a bitterly cold blast that whistled around the porch.

"Maybe I can give you a lift somewhere?" I offered, looking up at the sky. There seemed to be no let up in the weather. The snow was heavier than it had been earlier, and I noticed the tracks from Larry's car were all but covered.

"No thanks," she replied cheerfully, "I'll be fine." And she stepped out into the white swirl.

My phone rang as I closed the front door and I stepped back into the hall, closing the inner door behind me. It was Larry. As I answered I wiped condensation from the window and peered through it to ensure Madea was safe; but she was gone already.

"Madea gone?"

"Yes, she's just left."

"Right, of course. Can you do me a favour?"

"Sure."

"There's a special offer on bottles of craft beer at the supermarket, how are we off for stock?"

"Hang on, I'll check," I said and walked through to the pantry. "Right, we've got four boxes of six bottles here."

"I'd better get some then, it'll be Christmas in a couple of weeks. I'll get some more in case we decide to invite anyone over."

As Larry was talking, I slipped on my shoes and opened the front door. I was concerned about Madea and wanted to make sure she was safe. The falling snow hampered visibility so I could only see a short way down the drive, as far as the giant oak tree, which appeared as just a dark shadow.

I glanced down as I turned back to the house; the snow was heavy and I hoped she'd be alright. I kicked myself for not insisting she stayed until it stopped.

# Chapter Twenty-one
# Things That Go Bump In The Night

We probably drank more than we should have done.

Earlier in the day we'd gone out for some exercise and fresh air, trudging through the snow, which had deepened to about six or seven inches, making it a challenge to walk.

It was super-quiet. The snow seemed to have deadened all sound and even the birds seemed silent. Nothing much moved in that stark, white landscape. Everything was crisp to the touch and fresh to the smell.

As if by chance, the path seemed to lead us to the door of the Three Horseshoes and who were we to ignore the hand of chance? At the table to one side of the roaring fire we sat and indulged ourselves in home baked steak and ale pie with all the trimmings, and a couple of pints of locally brewed beer.

The bar area was warm, soporifically so, and apart from us, it was empty. As I approached the bar for a refill, the door flew open and the three old villagers, Colin, Jack and Bill, entered noisily, stamping their feet, rubbing their hands together and huffing loudly. I stood them a round and, as I sat down, they acknowledged the gesture by raising their glasses in our direction and muttering something unintelligible.

"Fen-speak," said Larry, as we drank.

"I never understood it," I replied with a smile.

"I don't think you're meant to."

We sat in silence for a few more minutes and I looked around the room. A large tree, tastefully decorated, stood in the corner by the door that led to the washrooms, and coloured tinsel, baubles and various other decorations were suspended from the blackened oak beams that crisscrossed the ceiling. Some of the tables had red candles with gold or silver tinsel wrapped around them, and a few seasonal cards were stuck to the wall above the fireplace.

"We ought to put our decorations up soon, you know," Larry said, taking a large sip of his beer and smacking his lips together with a satisfied sigh.

Something inside of me pricked at my heart. This would be the first Christmas I'd spent without Janet and mum and I wasn't sure how I was going to manage.

Larry leaned forward and gently held my arm.

"Don't worry, Jim, we'll get through it. I remember what it's like, I remember how you and Janet helped me cope with my first Christmas after Helen died. Now it's my turn to help you. We'll get through it, mate, I'm here for you."

I reflected briefly on the last nine months. He had more than been there for me and, despite my melancholy, I smiled.

"Thanks. I know you are, and I really appreciate it."

"Anyway, you won't have time to be sad once Harry, Leanne and the kids arrive. Grace and James will be hyper by the time they get here, and it'll be your job to entertain them."

"My job? Why my job?"

"I'll be cooking Christmas lunch, which excuses me. Harry and Leanne will be unpacking, so you'll have to be on granddad duty. It'll be great if this snow continues, you can take them exploring in the magical forest and winter wonderland."

Harry and Leanne planned to come to us on Christmas morning. Harry was working until Christmas Eve and wanting to unwind at home first, before having to go out again. They planned to stay with us until the 3rd of January, which meant we would get to see the new year in with them too.

As a precocious six-year-old Grace had lapped up all the Christmas hype; watched all the adverts on children's television and made an extensive list of all the toys she hoped Father Christmas would bring her. James, who was only three, had been wound up to a similar level of excitement by his big sister, although he wasn't entirely aware of what Christmas was all about yet. Still, Leanne had emailed their lists to us and Larry and I had chosen a couple of the more expensive ones; after all, they were our only grandchildren, so we were allowed to indulge them as we pleased.

After we had had our fill of pie and ale we wandered back to the Hall and, while I struggled to get the fire lit in the smoking room, Larry opened a bottle of wine. We rarely drank at this time of the day, but Larry said that if we were going to put the Christmas decorations up then we should open a bottle of wine and play a Christmas CD to help us with the task. However, it soon became apparent, as we drank our way through two bottles of red, that the decorations were going to have to be put up another time.

Instead, we attempted to finish the crossword but could only think up rude answers to each clue, so we tried charades instead. We were so bad that our sides were soon aching from laughing so much.

The evening drew late and by the time I went to bed I was in a relative state of sobriety. I quickly fell asleep once I turned out my light. In the early hours an almighty crash shocked me from my slumber. I was instantly awake and alert.

Sitting up in bed I wondered whether I had actually heard anything at all or whether I was dreaming. In the dark I sat and listened. The wind whipped around the house, making all sorts of strange whistling noises as it howled through the eaves and gables. Ghostly noises.

The room was freezing, and the old wooden beams creaked loudly as they shrank and expanded. I understood how people believed in the existence of ghosts when they woke in the dead of night and listened to noises like that.

I slowly moved my head from side to side to listen out for anything out of the ordinary.

The ticking of the Grandfather clock on the landing seemed louder than it did during the day.

The squawk of some night animal outside made me jump and I turned to face the window. The snow had finally stopped falling during the afternoon and the clouds had rolled away leaving a clear night. And a clear night meant a freeze.

The moon, three days since it was full, hung in the dark sky. A brilliant cold-hearted silver orb pouring its pale light over the glistening white snow that blanketed the wintry landscape.

Another crash rent the silence. In an instant, I was out of bed, pushing my bare feet into my cold slippers and pulling my dressing gown around me as I dashed along the landing. I was at the top of the stairs when I heard Larry's bedroom door open behind me.

"Did you hear it too, Jim?" he whispered.

"Yes," I replied, allowing him to catch up with me. I'm always a believer in safety in numbers.

With little thought for caution we both charged down the stairs, not caring about the noise we were making. Better to frighten off than confront was our motto.

"Any idea which room it came from?" Larry asked as we rounded the half-landing

"No," I panted. More from anticipation than exertion. "It seemed to come from across the hall." There were a half a dozen rooms off the corridor on that side of the hall, which meant we would have to search every one of them.

As I turned at the bottom of the stairs I caught a momentary glimpse, perhaps no more than a shadow, of what appeared to be the back of a woman's long skirt entering the library.

"Did you see that?" I yelled and set off at speed across the hall after her.

"What?" Larry called after me as he, too, set of in pursuit.

I threw the door open and rushed in, ready to confront whoever was there.

The room was full of dark shadows. Shafts of silvery light shone through from outside. Larry flicked a switched and the room was instantly bathed in bright light that temporarily blinded us. I blinked my eyes against the glare and saw that one of the windows was open, flapping in the wind, banging as it slammed shut and bounced open again.

"Intruders?"

Larry strode over and grabbed it.

"It's been open for some time," he said, "look."

He turned to me and in his hand he held the handle of the latch that fastened it. Or was meant to fasten it. The house was old, and the wooden window frame had rotted. In the strong winds we'd been having the screws holding the latch had worked loose and sometime during the evening they had finally relinquished what grip they had on the rotting wood and fallen, unnoticed, onto the sill. With nothing holding it, the latch had fallen too, and the window had flown open to be pummelled and buffeted by the wind, swinging freely on its hinges and crashing about as it did so. Snow, caught on the wind, had drifted against the sills outside and been blown through the open window and over the carpet.

"Shit!" Larry exclaimed. "The bugger's broken right off. Let's see what we can do to hold it shut now and we'll call up the carpenter in the morning."

"Probably easier to lean something up against it from the outside."

"Good thinking, Jim," he said, "you do that, and I'll make us a nice hot chocolate to warm us up when you've done."

"But…"

"No time for that," he said and disappeared through the door.

"Hell's teeth," I muttered, but realised there was no point in protesting, there was a job to be done and I seemed to have volunteered myself to do it. So, a few minutes later, wearing a warm coat over my dressing gown and a pair of wellington boots, I pulled back the bolts of the front door and ventured around the porch to the library window.

A cold north-easterly wind wrapped itself around me, finding gaps in my clothing to freeze me to the bone. Cold moonlight shone down over the house, casting long shadows cross the forecourt and the frozen fountain. High above a myriad of stars shone down from the black sky, their light having travelled for millions of years across unimaginable distances. All I was interested in right then, though, was far more mundane than trying to fathom the secrets of the universe. I needed to find something long enough and strong enough to prop against the window and keep it shut until morning when we could find someone to fix it. But I was having trouble finding anything beneath the thick piles of snow that were drifting across the forecourt.

As I stood wondering where to look, I had that feeling of being watched. The hairs on the back of my neck bristled.

Slowly, deliberately, I turned around.

On the opposite side of the fountain, bathed in moonlight, a woman, dressed in a thick cloth dress and wrapped in a dark, tartan patterned shawl, stood watching me. She peered at me from beneath the folds of the shawl that covered her head, and I was sure I saw her smile.

For what seemed like an age we just stood. The freezing wind blew through us. Bitter. Cold.

Slowly, she raised her hand and beckoned me to her.

I wanted to resist. I wanted to defy that beckoning hand, but I couldn't. It was insistent and I felt compelled to go to her. I felt drawn to her, as if we had some connection.

"Madea?" I said, thinking I recognised her as my counsellor, although I couldn't think for the life of me why she should be there. "Madea? What are you doing here?"

I struggled through the deep snow towards her. She looked like Madea and yet somehow, she didn't, and her image started to blur as I made my way towards her. The shadows cast by the statue on the fountain hid her in their darkness and, as I approached, she seemed to be pointing at something on the ground.

"Have you found anything yet? It's getting cold in here," Larry's voice called from the library window jerking me out of my reverie. I turned.

"It's bloody cold out here too," I shouted back. "Just give me a moment, I'm sure I'll find something."

I half expected him to ask what Madea was doing out here, but I knew he wouldn't. Deep down I knew she wasn't there at all; that she was just a figment of my imagination.

I turned back. She was gone, but there was a long, sturdy length of two-by-four wood where she'd been standing. Ideal for leaning up against the window and holding it shut until morning.

Despite the bitter cold I realised, when I had wedged the length of wood against the window and fastened it shut, that I was sweating, and my heart was thumping in my chest. I needed to get inside quickly and dry off before I began to suffer from exposure.

As I hurried back into the house one thought swirled around in my head. Had I just seen a ghost?

# Chapter Twenty-Two
## The Joiner

"Did I see what?"

The clock on the wall read twenty-five past one. A good seven hours before dawn. The kitchen lights seemed bright after being out in the moonlight and we sat, cradling mugs of hot chocolate for warmth. I'd just about stopped shivering when he looked at me across the breakfast bar and asked his question.

"Pardon?"

"Did I see what? When we were running down the stairs earlier you shouted, 'did you see that?' before charging off across the hall. What was it that I was meant to have seen?"

"Oh, nothing."

"Really?" He gave me that quizzical look, eyes wide and eyebrows raised, that suggested he didn't believe me. I shrugged.

"I was jumping at shadows," I told him, "I thought I saw someone, a woman, walk into the library."

"A woman again? And she led us to where the noises were. How convenient."

"Larry, don't," I said. I really wasn't in the mood for more suppositions about ghosts. Or insinuations about being haunted. Except I had seen something. Twice. At least, I imagined I had seen something and both times whatever it was I'd seen had seemingly guided me to find what I was looking for.

At our last therapy session Madea had told me to be open with Larry, otherwise he wouldn't be in a position to help me as he should, so I told him what I'd seen.

"Madea, eh?" he said. "So now you're being haunted by your grief counsellor. I'm sure that's not in her job description." He laughed, but I wasn't in the mood for jocularity.

"Mind you," he continued, "I did think for a brief moment that there was someone by the fountain when I popped my head out the window to see how you were getting on, but I think it was just a shadow of the statue cast by the moon."

There's always a rational explanation I thought and nodded.

"Of course," I said, "that's what it must have been." I felt a little comforted by the thought that he may also have seen what I saw by the fountain, be it shadow or something else.

He leaned forward with a conspiratorial look on his face, "I'm not saying it was or it wasn't Jim, I'm just giving you something that might help you to explain what you saw. Personally, I'd much rather it be a ghost, especially in the run up to Christmas. Let's face it, who doesn't love a ghost story at Christmas?"

I yawned and moments after, Larry yawned too.

"Come on," I said, "let's hit the sack, otherwise we'll be useless in the morning."

"It is morning."

"We'll be useless later on, then."

We left our empty mugs to soak in the sink and for the second time that night retired to our beds.


The pale sun hung low in the east heralding the late dawn. The pallid sky was clear, and the wind had dropped. The bare branches of the trees edging the lawn stood out dark against the virtually colourless background. A solitary bird flew over the woods and disappeared into the distance. The world outside was silent and still. As though it was holding its breath in anticipation of something about to happen.

From my bedroom window the garden twinkled with the reflections of the weak sun off the clean snow. Over its crisp surface bird footprints were haphazardly dotted about where a variety of birds had hopped across it in search of the fallen grain and sunflower hearts that we had put out for them.

A robin, all fluffed up against the cold, his breast a vivid red, hopped along the top of the wall and sang briefly before flying to the feeders hanging from a branch.

It was a Christmas card scene and I took a deep, satisfying breath in before turning away to get myself ready for the new day. I'd slept a restful and dreamless sleep after our night-time activity and I felt positive about myself, despite some of the things that seemed to be happening to me.

By the time I arrived downstairs not only was there coffee and toast ready in the dining room, but Larry had already found and phoned a

170

joiner in the village who promised to be here at nine o'clock to review the job and give us an estimate.

He arrived a few minutes after nine and I opened the door to a young man in his late twenties who told me his name was Jonathan Avery, the local joiner and carpenter. He was dressed in a clean set of navy-blue overalls and, surprisingly, he had brought a change of shoes with him so as not to traipse wet melting snow through the house and onto the rugs and carpets.

He looked at the large circular table in the centre, the full-length mirror hanging on one wall and paintings by long dead local artists over the others and let out a whistle of appreciation. Fair enough, it is an impressive hall.

"My whole house would fit in here," he remarked in awe.

I laughed. "You're not the first to say that," I told him.

Larry walked in from the corridor and introduced himself. They shook hands.

"Thanks for coming so quickly," he said.

"No problem, Mr Hilliard. To be honest," he said as we led him to the library, "I've always wanted to see this place. My Grandpa used to tell me how he worked here during the war and for a few years after. He worked on the farm, you know, when it was owned by your grandad and stayed on there after it was sold."

"I'll show you around when you've finished," Larry told him, "if you want."

"Thanks."

In the library Avery looked at the window, which was still held closed by the wooden prop I'd found, and said, "I can see the problem, rotten wood."

"Can you do anything?"

"No problem. I can replace the wood here and along here," he pointed along the frame to indicate where he meant, "and paint it up for you. You won't even know it's been repaired."

He quoted a price that seemed reasonable to us and Larry accepted.

"When can you start? Obviously, the sooner the better for us," he said.

"I can start straightaway. If you want me to, that is?"

Larry agreed and the lad went off to fetch his tools. As he made a start, Larry engaged him in further conversation.

"So, your Grandpa used to work for our Grandad, then?"

171

"Yes. He started working here during the war, when he was fifteen. He worked on the farm. When your Grandad sold it off, he continued working for the new farmer until he retired at sixty-five."

"Is he still alive, your Grandpa?"

"Oh yes," he laughed. "He's still alive and still misbehaving. He's ninety-two now but he's still active and still goes out every day with his two old mates. They've been friends since forever. They even have their own mugs at the Three Horseshoes."

"Not one of those three that're always there at lunchtime?"

"Yes, he's one of them. His name is Colin, Colin Avery."

# Chapter Twenty-Three
# Colin

"He's ninety-two. That means he was born in 1926, way after the murders took place."

We were on our way to the Three Horseshoes again, this time for the specific purpose of talking to Colin and his two friends. We left Avery working in the library; he reckoned he'd be finished by the end of the afternoon. We showed him the kettle so he could make himself a drink if he needed one and left him to it.

"Nevertheless," Larry said in reply to my objection, "he will certainly have something to say about it. This is a small village with a small village mentality, and back then it was even smaller. Everyone's business is everyone else's news and the Hall was home to people with money. You know what it's like, where there's money mixed with murder there's speculation and rumour. If I know villagers, great grandad's murder will have kept them all in gossip until the war broke out in 1939. He may not have been born when it happened but there's no doubt he'll have been told all about it, and even if what he heard was greatly exaggerated or distorted, there'll be an element of truth in it somewhere. We'll just have to sort out the wheat from the chaff."

As usual, the television was silently playing some lunchtime programme about how to sell your house, or spruce it up, or something like that. The landlady was avidly watching it despite the sound being muted. An old Christmas CD was playing the best-known seasonal tunes from the last sixty years at a volume that was loud enough to be annoying but soft enough to allow conversation.

Colin, Jack and Bill were sitting at their table near the fire, arguing about whose turn it was to buy the next beer.

"I didn't think they even paid for their beer," I laughed, watching them from the bar.

"They don't if there's someone else in the bar who'll stand them a round, but occasionally they have to buy their own and all three of them have got short arms and deep pockets," the landlady replied pouring our drinks. "You buying this round for them, then?"

I paid for their beers and carried them over. Larry and I sat down at the table next to theirs to greetings of 'cheers'.

"Your grandson, Jonathan, is doing some work for us at the Hall today," Larry said, by way of breaking the ice.

"Arr, and what do you want me to do about it?" Colin eyed him suspiciously.

"Nothing," Larry replied with a friendly smile, "I just commented. That's where we live, you see, and he's fixing one of our windows for us."

"I suppose."

"Didn't I hear that you used to work there?" I said, wondering if he was naturally reluctant to talk or whether he just didn't want to talk to us.

"Aye, I did too."

"How long ago was that, then?"

"During the war, and for a few years after that too."

"You must have seen a few changes over the years."

"Aye, happen I must have."

"Do you know about the murder that happened there?"

"Murder?" Jack butted in, "that was before he were born. Before any of us were."

"And there's not much around 'ere that happened afore he were born," Bill added and cackled. The other joined in, wheezing and coughing.

"Ignore the two kids," Colin told us, indicating the other two and tutting, "barely out of nappies them two and they think they know everything. I tell 'e this, though, they know owt, them two."

I looked at the three of them, causally hurling insults at one another in the way that only the best of friends can do and get away with. Bill and Jack can't have been much younger than old Colin; no more than a year or two at the most, I'd have guessed.

"What can you tell us about it then?" I asked.

"About what?"

"The murder."

"What do you want to know for?"

"Edward Hilliard was our grandfather."

"You brothers, are you? You don't look like brothers, if you ask me." He peered at us through bloodshot eyes. "I suppose there is a vague resemblance there."

"Cousins," Larry told him, "my dad was Anthony, and his mum was Clara, Anthony's sister."

"That explains it, then," he said.

"I remember them two," Jack chipped in.

"Me too," said Bill.

"'Ow are they? We 'aven't seen them in years."

"Dad died in 2009," Larry said.

"And Clara was killed in a car crash earlier this year. She was eighty-six."

"Sorry to 'ear that," Jack said. "She was quite the pretty one, if I remember right."

"She was out of your class," Bill jibed.

"Can't blame a man for havin' ambition." His whole chest seemed to rattle as he wheezed again in his attempt at a laugh. It felt a bit strange listening to these two nonagenarians talking about my mother as if they, and she, were still in their twenties.

"So, you remember them?" Larry prompted, trying to steer the conversation back to the subject on hand.

"Aye. I was in school wiv young David," Colin said, "at the village primary. We only had two classes back then; the little uns and the older ones. That was 'til he went off to some fancy boarding school. He were the eldest o' the brothers. Got hisself killed in the war, he did, along with his brother John."

"Tony, that be your dad, was a couple years younger than us," Jack pointed out, "so we didn't really know 'im so well."

It made some sense that Colin was in the same school as David if they were both born in 1926. I don't suppose we had really considered the idea of them attending the village primary school before being sent to prep school, but since prep schools typically started at eight years old it made sense. Uncle Anthony was born in 1929 which meant Jack and Bill must have been born in 1927. So, I was right, they were only a year younger than Colin.

"So, you all went to school together?"

"Aye, happen we did," Colin replied. "My old mum were the school ma'am in those days. She knew everyone in the village, an' everyone were afeared of her too. She didn't spare the cane she didn't, not her. She beat respect into every arse in the village, be they from the Hall or from the alms houses."

Colin drained his glass and rattled it against the top of the table.

"Drink up lads," he said to the other two, "I reckon these two'll stand another round or two to get the information they want," and he cackled again.

"Aye," said Jack, tipping the remains of his beer down his throat and looking between Larry and myself. "Looks like they can afford it too."

Larry went to the bar to get the refills. We had drunk barely half of ours, but we were here to listen to these three, not to imbibe. The beer was just the means to an end.

"You said your mum was the local schoolteacher?" Larry prompted, as they set about demolishing another pint of beer.

Another song that once topped the Christmas music charts thirty-odd years ago began to play and the fire burning in the hearth created a comfortable warmth as we settled down to listen to more reminiscences.

"Aye, taught everyone in the village, she did, rich and poor. She knew everyone and everything, and she 'ad a few tales to tell too, I can tell 'ee."

We waited while he gulped down a large mouthful of beer before resuming his tale.

"I remember her tellin' me about the happening at the Hall," he said after a few moments' reflection. "It were Christmas an' all. Christmas Eve of 1918, we'd just had a dose of the Spanish Flu and that buried a few of us from the village. Old Seth Chambers had bin drinkin' heavily in 'ere all evening and was that much the worse for his drink."

"I remember me mum tellin' us about Old Seth," Jack said, "a drunk an' a bully, so she said. Nasty piece of work, by all accounts."

"That's right," Bill added, "people used to cross the road to avoid him. Said 'e used to go home drunk and knock his wife, Beth, and 'is two girls about."

"That's what my mum used to say, too," Jack agreed. "'Not wishin' to disrespect the dead an' all,' she'd say, 'but old man Seth were a right, royal bastard', that's what she called him, a right royal bastard."

"It were the talk of the village right up until the war." Bill informed us and Larry gave me his 'I told you so' look.

"'And when war broke out the village had somethin' else to gossip about. We lost a good few men in the war, including those who would've been your uncles, and all mem'ries of Old Seth Chambers and the wife he murdered were forgot."

"So, what happened?" I asked.

"In those days," Colin said before the others could take over again, "it were customary to attend midnight mass on Christmas Eve. You'd be expected to be there and folks would turn out from the pub and pile into the church, but that Christmas Eve Seth were very drunk. More so than usual.

"He'd not had a job for months, see, and 'e hated being kept by what they paid Beth and Violet who both worked up at the Hall. Beth'd been the housekeeper there since before the first war and their youngest, Violet, she were employed as nursemaid to the boy, Edward, who was blown up in the trenches."

"Remember when 'e caught us scrumpin' that time?" Jack said.

"Aye, I do at that," Bill nodded, "chased us off with a gun, 'e did."

"No 'e didn't you demented old fool," Jack retorted, "'e could hardly chase us at all, could 'e, him havin' only one leg, remember?"

"I knows that, I'm not stupid," Bill replied indignantly.

"Yeah, right. He was a nice old boy, was Edward. He let us have them apples, didn't 'e?"

"He never did that," Colin said, "He made us give 'em all to his cook."

"That's right, 'e made us pick three more bags full," Jack said.

"And give 'em to the pub so they could make apple pie for the whole village. That was during the war, and 'e used to give food to everyone who needed it by givin' it to Daisy-Bell, she wot ran this place. Daisy-Bell used to cook it up for the workers comin' in off the fields for their dinner."

The three of them went off on more reminiscences and eventually Larry reminded Colin that he was telling us about Christmas Eve of 1918.

"Accordin' to my old mum," Colin resumed his story at last, "who 'eard it from me dad, who was told by Mick the milkman; someone in the pub that evening had suggested that Beth had become more than just the housekeeper up at the Hall since Lady Charlotte 'ad died. She was Sir William's missus," he added, in case we weren't sure who Lady Charlotte was.

"And Old Seth were the jealous type, as well as being a drunkard, and the thought of being a cuckold was more than he cared to 'ear, so he punched the bloke and soon they was fightin' like a couple of four year olds.

"That got him thrown out the pub. Mind you, it weren't the first time, he often got thrown out for fightin' an' he usually went home and finished 'is fightin' by givin' Beth a good beatin'. Her and the girls."

Colin took another long sip of his drink and looked around the bar. Apart from the five of us and the landlady, who was still engrossed in her silent programme, the bar was empty. My stomach growled with hunger and I coughed to try and cover the noise it made. Larry gave me an amused look and we waited for Colin to resume.

"After he was thrown out everyone expected he would walk around for a bit then turn up for midnight mass, where he'd fall asleep at the back like he usually did."

"But that's not what happened?"

"No. He disappeared and, as they were goin' up the street to the church some woman said she'd spotted him headin' for the Hall and wondered what was goin' on. Well, you can imagine, can't you? Those that'd been in the pub got worried. Well, he'd had a right skinful and some bugger'd just suggested that his missus was having an affair with Sir William. Talk about red rag to a bull an' all, no one knew what he might do.

"Anyways, off they went, up to the Hall, an' as they all piled up the drive someone saw a glow at the back o' the house. So they all charged round an' there was Old Seth, standin' in front of the chapel with a shotgun, with flames roarin' behind him."

"From the chapel?"

"Aye."

"Next thing Sir William is running out and confronting Seth, arguin' and shoutin' at him. A few moments later Edward is dragged out through the flames by some bugger no one knew yelling 'help us'. Then old Seth, he turns to Edward and fires his gun at him. Both barrels."

"At Edward?"

"Yeah, but here's the funny thing, he misses Edward and kills William instead."

"In front of the whole village?" I could hear the incredulity in Larry's voice.

"Aye, the 'ole village saw him do it," Colin asserted, and the other two nodded.

"Even the vicar were there, bein' as the 'ole village were up at the Hall and no one 'ad turned up for midnight mass," Jack added. "He knelt down in the snow beside your great grandfather, took his hand and administered the last rites to him there an' then."

"Then it all kicked off by all accounts. Some grabbed Old Seth,

178

others set up a human chain to dowse the fire with buckets o' water, 'til the fire brigade come an' put it out, proper."

"What became of Beth?"

"No one knows," Colin said. "It were assumed that Seth murdered her too, but her body were never found. He was found guilty of her murder nonetheless and he were hanged for both murders."

"You said there were two daughters?" I said.

"Aye, Gwen and Vi," Jack said.

"Vi married Edward," Colin said, "not long after Old Seth's hanging. Imagine wantin' to marry the daughter of the man who murdered your father. She were your gran, weren't she?"

"Yes," said Larry.

"And the other daughter?"

"Gwen? She'd already left home," he replied. "No one ever heard from her again."

Violet had said to Edward, admittedly in my dream or whatever it was, that her sister had died from Spanish Flu after running away to London.

"Of course," Colin continued, "she may never have left at all."

"What do you mean?"

He paused and looked at each of us in turn, then smiled.

"Maybe Old Seth killed her too."

"Aye," said Jack, "there's plenty around here who said he did."

# Chapter Twenty-Four
## The Ties That Bind

"So, the whole village was there to witness our great grandad's murder?"

We wandered back through the village, enjoying the fresh air. After the stuffiness of the Three Horseshoes which had seemed to suit the three old boys, the cold air blowing against our faces was a pleasant relief. As we walked along the icy path, we could hear the background thrum of traffic driving back and forth along the busy A10 between Cambridge and Ely.

"Remember when all that traffic used to come through the village?" I said as we passed a house that had so many Christmas lights decorating its frontage that it must have been a drain on the national grid when they switched them on in the evening.

A bedraggled blackbird hopped along the verge ahead of us, searching for any titbits on the frozen ground. It hopped away as we approached and then, with an angry tweet, it flew up and perched on one of the telephone wires that criss-crossed the road and waited for us to pass.

The crisp snow crunched noisily beneath our feet and our breath formed clouds of condensation as we walked along in silence, considering the tale Colin had related.

A thought was buzzing around in my head. A ludicrous, but persistent idea. One I couldn't shake from my mind. The other daughter. Had she been murdered, or had she run away?

Our cheeks were rosy red from the cold, and I had to blow my nose several times as we walked up the long, winding drive back to Rosehip Hall. The Hall's stone brick work always seemed to reflect the sky, and in doing so seemed to reflect one's mood. Right now it seemed grey and foreboding, whereas in sunlight it would appear bright and inviting, more a pale sandstone in colour.

"Penny for them, Jim?" Larry said as we approached the house. We could see Avery hard at work fixing the window. He waved and smiled, and we waved back. "He's doing a good job of that."

"I was thinking that Grandad Edward married the daughter of his father's murderer," I lied.

"I was thinking the same thing, Jim. It sounds a bit complicated, doesn't it? Our great grandfather is rumoured to be having an affair with his housekeeper, so her husband murders him, and then his son ends up marrying their daughter, our grandmother. Meanwhile, our grandmother's sister disappears. Did she run away or was she murdered too? What a strange turn of events. Sounds like something from a Jane Austen book."

"The sister was called Gwen."

"That's right."

"Short for Gwendoline."

"So?"

"My mother's mum was called Gwendoline. Gwendoline Butler."

"Butler, the butcher's wife," he smiled. "What of it? Plenty of women were called Gwendoline back then, it was a very common girl's name. Anyway, I thought you said the sister had died from Spanish Flu during the autumn?"

"But what if she didn't? What I saw in whatever it was I did see might not be right?"

"That's ridiculous, why would she be reported dead if she wasn't?"

I thought about that for a moment then said, "to keep her safe from her father. Maybe Beth was protecting her daughter from Seth for some reason. Remember, he did beat her up, maybe he tried to rape her, or something."

"I don't know, it all sounds a bit far-fetched."

"For God's sake, this whole episode is far-fetched. There's just as much chance that Gwendoline didn't die as there is of us seeing ghosts in this house."

We made our way into the kitchen for some hot soup. Our conversation with Colin, Jack and Bill had been the main reason for our visit to the Three Horseshoes and not, as in our previous visits, to enjoy the victuals.

Deep down I agreed with Larry. It was a ludicrous idea and, I suspected, simply a straw clutching exercise on my part. It was like Madea had said, I was still searching for answers, and this was one of them. I just couldn't get the idea out of my head.

What if …?

"Look," said Larry, peering through the steam rising from his bowl, "after lunch we'll have a look, shall we?"

"How?"

"We'll go on-line. There are public records going way back that are all being put on-line these days. We might find something."

I wasn't sure. I've never been into genealogy, and my impression was that the ancestry sites were difficult to navigate unless you actually knew what you were looking for. In my case I didn't know much at all. Despite that, I agreed with Larry's suggestion. If we didn't find anything, and I was certain we wouldn't, then all we'd lose were the few hours we spent trying and my adoptive dad always used say, 'people who never fail are people who never try'.

I cleaned up while Larry went into the drawing room to fire up the laptop. Normally we would have gone into the library or the smoking room but, with the windows open in the library, both rooms were chilly and there was a howling draft blowing through the secret door.

The dulcet tones of Avery singing along to a song playing on his radio greeted me as I left the kitchen and I smiled. Like most of us who liked to sing along to songs, he sang slightly different words to the original.

"How are you getting on?" I asked Larry as I walked in and stood in front of the fire. The drawing room, which was at the end of the corridor on the left, looked out the back of the house, overlooking the chapel and the kitchen garden. This was a room we hardly ever used. Kept for entertaining guests rather than everyday use; which was what the smoking room was for. A large, L-shaped Chesterfield sofa took up one corner of the room with four matching armchairs placed around the room. The general shape of the drawing room, in the south-west corner of the house to capture the afternoon and evening sun, was almost a mirror image of the morning room in the south-east wing. Next to it, but without an adjoining door, was the billiard room that overlooked the front of the house.

"I've switched the laptop on," he said, "and then I laid the fire while it was starting up. As you can see, it's nearly ready."

I sat next to him on the sofa and watched the little circle spin round, disappear and then re-appear, still spinning. Eventually Larry opened the browser window.

"Where to start?" he muttered, more to himself than to me.

"National Archives?" I suggested after a moment's thought.

"Worth a try," he said, and soon we were scrolling down their website.

"What are we actually looking for?" I asked. "We don't need birth certificates, and anyway, they'd be easy to find because we know they were born around here, so they'd have been registered in Ely or Cambridge."

"I don't know. I suppose we should look for something on Gwendoline, see if we can find a death certificate for a start. Look, here we are, 'Births, Marriages and Deaths in England and Wales. Oh."

There was a disappointed edge to his voice.

"What's the matter?"

"It says records of births, marriages and deaths in England and Wales are kept in various places but not usually at The National Archives."

"Why don't you follow some of those links? How about that one?" There were several links on the page, most were commercial sites, but there was one that looked as though it might be a free site and I pointed to it. Larry clicked on it and the page changed.

"Here we go," he said and clicked on a link titled 'search deaths' and typed Chambers in the surname and Gwendoline in the first name boxes. "According to what you said Violet said she died in the autumn of 1918 somewhere in London."

"Yes."

He clicked on the search button and the page displayed 'No Results Found'. He expanded the search by changing the range of years from 1916 to 1924. It still came up 'No Results Found.'.

"Well," he said, "there's no record of her dying in that time so let's see if we can find a record of Gwendoline Chambers marrying James Butler. What year should I choose?"

"Well, we know that my mum, Caroline, was born in 1934 and she had a brother who was ten years older.

"We also know that she left home in 1918 so why not search from January 1918 to December 1924 and see what we get."

He typed it in and pressed search and there it was amongst a record of some seven women called Gwendoline Chambers who had married in England and Wales in that same six-year period.

### Marriages June 1923

| Surname | First name(s) | Spouse | District | Vol. | Page |
|---------|---------------|--------|----------|------|------|
| Chambers | Gwendoline | Butler | E.Tilbury | 4a | 1564 |

"So, she didn't die," Larry said, turning to me.

My heart skipped a beat. A piece in the jigsaw of my life had just appeared on the screen in front of me.

"If this is correct," I spoke slowly, my head spinning with implications, "then my grandmother was grandmother Violet's sister."

"Which means we really are related."

"What does that make us?" I said but Larry was ahead of me and was already doing a search. In a short while he had opened a neat infographic that gave the list of relationships.

"Let's see," he said, "we share common great grandparents, Seth and Beth Chambers, which makes us … second cousins."

"That means that my real mother and my adoptive mother were actually cousins. And they never even knew it. How cruel life can be sometimes. They never knew they were related. No wonder they got on so well."

To verify our findings Larry did another search under 'search marriages', this time using James Butler as the search subject and found the same result.

### Marriages June 1923

| Surname | First name(s) | Spouse | District | Vol. | Page |
|---------|---------------|----------|-----------|------|------|
| Butler | James | Chambers | E.Tilbury | 4a | 1564 |

He then searched birth records for Caroline Butler, which gave mother's surname as Chambers. Finally, we searched marriage records for Caroline and found record of her marriage to Christopher Walters in 1955.

"That's pretty conclusive," I said, sitting back.

"Jesus," Larry exclaimed, "I'm glad we didn't discover we were more closely related than that."

"Why?"

"My son is married to your daughter, don't forget."

I hadn't even considered the effect it might have on Leanne and Harry. To be honest, I was a bit shaken by the find to think about any other implications.

"Christ, yes. That could have been rather awkward."

"Fortunately, it's not."

"No. What does that make them?"

"Er, hang on. Here, look, third cousins, because they have common great-great-grandparents."

"Complicated."

"Could be, but it's four generations. Way too distant to be an issue."

"Yeah. We'll have to tell them."

"Let's not yet. Let's try to work out how best to do it first."

"Should it actually matter?"

"It shouldn't. They've been in love since they were kids and anyway, they've got two children."

A maelstrom of thoughts possessed my mind as we sat down for our cup of tea that afternoon. In discovering we really were related, albeit second cousins are quite distant relatives, we had also discovered that the great grandfather we had in common was a murderer, who had murdered Larry's other great grandfather.

We had also discovered that Larry's son and my daughter, who are married to each other, are third cousins, which could be complicated. Hopefully, it wasn't. Certainly, it was neither illegal nor immoral, nor was it genetically a potential problem.

I just hoped that it wouldn't cause a problem to Leanne and Harry. I didn't expect it would, but you never know.

# Chapter Twenty-Five
## Sweet Dreams

Night has a habit of mixing up that which in the day appears simple and ordinary to make it confusing and occasionally frightening.

I was in the library with Grandfather Edward. The room was in darkness with the exception of a candle burning on the occasional table that lit up grandad's face. The big window was open. The flame of the candle flickered, casting eerie shadows across grandad's features and around the room. He sat in his wheelchair with a red tartan blanket wrapped around his legs, reading to me from a copy of his diary.

I was dressed as a child in my Prep School uniform. Grey flannel short trousers, knee high grey woollen socks held up by elastic garters that were so tight my legs were all tingly below the knee, a pale blue aertex shirt and a navy woollen jumper with holes in the sleeves through which I had stuck my thumbs. I was dressed as a schoolboy, but I was me, an adult of sixty-one.

"Now then, boy," Grandfather Edward said in that voice he used to use when he was about to impart some of his knowledge to me, "if I killed you, where would I bury you?"

I was about to tell him I didn't know when a cold breeze blew over me and I noticed the snow. It had piled up against the front of the house and was now pouring into the room like water flowing down a waterfall. It rolled across the library floor, over the oriental rug and on towards the table.

"Somewhere they won't find you of course, boy," Grandad said, laughing. I was lying on my back with my arms folded across my chest beneath the table with the snow forming a wall around it. Grandad stood on the table and laughed. His wooden leg became one of the table legs, and he banged his other foot down heavily on the polished tabletop.

"What are you doing, Grandad?" I said and started snivelling as he began shovelling piles of snow over me. As it poured over my body it turned to thick, slimy clay that stuck to my clothes and oozed down between my legs and covered my arms, trapping them in place so I couldn't move. I tried to lift my leg, but the mud sucked it back, making a loud slurping noise as I was pulled in.

With a maniacal roar, Grandad Edward pushed great grandfather William beneath the table with me. Only I was no longer beneath the table, I was in a deep hole with wooden sides, barely wide enough for my shoulders, looking up at the old man who now lay on top of me, trapping me at the bottom of the hole. He was heavy and my chest was constricted, pushing the breath from my lungs. I didn't have the leverage to push him off and, as I struggled, more mud poured over me, gradually rising up the sides of the pit. Covering me.

Larry was standing beside Edward carrying the lifeless form of a woman.

"Don't worry, Jim," he said, pushing his face right up against mine. I could feel his hot breath blowing against me as I struggled to breathe. "She'll help you."

He stood back and dropped the woman's body on top of us, weighing me down still further. In desperation, I gasped for air.

I was beginning to panic. I suffer from claustrophobia and here I was, lying on my back in a tiny box, beneath two bodies. I was wet and cold from the claggy mud pouring in over me and I felt I was being crushed by the weight bearing down on me.

The woman's body flopped over and lay facing down on me and I was staring up into the lifeless eyes of Madea Down. She smiled at me and opened her mouth in a rictus grin. Her tongue poked out between her teeth and insinuated its way into my mouth, forcing my lips apart and pushing in right to the back of my throat. I gagged.

Piece by piece, the skin around her eyes began to flake away. Her lids peeled back, turning to clouds of grey dust and her eyeballs plopped out of their sockets and hung suspended, dangling on the end of a ganglion of stringy nerves and blood vessels. Seconds later her whole face disintegrated into dust that poured down my throat and up my nose. Blocking my airways. Choking me.

I gasped for air, but her tongue was still lodged in my throat, pushing down further, deeper, entering my lung, filling my chest. I struggled to get out; desperate to escape. I was stuck.

My arms were trapped beneath the sheet, pinning me to my mattress and preventing me from moving. I was lying on my back and the heavy duvet had flopped over to cover my face, weighing down on my nose and mouth.

In a desperate panic I kicked my leg and wriggled my body in an effort to free myself from the bedsheets. The more I struggled the more I seemed to be trapped.

I was choking, suffocating. I couldn't breathe. I was going dizzy through lack of air and I could feel a black mist rising before my eyes, wrapping its arms around me, ready to take me away.

But I was not ready to go and with a final manic effort I felt the edge of the sheet finally pull free from the mattress and release me from my bondage.

I sat up in bed, gasping and choking. I was wide awake. In my panic I threw off the bedsheets and leapt out of bed, doubled over, frantically fighting to draw air into my aching lungs. I was dizzy from lack of oxygen and I struggled to draw in a deep breath.

Eventually, still coughing and gasping, I sat on the edge of my bed until my breathing returned to normal; then I put my head in my hands and cried.

# Chapter Twenty-Six
# Affairs in the Dark

I sat on the edge of the bed for what seemed ages, bent forward with my elbows on my knees and my head in my hands. The dream had got me rattled; it had seemed so real and I honestly thought I was going to die in a most horrible way. It had no rationale; it was just a bad dream. I kept on telling myself that nightmares don't repeat themselves, but I was too scared to lie down to try and go back to sleep.

Why did I have to have such vivid dreams about suffocating in a confined space? My worst nightmare. Surely my brain wasn't so cruel to subject me to nightmares like that.

What I remembered of the dream seemed like a mash-up of everything I'd learned that day, mixed with random ideas and people, but with everything wrong. In the dark of night, it all seemed to be much worse than it probably was.

The room was cold, and a shiver went down my spine. I switched on the bedside lamp and searched for my dressing gown.

The silence was eerie.

I stepped into my slippers, pulled my dressing gown tightly around me, crossed to the window and peeped through the curtains. The moon was hidden by a blanket of cloud and, though it was dark as pitch outside I could see flakes of snow falling past my window. With a week to go until Christmas it looked as though we might, finally, get a white one this year.

I thought to myself that we still hadn't got around to putting up the decorations yet; something we needed to do in the next couple of days, so we didn't leave it until the last minute.

As my eyes became accustomed to the darkness outside, a movement on the lawn caught my attention. I tried to look directly at it, but I could see nothing, so I looked to one side instead. There it was again. A fox struggling through the snow. The snow was deep and came up to its stomach, so it had to cross the garden in a series of leaps.

It became clear to me that I wasn't going to get back to sleep, so I decided I needed a cup of tea.

As quietly as I could I crept along the upstairs landing and slowly descended the stairs. The third step down began to creak, and I quickly lifted my foot and stepped to the edge.

Downstairs I headed for the kitchen and the kettle.

As I passed along the corridor from the hall, I noticed a sliver of light shining beneath the door to the smoking room. For a brief moment I wondered whether we had left the light on when we went to bed but then I remembered we had spent the afternoon in the withdrawing room and the evening playing snooker, so we hadn't been in the smoking room at all. I hesitated. Perhaps the light had been on all day, we had been in there first thing, before Avery arrived to fix the window in the library.

Cautiously I turned the handle and pushed the door.

The room was bathed in dim light and looked as it had when I'd seen it the other night. The dark wallpaper, the thick curtains, the oriental rugs, the armchairs and the drinks table were transformed as they were before.

A man and a woman stood in a romantic clinch in front of the fire, seemingly oblivious to my presence. I recognised Edward and Violet from before and there was an obvious passion in their embrace. As the door closed behind me with a sharp click, Violet suddenly jumped back looking startled, and glanced in my direction.

"What is it, my love?" Edward asked, holding onto her hand.

"I heard something." She looked anxiously around the room, but I was clearly invisible to her.

"What? What did you hear?"

"The door shut."

"The door's been shut all the time."

"Maybe someone came in, saw us and left again." Her eyes darted around the room in fear and I thought once again how beautiful she looked.

An involuntary shiver ran through her.

"It feels like someone's watching us," she whispered.

"Who?"

"Can't you feel it?"

"The only thing I want to feel is the welcome warmth of your body pressing against mine," he said, pulling her towards him, "and I want to feel it now."

She pulled back, released herself from his grip and moved away from him.

"No Edward, it's late. I must get ready to go home. Mama will be through in a minute."

"But ..." He took a step to her and slid his arm tenderly around her slender waist.

"No, Edward. I'll see you in the morning."

"I look forward to the day when we don't have to say goodbye when we say goodnight, Violet."

"So do I, my love, but we'll just have to wait. We'll have a lifetime of goodnights to look forward to. Now, unhand me, Sir." She giggled and, like the gentlemen he was, he withdrew his hand and Violet, with one last nervous glance around the room, made to leave.

As I too like to think of myself as a gentleman, I was about to open the door for her, but thought better of it before I frightened the girl half to death. I did step out of her way though.

She walked out and I turned back. Edward filled a glass from the whiskey decanter, lit a cigarette and limped to the fireplace. Then he crossed to the window where he peered through the closed curtains before returning to the fireplace.

He was about to sit down when the door opened, and William came in.

"I was just leaving," Edward said on seeing his father enter the room.

"Really?"

"Yes," he said, draining his glass and throwing his barely smoked cigarette into the fire. "I'm going to bed."

"It's early."

"I'm tired."

Before the conversation could develop into another argument Edward placed his empty glass on the mantlepiece and strode out of the room as best as he could with his prosthetic leg.

William stared at the door for moment after Edward had left, with a look of anger on his face. There seemed as though there was no thaw in the relationship between father and son. I saw in William a typical wealthy Victorian father; disapproving of a son who would never exceed his expectations. Distant because that was the Victorian way. To him children were just a means of continuing the family dynasty and keeping a simpering wife happy; where sons were valuable and daughters an expense to be married off to the highest bidder as soon as possible. Sons were expected to grow up and fulfil their responsibility. Their fathers were there to give guidance. The very idea of showing anything akin to love and affection was anathema to them. I reflected that, according to what Edward had written in his journal, William had forced him to join the army when he could have used protected job status to stop him going. I recalled his somewhat dismissive reaction to the deaths of his wife and three of his children from the Spanish Flu and I understood Edward's feeling towards his father. In fact, I empathised with those feelings.

With a sneer, William turned and poured himself a drink, sat down in one of the armchairs and started lighting a large cigar. As he disappeared in a cloud of blue-grey smoke there was a knock on the door behind me.

The door opened and in walked …

"Madea?" I exclaimed, loudly.

"Ah, Beth," William said from beneath his cloud of cigar smoke, "all finished for the day?"

"Yes, sir. I'll be heading home now."

She even sounded like Madea. Except she couldn't be. She looked different. Except she didn't, not really. It dawned on me that it was the way she was dressed that made her look different.

She wore a plain, beige cloth blouse with a wide pale-grey collar, buttoned to the neck and tucked neatly into the pleated waist of her thick, dark-grey calf length skirt. The skirt was fastened at the side with half a dozen pearl buttons and was tailored to accentuate her slender waist and full hips.

My mind was in a whirl. Her clothing aside, this woman, who William called Beth, was the spitting image of Madea Down. I wondered whether Madea was a descendant of Beth. If she was it meant that she would be related to me in some way since Beth was my great grandmother.

"Before you go, Beth," William said, "I want to ask you something."

"Sir?"

"Tell me, is there anything going on between Edward and Violet?"

"What do you mean?"

"Are they getting … ahem … er, close, do you think?"

"I don't know what you mean, sir. She's employed as his nurse; he's been through some tragic events this last year and she's helping him."

"You don't think there's … er … anything more?"

"No, sir."

"She hasn't mentioned anything to you, then?"

"No, sir, she hasn't. She respects her professional confidentiality, and

192

so do I, sir."

"Good. Capital. Right." William looked slightly awkward, as if there was something more that he wanted to say. "Well then," he continued, "perhaps you might remind her of her position."

"Sir?"

"As a servant. In case she has any thoughts."

Madea ... Beth stood staring at her employer with a look of disbelief on her face. I found it hard to imagine that there might be any truth in the rumours of any relationship between them.

Beth drew herself up, clasped her hands together and said, "Well, if that'll be all, sir, Miss Violet and I will head off home."

"Yes, yes, of course."

"Goodnight, sir."

"Yes."

Beth turned and, with her head held high, she walked from the room...

... And straight through Larry, who was standing, wrapped in a warm dressing gown, in the open doorway.

# Chapter Twenty-Seven
# Dead Woman

As she passed through him, something dropped from her hand unseen by anyone but me. It fluttered to the ground and, unknowingly, Larry kicked it along the floor where it slid beneath the corner of the rug.

"What's up Ji… Whoa, what the…?"

A look of incredulity passed across his face and he spun around and looked behind him. All he could see was the darkness of the corridor.

"What the …? What was ….? Did I just …?" he stammered and stuttered, shaking his head and whirling about with his eyes nearly popping out of his head. Eventually he seemed to pull himself together. "What just happened there?"

I looked at him as he shook his head, then turned back to the room. It was changed back to its normal twenty-first century look. I felt a bit light-headed and staggered to the sofa that had reappeared with the rest of the room and sat down heavily. It had been a God-awful night so far.

"Did you just see that?" I indicated the room that was now back to normal.

"I-I think so," he said, "unless I was dreaming."

"No," I said, shaking my head slowly, gazing down between my knees. My voice was steadier now that I knew that I wasn't going mad. Larry had seen what I had seen meaning something really was going on and apparently, it was nothing to do with my illness. "No, you weren't dreaming."

"Were they … your ghosts?"

"If that's what you want to call them, I suppose they were."

"What do you call them then?"

I looked at him. I must have looked terrible because he stopped asking what he was about to ask and instead said, "I'll make us a cup of tea."

Warily I looked around the room, half expecting it to change back again, but whatever it was we had seen was gone. At least, for the time being.

In a way I was glad Larry had witnessed it too, or at least had had a glimpse of it, because it validated my sanity. It proved that I wasn't going mad after all, that this wasn't some manifestation of my fragile mind or an indication that my depression was returning, and yet, unreasonably, a part of me regretted that he had shared it. I couldn't understand that part; it was as though I wanted to keep it all to myself, that it was my own haunting, not to be shared with others. What made me feel that way? It didn't make sense, yet nothing about this incident made any sense.

"So," said Larry, returning with two mugs of tea, "can you explain to me what just happened?"

"Not really, no," I replied, cradling the hot mug in my hands, feeling my palms burn from the heat.

"We're seeing ghosts," he said, and I could see that the twinkle had returned to his eyes. The excitement of what we had seen was apparent, and I looked at him wearily. I was tired, already shaken from my nightmare and then this, and I couldn't think of anything more rational to explain it than his damned ghost theory. "I'm sure we are, Jim. Think about it. At first, we thought it was just a side-effect of your depression. Things were happening to you. You saw things, you saw people that I didn't, so we assumed it was all down to your illness. But I just saw a woman walk right through me just now. For fuck's sake, Jim, she walked though me. Real people don't do that, it doesn't even happen in dreams. At least, not in my dreams"

He hesitated. "That is … that was what you saw, wasn't it?"

"Yes," I said, "that was exactly what I saw."

"There you go then. Explain that if you will."

I swear he was enjoying it. The nightmares aside, which had been as vivid as they were frightening, neither time when we had seemingly looked through a window into the past had I felt fear or felt threatened. It was a bit like watching a period drama on the television; we could see them, but they couldn't see us.

Except Violet had heard me close the door and she had said she felt as though she was being watched. Now that was odd.

"I can't," I said, rubbing my face in the palms of my hands. "When I was the only one seeing things it was easy to explain. We simply put it down to my illness. But now that you've seen it I can give you no explanation."

I felt utterly bewildered. It was the middle of the night; I'd been woken by a nasty nightmare, then come downstairs to find myself projected a hundred years into the past. If it weren't for the fact that Larry had seen it too, I could have accepted that I was experiencing a dream within a dream, but now I didn't know what to think.

"Don't be scared, Jim."

"I'm not scared. No, correction, I am scared. I'm scared of what's happening to me. To us. Why is it happening? And why now?"

Larry shrugged and sipped his tea.

"In all the years I've stayed in this house there's never been any signs of ghosts."

"Maybe …" Larry began, "maybe they've been here all along and your illness has just made you more susceptible to seeing them. More … sensitive."

I snorted. "And what about you? How come you're finally seeing them too?"

"Ah, well, that's because …"

"Yes?"

He was thinking and I could almost see the straws he was trying to clutch. "Maybe, because you've been seeing them it's opened my mind to being able to see them too. You know, somehow you've brought them into the house and now I can see them."

"That doesn't make any sense," I told him.

"No," he agreed, "it doesn't, does it?"

I yawned, feeling absolutely drained of all energy. I sipped my tea and felt its warmth flowing through my body. Sitting back on the sofa I rested my head gently against the soft cushion and, just for a second, I closed my eyes. They felt hot and closing them seemed to relieve the burning sensation.

Thoughts of Madea and Beth floated around in my head. Was Madea her great-granddaughter? Was she another second cousin to Larry and me who we knew nothing about?

I mentally drew the Chambers' family tree but couldn't reconcile Madea into it through the lines I now knew. Unless Gwendoline and Violet had had a brother or another sister, which I was certain they hadn't. Maybe she was descended from a cousin, from a brother or sister of Beth, for instance. That could make sense. It was quite likely Beth had had a sibling of some sort. In those days it was quite rare to travel very far from your home village or town, and we had only recently spoken to three examples of that in Colin, Jack and Bill. Mind you, I thought, look at the Hilliards. Generations of the family had lived in Rosehip Hall since it was built in the 18th century.

The more I tried to focus my mind the more it wandered. I thought about the Christmas decorations and how we needed to get them up soon otherwise we wouldn't be ready for when Leanne and Harry arrived on Christmas morning; a line from The Beatles' song Yesterday popped up out of nowhere and I couldn't stop the line repeating over and over again; I just couldn't get past that one line about my troubles seeming so far away.

My thoughts became confused, a jumble of half remembered places and happenings and I was unable to control the chaos. Round and round they whirled like a carousel, muddled and out of control, until a welcome black mist enveloped me and carried me away on the wings of oblivion.

I awoke to the chill of a cold winter morning. Larry had covered me with a blanket and left me to sleep on the sofa where, exhausted, I had finally nodded off in the small hours of the morning.

I had had no further dreams but as I sat up it seemed to me that every joint and muscle in my body ached or creaked. Sofas are not the ideal place to spend the night, being designed for sitting or lounging rather than sleeping on, but Larry had not wanted to disturb me once I had fallen asleep. He assumed I might wake in the night and return to my room, but I didn't, I had slept deeply.

I eased myself upright, bleary eyed, and stretched. I rolled my head from side to side to try and work the stiffness from my neck and I yawned loudly, which seemed to give me enough energy to get me to my feet.

The room was cold, and I tightened my dressing gown around my shoulders. As I stood up, I noticed the newspaper on the coffee table that Larry had been scribbling on. It was open at the crossword page and I noticed, amongst all the scribblings, that he'd written MADEA DOWN in the centre. Underneath he'd rewritten it as a simple series of letters; M A D E A D O W N and in brackets he'd written '?anagram!!!'.

By crossing out the first two and the last three letters he was left with DEAD and the remaining letters he had rearranged into WOMAN.

DEAD WOMAN.

# Chapter Twenty-Eight
## Violet

"The fact is," Larry explained as he bit into his toast and marmalade, "I've never seen her."

I looked at him, sceptically.

"Honest," he said. "The times she's come to the house when I was here I was busy in the some other part of the house and she came and went before I saw her. All the other times she's been here I've been out. So, I've never actually seen her."

"But she must exist, I've sat with her, talked with her. She's my therapist, for God's sake, she's been helping me."

"Remember the first time she was here. She'd just left and I joked that she must have sprinted up the drive because we didn't hear a car?"

"She cycled."

"She could have done," he said, "but who comes to visit a client in a remote village on a bicycle? And have you ever seen her arrive or leave?"

"I've never seen her arrive, I must confess, but I've always been there to let her out when she leaves."

"So, you've seen her cycling up the drive?"

I thought for a moment, then said cautiously, "Well, er, no. Not exactly."

"When you say, 'not exactly', do you mean you've never actually watched her go up the drive either walking, on a bike or on a broomstick?"

The more I thought about it the more I realised Larry was right, I couldn't remember a time when, having closed the front door, I'd actually watched her leave the grounds and I admitted as such to Larry.

"There you go then," he said, "case proven, she's a ghost."

"No, she's not."

"Why don't you phone her."

"What?"

"Why don't you phone her?"

"Right." I stood up and then sat down again.

"Well?"

"I – I don't have her number."

"You've spoken to her on the phone, haven't you?"

"Yes, but she's always phoned me."

"So, she's a ghost."

"Are you trying to tell me that the ghost of my great-grandmother has just spent the last three months giving me therapy – something I'm sure she wouldn't be qualified to do – because I was suffering from depression over the death of her granddaughter, my adoptive mother? That's ridiculous."

"So, she's a nice ghost," he said, shrugging, "ghosts can be nice, you know. It's only in Hollywood films and sensational books that they're malevolent entities. Real life ghosts are more …"

"Real life ghosts? Really?" I said, interrupting him, "Larry, listen to yourself. You're talking about ghosts as if they are an everyday occurrence like trains and buses."

"That's not what I'm saying, Jim, I'm just saying that hauntings don't have to be a revenge thing like in The Exorcist or The Omen. They could be more like Casper, the Friendly Ghost."

I burst out laughing.

"And how much experience do you have of everyday ghosts, friendly or otherwise?"

"Well, none, of course. You'd know if I had because I would have told you. Aren't you even a bit curious about this?"

"Curious, yes. But ghosts? That's impossible and just because I can't explain it… Christ, I don't even understand it, but that doesn't mean there isn't an explanation of some sort."

"You know," he said after a few moments silence, "I once read an account of a supposed true story about a haunted Inn in Devon where the ghost of a dead barmaid would occasionally appear and make passionate love to a guest staying there. It was a popular place to stay."

"Are you suggesting that the ghost of our great-grandmother is haunting me because she wants to have sex with me?"

"No, of course that's not what I'm suggesting. What I'm trying to show is that ghosts can be nice, even helpful. Look what she's done for you, after all. Maybe she was just helping you through your illness. Maybe now you're better she'll go and leave us in peace.

"Maybe," I said, "let's hope."

"Or maybe she wanted to help you find out who you really are after Aunt Clara was killed."

"Can we please change the subject? I've had enough of ghosts."

"Of course, we can," he said, "for now. But I've got a feeling we haven't seen the end of them yet. Right, our task for today is ..." and Larry tattooed a drum roll with his hands on the table, "Christmas decorations."

To the right at the end of the first floor landing a set of stairs, smaller than those of the main staircase, leads to the upper landing from which a number of attic rooms are accessed. These rooms, which once housed the servants employed at the Hall, were nowadays used for storage, and the Christmas decorations, amongst other things, were kept in the third room along overlooking the front of the Hall.

Several boxes full of decorations were stacked on shelves in the corner of the room and I blew a thick layer of dust from the top box that had accumulated since last January.

Traditionally, we put presents beneath a main tree in the morning room; then we had a big tree in the hall and another smaller one in the smoking room. Many years ago, when Larry and I stayed as children, the trees were always real, but Larry's mum had banned them from the house a few years after Edward died and the Hall had passed to Uncle Anthony, because they made too much mess. Besides, she argued when we pleaded with her to change her decision, fake trees were just as realistic as real trees nowadays.

We checked in all the boxes then readied to take them downstairs.

"I'll bring the duster and vacuum up when we come back for the rest," I said, as we carried the first few boxes downstairs, "that room needs a bloody good dusting and if I don't do it now it won't get done for another year."

"There's a vacuum cleaner in the next room," Larry told me, "I bought one to save having to carry it up and down stairs all the time."

I laughed and looked around at the layer of dust, "Is it still in its box?"

"I've used it," he protested.

"Once?"

"More than that. Twice, I think."

I left Larry sorting out the tree downstairs to go up and quickly run the vacuum over the room. It wasn't very dirty, just dusty with a few cobwebs. The cleaner would soon pick it all up.

Using the nozzle attachment first I quickly ran it over the numerous shelves containing books, binders and box files. I recognised mine and Larry's University files and, as I pulled one off the shelf to look at it the whole pile came down with a crash, spilling their contents out all over the floor.

"Bugger," I muttered to myself, then knelt down to pick them up. I scanned through each piece quickly to try and identify in which box they belonged and rapidly put them back. One sheet was wedged beneath the corner of a rug and I remembered Beth dropping something last night as she left the room. I wondered if it really was there. If it was it would prove Larry was right about ghosts.

I stacked the box files back in their place and hurried downstairs.

Larry had finished putting up the trees by the time I came down and he was now in the process of untangling metres of tree lights. Miraculously they all worked and, after wrapping them around the first tree, we decided to stop for coffee.

On the way to the kitchen I stepped into the smoking room. My heart leapt as I saw something tucked under the corner of the rug. The edge of a piece of paper. I bent down and retrieved it. It was a sealed envelope, crisp and new, addressed to Violet.

"What's that?" Larry asked as I came in staring at the envelope as I held it in front of me.

"Last night when Beth left the room, in 1918, she dropped something as she walked through you. You didn't see it and before I could do anything, you'd kicked it under the rug and the room had transformed back to today. I'd forgotten about it until just now and I wondered if it was still there, and it was. Look"

"What it is?"

"A letter. To Granny Violet."

"Let's have a look." I handed him the envelope. "But this is new," he said, turning it in his hands.

"She only dropped it last night," I said. "Is it possible that it dropped through time with us when it wasn't meant to?"

He picked up the letter opener and tore it open. He withdrew a short, handwritten note, scanned it and let out a low whistle. "Listen to this," he said and started reading.

*My dear Vi*
*I don't know how to put my feeling into words. I have hidden a lie*

201

*from you, and it is weighing on my mind. I can't speak of it so I'm writing this note and will have to hide it, so you find it sometime. The lie I have hidden is to protect you and your sister. You see, I have made up the lie that Gwen is dead from the Spanish Flu, but that's not true. I made it up and I'll tell you why.*

*In August your father came home from the Three Horseshoes much the worse for drink. You'd just started working up at the Hall then as Master Edward had just returned from the war and you were staying on there for a few days to settle him. Your father was angry, drinking always made him angry and when he got home he started beating me. Gwen heard and came rushing downstairs and tried to stop him. He knocked me down and I think I was knocked out for a few moments, because when I looked at him next he was holding Gwen and ripping off her bodice. She had a big red mark on her face and she was sobbing. He was just about to pull off her skirt when I crashed the big vase over his head and he collapsed on the floor. I thought I'd killed him at first but he was still breathing, so I got Gwen upstairs and while she dressed herself I packed her clothes into a suitcase. Then I took her round to Mrs White next door who agreed she could stay overnight. Gwen caught the train to London the next morning and I never told your father where she went.*

*When I went to see her a few weeks ago I told her she must never contact us again for her own safety and when I got home I told everyone she'd died of the Flu.*

*I had to tell you the same lie because your father would notice if you weren't a-grieving and he'd make you tell him the truth. He does that. But I want you to know that she is safe and has secured a position as a school mistress at a school near London, in a place called Tilbury.*

*I've done this for the best, to protect both of you and I hope, one day, you will be able to find her again and forgive me my lies.*

*Mum*

We sat in silence contemplating the letter.

"So, Seth tried to rape his own daughter," Larry said, "what a bastard."

"And Granny Violet never knew her sister was still alive because she never got this letter as Beth dropped it when she walked through you. She must have taken it from her pocket to give to Violet as they were about to go home together, and she dropped it just as the room went back to our time."

202

"So, it's been under the rug for a hundred years?"

"No, it's been there since she dropped it last night. It must have come back with us somehow."

"A time travelling letter?"

"I saw it," I said, "I can't explain it, but I'm sure as hell it shouldn't have happened."

"So, do you believe in ghosts now?"

"I don't know. No. Yes. Whatever." Truth is I was more confused than ever. This letter should have made all the difference to the lives of those two women. With it Violet would have known about Gwendoline. She would have gone to find her.

"It seems to be an important letter," Larry said, echoing my own thoughts, "do you think we can send it back somehow?"

"I don't know," I replied. I felt I was losing my grip on reality again. "If Violet had received the letter then she would have found Gwendoline, wouldn't she?"

"Yes."

"And if she had found her sister," I reasoned, "Gwendoline would have returned home."

"Yes."

"And if she had returned home then she probably wouldn't have met and married James Butler and had her children, in which case I would not have been born. So no, I don't think we can return that letter, because we can't change history. Obviously, because I am still here."

"So Violet married Edward, left her old life behind her and lived happily ever after, never knowing the truth about what really happened to her sister."

"And I don't suppose Gwendoline ever knew about what happened to Beth and Seth either because there was no television and being a schoolmistress, she wouldn't have been allowed to read daily newspapers.

"What a messed-up family," I said.

I felt a need to talk to Madea, but if it was true that Madea was really Beth, and I was slowly coming around to that conclusion, then I knew I'd never see her again.

"Oh, I don't know," he replied cheerfully, "I think we've turned out remarkably well, considering."

I took the letter from him and read it again. The writing was elegant, even if the words were a bit clumsy in places. Beth's writing sloped to the right with lots of loops, a script no longer taught in schools, the importance of writing having been replaced by the importance of typing. I looked up from the letter, "do you think this is another piece to the puzzle? We now know why Gwendoline and Violet lost touch. Maybe that's the end of it."

"Poor Violet."

"Poor Gwendoline."

"One thing we still don't know, though," Larry said, turning to rinse his empty coffee mug.

"What's that?"

"We don't know what happened to Beth."

"She was murdered by Seth."

"We know that. But we don't know what happened to her. They never found her body, did they? When Seth went to his grave, he carried his secret with him."

# Chapter Twenty-Nine
# Christmas Eve

The next few days were spent busily preparing for Christmas. We finally managed to get the decorations up, cards were displayed on various shelves and windowsills around the house and vast quantities of food and drink, enough to last several people for several months, were stored in fridges, freezers, cupboards and in the cellars below the house.

It was Christmas Eve.

Fresh snow had fallen, and it looked as though we were in for a picture postcard Christmas, something we hadn't enjoyed for several years. I took loads of pictures of the grounds and of the Hall in the snow and sent them to Leanne who replied with comments like '*looking forward to seeing you on Christmas day*' and '*the kids are excited, I hope you are!!*' all signed off with a variety of festive emojis. We spoke every few days and she told us how hyper the children were getting and how much they were looking forward to seeing Father Christmas and their grandads; and in that order, I suspected.

For me there were mixed emotions. I've always loved Christmas, and in many ways, I was just as excited as Leanne and the grandchildren, but this year it was tinged with sadness too. This would be my first Christmas without Janet and mum – I still called her mum despite everything I'd discovered in the last few months. The sadness was just that though and nothing more; it was no longer underpinned by my depression; I'd moved on from that. I'd done everything that Madea had instructed me to do and I was totally grateful for her support, even though it seemed she may have died a hundred years ago.

I'd even come to terms with that, too. Perhaps I had been swept along by Larry's enthusiasm for ghosts, but it was clear that whatever we had seen wasn't harming us. Anyway, there had been no sign of them since we'd found Beth's letter – and there was no disputing the reality of that – so perhaps the hauntings really had finished as Madea had suggested they would. Perhaps the letter was the final piece of a rather complicated puzzle, although Larry's point about the mystery of what happened to Beth's body weighed on my mind. It remained unresolved.

"Fancy a walk? A bit of fresh air, topped off with a nice stodgy pie and a pint of the finest at the Three Horseshoes?" Larry suggested, folding his paper and looking at his watch. "We haven't had any exercise today and it'll do us good; blow away a few cobwebs and fill our stomachs."

"Sounds like a plan," I replied. I was taking Madea's advice and writing a journal of everything that had happened since that fateful day last spring and I had just reached a suitable place to stop. I was ready for a break I must confess, although I was finding the process quite cathartic.

Eight months had passed already. At times it seemed like it had happened only yesterday and at others it seemed like a lifetime ago; isn't time a strange concept?

It was wellington boots weather and soon we set off through the back door. We intended to check on the kitchen garden before walking to the pub; that way we'd get some exercise and work up an appetite.

For the first time in many days the sun was shining, although it was very low, barely above the horizon, and it cast long shadows on the clean white snow. It wasn't warm, but it was bright, and it reflected off the snow, dazzling us as we walked across the back lawn. We wore sunglasses, which seemed a bit incongruous alongside our woolly hats and scarves, but they did the job. A few icy flakes fluttered down over us, blown by gentle breezes off the overhanging branches.

"I reckon, if we put the turkey on about ten," Larry said, "that'll give it three-and-a-half hours cooking time and thirty minutes resting time, which should be plenty. Harry and Leanne reckon they'll be here between twelve-thirty and one, depending on traffic..."

"And the kids."

"Them too," he said with a laugh, "so we should be ready to eat between two and half past."

"Perfect."

Unlike both their siblings, who were always late for everything, Leanne and Harry were habitually on time. Even with the children they had managed to maintain that discipline.

"The Hall looks really festive," I remarked and we both turned and looked. The low sun shone directly onto the back of the Hall lighting the windows golden and the walls a pale yellow. So peaceful I thought, as I gazed back; peaceful and inviting. So different to the way it had appeared the other day when I had felt the coldness in its soul.

"Look at that robin," Larry said, pointing out the small, red-breasted bird hopping about beneath the feeders, picking up fallen birdseed. He stopped, cocked his head to one side and looked at us for a moment. It was as if he was weighing up the level of threat we posed and, deciding we offered none, carried on as though we weren't there.

We walked into the kitchen garden. Since the snow had fallen we had done very little work on it, but before then we had made good progress having finished cultivating two of the big beds. We had also harvested brussels sprouts, carrots, cauliflower, and parsnips ready for tomorrow's feast.

"After Christmas," Larry said, as we walked along the wall, "when everyone's gone, we can get started on this bed." He waved his hand over the mass of brambles and dead weeds covered by a thick layer of snow.

"Absolutely," I agreed with enthusiasm. I had enjoyed the work we had done so far, and looked forward to when we could continue, "and we'll need to do something to help rid us of all that extra weight we're going to put on over the next few days."

Larry looked at me with a smile and said, "I don't think you've got anything to worry about, Jim. Look at you."

Before Janet had died, she was on at me to lose a bit of weight. Not a lot, maybe a few kilos to trim me down a bit and take a little off around my stomach, but during my illness I had lost nearly fifteen kilos, which is over two stone in old measurements. Since staying with Larry I had put some of it back on. I felt physically fit and my mental health was much improved despite recent happenings.

"I'm fine."

He put his arm around my shoulder in a gesture of companionship. "You look good, Jim, you look really well. Leanne will be really impressed when she sees how good you look right now."

"I feel good too, and it's all thanks to you, Larry."

"It's not down to me," he protested, "we're family."

"We really are," I laughed.

"Exactly, and you were there for me when Helen died, I just returned the favour."

"Thanks."

He bent down, scooped up an armful of snow and dumped it over my head.

"Hey."

"That's for getting all soppy with me," he said and set off through the gate into the main garden. I grabbed a handful snow and chased after him across the lawn. We were laughing as he tripped and fell. I jumped to avoid his flailing legs, caught my foot on them and fell in the snow beside him. The snow was soft but crisp. Laughing like schoolboys, we lay on our backs looking up into the pale grey sky and made snow angels with our arms and legs; watching the steam from our breath dissipate into the air.

After a while we sat up, glowing and exhilarated.

"Come on," he said, "let's go and find some lunch."

The gloom of missing Janet and mum remained in the back of my mind but I knew I was going to spend Christmas with people who loved me and who cared about me, and I knew that when I fell into moments of melancholy, which I inevitably would, they'd be there to raise my spirits.

The Three Horseshoes was remarkably packed, and the atmosphere was vibrant. Clearly many people had taken the day off work, or had finished early, in preparation for Christmas.

A couple who were just leaving offered us their table and Larry sat down as I pushed my way through the crowd to the bar. As usual the television was on but no one was watching; the landlady was too busy serving the throng of revellers to have time to watch, and the usual Christmas CD was playing, but no one was listening. The festive choruses were lost beneath the noisy banter and raucous laughter. I ordered our usual and made my way back to Larry who was chatting to a couple of villagers on the next table.

A couple of hours, a couple of pints and a pie later and we headed back. The sun was now a pastel pink as it sank slowly in the west to make way for the blanket of darkness sweeping in from the east.

"It's getting dark already," Larry said, looking at his watch, "and it's not even three o'clock yet."

We stepped back hurriedly, as a car speeding through the village towards the A10 sprayed filthy slush over the edge of the pavement.

At this time of the year the heating in the Hall was left on all day. It was a big, drafty old house and the central heating barely managed to take away the worst of the chill. The Hall was always cold this time of year so, when we had removed our boots and coats, I went into the smoking room and laid a fire.

While it roared into life and began to warm the room, Larry and I spent the afternoon checking our preparations and making sure that we had done everything we could to make tomorrow morning as stress free as possible. Presents were laid out beneath the tree in the morning room, stairgates for the children were put out in readiness at the top and bottom of the staircases and fire guards were placed by hearths. After a light supper of bread and cheese accompanied by some fruit, we settled down in front of the fire with a welcome glass of whiskey.

The flames threw flickering shadows of yellow and orange around the room. Their warmth created a soporific stuffiness, so I opened the door to let some cooler air flow in. A welcome draft blew across us and fanned the flames which momentarily flared up, brightening the room with their merry glow. We sat facing one another on the comfortable sofas, mesmerised by the intimate writhing of the flames and sipped a fine twenty-year-old malt. I stared deep into the heart of the fire and felt relaxed.

Larry muttered something but his voice seemed to come from far away, and then only as a vague noise. I felt myself drifting away on a gentle wave of sleep, carried to that peaceful semi-conscious state between sleeping and wakefulness. I felt the heat of the fire stroke my face with its gentle fingers and my mind wandered pleasantly into a land of sweet dreams.

I closed my eyes, let out a satisfied sigh and smiled. All seemed good with the world.

# Chapter Thirty
## Seth Chambers

A loud crash jolted me from my reverie and a loud voice yelling "Hilliard. Come 'ere, Hilliard," made us both leap to our feet in a state of confusion.

"What the hell was that?" Larry demanded and rushed to the door with me hot on his heels. An almighty rumpus was coming from the main hall and we dashed along the corridor to see what was going on. My heart was racing from being wrenched so suddenly out of a state of deep relaxation.

"You're no more than a cheap whore," a man's gruff voice growled, followed by a slapping noise, a crash and a yelp of pain.

In the hall a man dressed in a black reefer coat and felt cap stood menacingly over Beth. He was tall and beefy with a round face, red from the cold wind and with a purple hue from years of alcohol abuse; not the sort man you'd want to pick a fight with.

"What are you talking about?" Beth shouted back from where she had fallen beneath the big round table. I noticed that it was the same table we have there today, even though the rest of the room looked different and I realised we were once again witness to a previous time.

Beth held her hand to her cheek covering the angry red weal caused by Chambers' hand. He bent down, grabbed her by the throat and pulled her upright. She gagged, trying to scream but the pressure around her neck stopped her.

Instinctively both Larry and I rushed forward to help her, but we were invisible to them and unable to interfere. We were just observers, as if we were experiencing some bizarre immersion video. Chambers pulled Beth to him, holding her by her neck in his vice-like grip. Her face was turning purple as she gasped for air.

"I'm talking about you and Hilliard," he shouted right into her face.

"Wha.. ..bout ..s?" Beth gasped.

"You're having an affair with him, aren't you?"

"Le.. me go, Se..." she pleaded.

210

He pushed her violently away and sent her clattering across the marble floor where she crashed against the far wall. She forced herself up, rubbing her swollen neck and gasping for air.

Larry and I stood by helplessly, only able to watch this dreadful scene unfold.

"I think we're about to witness Beth's murder," I whispered. My voice was shaky, I didn't want to be a part of it, but we were powerless.

"Can't we do something, Jim? Can't we stop it?"

"I don't think we can. They can't see us, we're not part of it. It's already happened."

"Then why?"

"Do you deny it?" Seth shouted across the hall at his wife.

"Sir William and me?" she rasped. A thin line of blood trickled down her cheek from a cut below her eye and mingled with her tears. "What a ridiculous idea! How can you even think something like that?"

"It's all the talk in the village."

"In the pub, you mean." Beth struggled to stand up. Her left ankle was swollen, probably sprained when she fell, and her face was a mess of blood and tears. As she stood, Chambers stepped forward, raising his hand to hit her again. A look of defiance came to her face; she'd been through this abuse dozens of times before and had become hardened to it.

"That's right," she spat at him, "hit me, like the big man you are, but it won't change anything. You won't believe me because you don't want to believe me. You want to think I'm having an affair because that's your justification for hitting me. You are a stupid, stupid man who'd rather listen to a bunch of ignorant drunks than hear the truth. Well here's the truth, Seth. I've had enough. I've had enough of your petty, unfounded jealousy. I've had enough of your drunken rages and your self-pity, and I've had enough of your beatings."

"Silence, woman," he yelled, slapping her with the back of his hand. She fell.

"It's all because of you that Gwen left. Do your ignorant friends know what you did? What would they think of you if they knew the truth about you? That you tried to rape your own daughter. Would they still want to know you then?"

"I'll kill you if you don't shut up."

"I'm not afraid of you," she said, a calmness in her voice. It was almost as if she knew what was going to happen to her and she'd resigned herself to her fate. "But I have had enough, do you understand? I want you to leave, pack your things and go. I don't care where, just go."

Both Larry and I winced at the sound of his fist as he hit her again. She screamed in pain and fell back. Instinctively she curled into a ball and raised her arms over her head to protect herself and he kicked her in the back.

"We have to do something," Larry shouted above the noise.

Chambers was squaring up to hit her again and I stood in his way, knowing that my action would be useless, but I had to try.

"What the hell is going on here?" a man's voice yelled from the corridor. Edward appeared from the smoking room. On seeing Chambers standing there he stopped, "Who the hell are you?" he demanded. "And what are you doing in my house?"

As the two men faced each other I knelt to Beth and whispered urgently, "Run." She turned to look at me with a puzzled look. It was as if she had heard my voice but couldn't see me. I reached out, wanting so much to help her as she struggled to her feet. Edward and Chambers circled one another with angry looks on their faces. I thought of David and Goliath, but I really didn't rate Edward's chances against Seth who looked like the type to enjoy the pain of a fight.

Although she was unsteady on her feet, Beth limped along the corridor as fast as she was able. In that same moment Chambers stepped forward and swung a punch at Edward. He was still drunk, and the punch was wild. Edward caught hold of his arm as it swung at him; but its force took him by surprise. He lost his footing and fell heavily to the floor.

Before Edward could react, Chambers grabbed a shotgun that had been left leaning against the wall and set off after his wife.

"Damn and blast," Edward shouted, sitting up. He ran his hands down his right leg and quickly adjusted the fastenings of his prosthetic leg, it must have come lose when he fell. Not waiting for him, we dashed down the corridor after Beth, hoping that somehow something would happen to let us help, but in my mind, I doubted it. I still didn't understand why we were there.

A cold breeze blew over us and we caught sight of Chambers as he rounded the corner towards the backdoor.

"Stop, you bitch," he yelled, charging into the deep snow that covered the back garden.

Even though we weren't really there; I mean we could see what was happening and we could hear what was being said, but we couldn't touch anyone and they couldn't see us, I felt the coldness of the air and I could touch the walls and, bizarrely, I could touch the backdoor. It was swinging shut as I reached the end of the corridor and I put my hands out, not sure what would happen, but it was as solid as it usually was and I pulled it open. Larry was with me and we could hear Edward running behind us.

"You realise," Larry panted beside me as we waded through the snow, but his words were lost as he tripped and fell. I stopped to help him up.

"What did you say?"

But his reply was lost beneath a rising cacophony of noises. Ahead, Chambers was yelling at Beth; behind us, Edward was shouting for everyone to stop, and in the distance I could hear the shouts and calls of a crowd of people, presumably the villagers who were meant to be going to midnight mass but had realised that there was likely to be something more interesting to watch at the Hall.

"They're heading for the chapel," I yelled, pulling Larry out of the snow and stumbling forward. A freezing gust of wind blew snow over us, making my shirt damp. Neither of us was wearing a coat and the air was bitterly cold, but despite that I was sweating from our exertions.

The night was dark. The moon was hidden by a heavy blanket of cloud, but the white snow lightened our surroundings from pitch black to a dark grey. Wading through the snow was like trying to run through treacle and we were struggling to catch up with Chambers.

Before us the chapel loomed out of the gloom, a black shadow against a dark colourless backdrop. My eyes gradually became accustomed to the dark and shapes took on form around me.

Ahead of us I heard the chapel door slam shut.

"You can't hide," Chambers yelled from inside the building. There was menace and anger in his voice.

"You leave me alone, Seth Chambers, you drunken bully."

From the other side of the door we could hear the scraping of furniture.

"Sounds like he's moving the pews."

"Maybe he's trying to block Beth's exit."

"What a bastard. Let's go in."

I turned the handle and, with Larry's help, pushed the door open, forcing aside the pews that Chambers had piled against it.

The darkness inside was almost impenetrable, but the faint light caste through the windows highlighted the black shadow of Chambers as he moved around the room in his search for Beth.

We heard a cry.

"Gotcha."

"No Seth," she pleaded, "let me go."

"Leave her be, you bastard," Larry shouted, rushing forward into the dark and clattering into the pews that blocked the entrance. He went crashing over it and tumbled forward.

"What was that?" Chambers called.

"Seth, you're hurting me."

"Who's there?"

"Please, let me go."

The room was suddenly bathed in bright yellow light. Edward ran into the chapel holding an oil-fired storm lantern whose flickering flame penetrated the thick darkness inside.

Near the altar Chambers held his wife tightly, pinning her arms to her sides. Her face was a picture of pain and defiance, covered as it was in cuts and bruises. Chambers shook her and Beth struggled to free herself. She kicked out.

"Stop this at once," Edward commanded, dashing towards Chambers.

"Yeah? Or what?" Chambers demanded, throwing Beth across the chapel like a child might throw an unwanted toy. She crashed against another pew and it clattered to the floor. The back of the pew knocked her legs from under her and she tumbled down and lay there, in a crumpled heap.

Quick as lightning, Chambers picked up the shotgun from the altar and swung it at Edward. Caught off guard it smashed against the side of his head with a loud crack and Edward fell lifeless to the floor. The lamp flew from his hand and smashed against the far wall where it exploded in a flash of light and flame. Burning oil sprayed over the wooden pews and splashed across the floor; a liquid line of fire. It reached a wooden plinth carrying a stone bowl. Dry from centuries of neglect the base flared up. In seconds flames snaked up the column and licked at the bottom of the stone bowl. Tongues of orange and red jumped from pew to pew and the fire rapidly spread through the chapel.

Regaining her feet, Beth grabbed a brass candlestick from the altar

214

and leapt at Chambers, but he saw her as she swung it at him. Instinctively he dropped to his knee and turned to face her, throwing his arms up in front of him. The candlestick glanced harmlessly off his arm and immediately he sprang up and grabbed her, his right hand snaking out and clamping around her throat.

I heard Beth gasp as he tightened his grip, restricting her windpipe and cutting off her air.

Beth struggled, frantically, but he was too much for her. She grabbed hold of his wrists as he lifted her from the ground. He was a strong man and his strength was fueled by his anger and jealousy; that and the alcohol he had consumed.

Beth's face was turning blue as he held her by her throat, dangling in the air; slowly squeezing the life from her.

The heat from the burning pews intensified as it spread throughout the interior of the chapel, but with no fire safety equipment, buckets of water or sand, we were unable to douse it and I backed towards the door, glancing around the room.

I couldn't see Larry.

Edward lay on the floor, still and lifeless. His unconscious body was surrounded by flames that were slowly creeping towards him.

Chambers let out an almighty roar as he shook Beth. She dangled from his hand like a rag doll in a dog's mouth, clinging to his wrists, desperately trying to pull his fingers apart and relieve the pressure as he crushed her throat. I could see she wasn't going to last much longer.

What could I do?

As I stood helplessly in the entrance to the chapel something crashed into me from behind, catapulting me forward. I tripped over a broken pew, flew forward and crashed against Chambers.

Instead of passing through him I collided with him. It was like crashing into a wall, but I knocked him off balance and, in his surprise, he dropped Beth who fell against the back of the altar.

As she fell crashing to the floor her elbow knocked against the back face of the stone edifice and a panel sprang open at its base. I reached out to her as she rolled forward and fell through the opening, dropping into the pitch-black pit below.

It was an entrance to some sort of vault; a crypt perhaps.

I turned to see Sir William rushing at Chambers and I wondered if I had fully crossed the timeline to 1918 and that was why I had been able to touch them both just now. If so, was that the reason I could no longer see Larry; he hadn't crossed with me.

William confronted Chambers and although I didn't hold out much hope of him overpowering him, I knew I had to get to Edward and this diversion offered me that opportunity. The sleeve of his coat was smouldering, and he remained still. A nasty bruise had welled up on the side of his head where Chambers had hit him with the butt of the shotgun.

I rushed over, keeping low and out of sight, and pulled Edward back, away from the fire, quickly beating out the flames that had broken out on his sleeve. As soon as he was safely away from immediate danger, I checked him for life signs. He wasn't breathing. Without another thought I loosened his tie and ripped open the collar of his shirt.

As Sir William fought with Chambers behind me and the fire burned on either side of me, I tried to remember the basics of CPR. Nothing came to mind, so I rolled him onto his back and, kneeling over him with both arms outstretched, started pumping his chest to the rhythm of Nellie The Elephant, which was the only bit of my training I remembered.

I pumped hard and, after a short time Edward gasped in a deep breath. Quickly, I turned him on his side to the recovery position in case he was sick. He was still unconscious, but I had to leave him to try and help Sir William.

When I had knocked into him Chambers had dropped the shotgun and I grabbed it, with the intention of threatening him with it as I was sure he could see me now.

William held Chambers from behind with his arm wrapped tightly around him. Chambers struggled and seemed to be smiling, as if he knew he hadn't lost. On seeing me aiming the shotgun at him he let out a roar of rage and suddenly ran backwards, taking Sir William with him and ramming him against the altar. With a howl of pain William let go of his grip and in one fluid movement Chambers bounded forward, grabbed the barrel of the shotgun, ripped it from my hands and swung it through the air in a wide arc.

I ducked and felt its breeze as it passed above my head. It gained momentum and caught Sir William on his shoulder. I heard the crack of breaking bone and Sir William cried out in pain and fell back against a pile of burning pews.

Still seething with anger, Chambers turned and faced me. A brief look of confusion crossed his face for I was unfamiliar to him, but then he sneered. Compared to him I was a lightweight and he could see I posed him no real threat. Demonstrating agility that belied his bulk he leapt at me, swinging his fist. This time he was too quick for me and he landed an almighty punch on the side of my head. I felt like I had been hit by a freight train, it was so powerful. I staggered away from him, reeling from the shock. My head was spinning, and stars danced before my eyes. For a second, I just stood there, staring at his ugly, leering face. My legs seemed to turn to water and they gave way beneath me. I dropped to the floor.

I must have briefly lost consciousness for the next thing I remember is being carried across the chapel to the back of the altar. Then Chambers knelt and silently dropped me through the entrance to the vault where I rolled into the darkness and landed with a dull thud on top of Beth. I could feel both sides of the tiny hole, which were barely wider than my shoulders, pushing against me and I scrabbled to get up, to get out. But before I could do either I was knocked back with some force as something heavy landed on top of me and knocked all the breath from my body.

Then the hole was plunged into total darkness as Chambers closed the panel.

# Chapter Thirty-one
# The Vault

Every cell in my body was seized with uncontrollable panic. It gripped every nerve and sinew, and screamed at me to get out, telling me I was going to suffocate and die in this tiny hole.

I tried to draw breath, but I couldn't.

I was stuck. I couldn't move; I was sandwiched between Beth beneath me and Sir William on top of me. William, a big man who clearly enjoyed his food, was a dead weight on top of me, unconscious and unmoving.

I was winded from when he landed on me and I was struggling to breathe. In the desperate battle between my rising panic caused by my irrational fear of enclosed spaces and my rational attempt to keep calm. Panic had the upper hand.

I bucked and wriggled to try and dislodge the heavy weight that pinned me down.

It was pitch black. Not a single sliver of light entered this hole of hell and I could feel the walls on either side of me, trapping me, crushing me, reminding me just how small and confined this tiny space was. Even if I could move William was there enough room for me to move out from beneath him?

I was convinced the air was being sucked out of the hole and again, I had to fight to control my fear.

Catholic priests, I reasoned, had hidden in places like this, sometimes for hours on end, whilst their persecutors searched for evidence of their presence.

It was no good, no amount of reasoning could stop me losing control and I struggled frantically, trying to move and trying to breathe.

From out of nowhere I seemed to find a burst of almost superhuman strength and finally, I felt Sir William's body shift enough for me to be able to push him upright. I then struggled to free myself with one hand while having to hold him away from me with the other. As I moved, Beth let out a barely audible groan.

She was alive.

Trying my best to avoid treading on her I wedged William against the end wall and reached up to run my hands along the inside of the panel, searching for a button, switch or latch; anything that would release the door and allow us to escape.

I couldn't find one, and immediately started to panic again, fearing that we would be trapped here forever. I reasoned that while the switch on the outside would be hidden, the one on the inside should be obvious.

But what if there was no way of opening it from the inside? What if it was designed only to be opened from the outside? It made sense, my irrational sense told me as my fumbling became more urgent, there should be no way of opening it from the inside. Why would there be? It was a vault. No one alive should be in there. Unless it was a vault that doubled as a Priest's Hole.

I realised then that I was going to die in there.

I pounded on the panel with my fist and yelled for help. The panel was solid and I hurt my hand as I thumped it. Obviously, it was going to be solid, I argued, it needed to sound solid to anyone outside who knocked on it.

Something in the back of my mind chose that moment to remind me that the altar stone was a solid piece of granite weighing over one hundredweight and another wave of panic gripped me. I convinced myself that not only was I trapped down here but the fire was going to cause the altar to collapse into this hole and it would slowly crush me to death.

In anger and frustration at my dilemma I banged my fists on both panels. The panel behind me reverberated with a hollow knock. My fear had stopped me thinking straight; I had been facing the wrong way. I turned around and ran my hands swiftly along the opposite panel. At last my hand found a catch and, with a satisfying click, the panel opened once again.

A flood of flickering light flowed into the vault followed by a wave of searing heat. The fire had taken hold inside the chapel and, looking through the narrow entrance I could see flames licking up the walls.

Without hesitation I pushed myself out and then grabbed Sir William to pull him out after me. He had regained consciousness while I was searching for our exit.

"Where the bloody hell am I?" he demanded.

I grabbed his arm and he cried out in pain.

"Careful of my arm, you bloody fool."

"Sorry."

"Who the hell are you?"

"No time for introductions," I replied, "we've got to get out and stop Seth Chambers."

"That bloody idiot? Where is he?"

"He's probably escaping."

"Bloody Hell!"

I peered around the altar stone to see that Chambers was still in the chapel. Because the panel opened at the back of the altar, we were hidden from him. He still held the shotgun as he headed for the door.

"We've got to stop him," I shouted to make myself heard above the crackling flames. "Give me your hands."

"My arm is broken," he shouted back, "here." He raised his left arm and I grabbed him by his wrist. With all the strength I could muster I pulled him up and out of the hole.

"Where is he?" William demanded, holding his broken arm with his good hand. The panel door snapped shut as he stood up.

"He went outside," I said, and he ran off. I followed after him but was stopped by a cry for help. Edward was waking and was surrounded by a wall of fire. The intensity of the heat was nearly unbearable as I dashed through the flames. Smoke was filling the chapel and I had to crouch low to keep from choking on it. The wood in Edward's prosthetic leg was burning and I looked around for something to smother it.

Edward opened his eyes and I could see the fear in them. I guessed he was having flashbacks.

By the door was a table covered with a thick cloth and I reached over and grabbed it. A couple of silver candlesticks, a wooden cross and a collection bowl clattered to the floor. I threw the blanket over Edward's leg and patted it down. It was an effective fire blanket and once I had extinguished the flames I helped him up. He was wobbly on his feet, so he put his arm around my neck and together we hobbled to the door.

Flames licked angrily around the chapel, everything flammable was burning fiercely, and the heat blistered our skin. Thick, choking smoke billowed over us and the bitter, acrid smell of burning wood and melting metal filled the air. Orange and yellow fingers licked up the curtains and engulfed a large cross holding the crucified Jesus. It tumbled forward, crashing through burning pews and the effigy of Christ bounced across the room, where it lay burning by the altar.

"Come on," I said, pulling Edward forward, "this way."

A burning banner crashed down just in front of us, roaring flames exploding in a blinding fireball. I felt rather than heard Edward's reaction. He was beginning to panic as he was beset by flashbacks of exploding bombs and gas attacks. I needed to get him to safety quickly.

Our way to the door was obstructed by a huge wall of flame and the only way out was to go through it, but Edward was backing away in fear.

"We have to go through," I urged him.

"I can't."

"You must. It's the only way."

"No." He was struggling to get away. I had an idea.

"Captain Hilliard," I ordered, "lead your men through that door. That is an order. Now."

Having spent so long in the trenches obeying orders, he snapped to and, leaning heavily on me, we ran through the fire and pushed through the door. The flames scorched my face but, by some miracle, we made it through and the cold winter air blew a welcome blast against our burnt skin.

A crowd had gathered outside. The villagers on their way to midnight mass, just as Colin had told us, were gathered around Sir William as he confronted Chambers.

"Help us," I called, trying to be heard above the shouting voices and the crackling flames.

Edward caught sight of his father and, with a huge effort, pushed away from me and struggled over to him.

"Father."

Chambers swung around to face Edward and raised the gun.

The villagers fell silent. People who were standing behind Edward moved quickly away, getting out of the line of fire. For several moments we all stood still; watching and waiting.

Edward stepped forward.

"Stop," Chambers demanded, "or I'll shoot."

Edward laughed. "I've spent three years being shot at and blown up by better men than you. Do you really think I'm scared of some drunken village idiot?"

"Edward, don't!" Sir William pleaded, stepping toward his son. "Don't antagonise him. He's not worth it."

There was a madness in Chambers' eyes as they flicked rapidly between father and son. He kept the shotgun aimed at Edward's chest and I watched in horror as he began to squeeze the trigger.

I knew what was meant to happen. It cannot change I told myself. But of all the people who were standing watching I was the only one there who knew this truth.

This was wrong. Chambers was pulling the trigger, he was firing the gun, but the gun was pointing at Edward. He was about to shoot the wrong man.

Was that why I was here? Was I meant to stop Edward from being killed?

If not me then who else?

If Chambers killed Edward, that would mean Larry would never be born and the Hilliard family would cease to exist.

Although I couldn't see him, I heard, or thought I heard, Larry whispering urgently in my ear, "Stop him, Jim. You have to stop him."

Without considering the consequences I leapt at Chambers just as he pulled the trigger.

# Chapter Thirty-Two
## Slow Motion

It's true what they say about time. It really does appear to slow down in moments of major trauma.

With my eyes fixed on Chambers' finger as it tightened its grip on the trigger, I threw myself at him. As I flew through the air, I distinctly heard the loud click of the trigger as it released the firing pin.

My hand moved slowly, reaching before me, reaching for the barrel of the shotgun.

The sound of the pin punching the detonator in the centre of the cartridge was a prolonged wavering bass, like a slowed down record and at the same time my hand grasped the cold metal muzzle.

In fluid slow motion the shotgun arced away; simultaneously a blinding flash erupted from the end of the muzzle. Searing heat burned the palm of my hand as several hundred tiny lead pellets fired out of the gun in a puff of grey smoke.

Time returned to normal. I fell crashing to the ground with my ears ringing from the loud blast and heard a gasp of horror from the villagers. My hand hurt like hell and I plunged it into the freezing cold snow, and I lay there, dazed and confused, not knowing whether I had saved Edward or not.

With an effort I pushed myself up and looked around.

A group of villagers had grabbed Chambers and were struggling to restrain him.

Edward stood there, transfixed with a look of horror on his face.

Sir William lay at his feet, close to where I lay. A dark stain seeped through his white shirt from a hole in his chest, staining the white snow a deep crimson.

I had saved Edward but in doing so I had caused William's death.

I felt exhausted. My hand was red and blistered; burnt from holding the muzzle of the gun at the moment of firing. My ears were ringing, and I felt a trickle of blood oozing from the right one, and the side of my head felt swollen from where Chambers had hit me.

There was a loud crash from the chapel as one of the windows exploded, showering us with shards of glass, and tongues of bright orange and yellow flames licked up the outside wall.

The villagers leapt into action, but there was something else for me to do; Beth was still in there.

I couldn't be certain if she was still alive, but she had shown signs of life when I rescued William. I had to try.

The heat of the fire held me back. The smell of burning was pungent, and a thick cloud of black smoke billowed through the shattered window. I pushed myself up.

I staggered as a wave of dizziness swept over me and I stood still to steady myself. It passed and I made a dash for the door. I stumbled though it and ran into a wall of heat, intense and impenetrable. The chapel has completely succumbed to the fire and there was nothing I could do. Tears of frustration filled my eyes as I stood there, helpless.

"Beth," I called, "I'm sorry."

Then I saw her, through the blinding intensity of the flames. Only it wasn't her, it was Madea, dressed in her modern clothes. Her outline was blurred, and she knelt before the altar. She genuflected, stood up and then turned to me. A smile spread across her face and she smiled at me. Then, almost imperceptibly, she faded into the background and was gone.

"Jim."

I turned to see Larry running towards me through the dark, stumbling across the snow.

"Larry?"

"You're back. Oh, thank God you're back."

"What?"

I looked around. The fire was gone, the villagers were nowhere in sight and Edward had disappeared.

I was back in 2018.

The dizziness returned and the last thing I remember was falling into Larry's arms.

# Chapter Thirty-Three
# Christmas

I looked worse than I felt.

I looked like I had been set upon by a gang of thugs and beaten up. My face was swollen, I had bruises on the side of my head and my right eye was a livid purple. My forehead was red and blistered and my eyebrows had been singed off. It felt like I was hearing through wads of cotton wool that had been stuffed into my ears and my hand was stinging from the burns on my palm.

"Jesus Christ," Larry said, "Leanne is going to go ape when she sees you."

Having half carried and half dragged me back to the house Larry had put my hand under the cold tap for twenty minutes while forcing brandy into my mouth to help me recover. The burns to my hand were superficial, and after he had covered it in antiseptic cream, he'd wrapped it in a bandage.

"It looks a lot worse than it is," I replied.

"Thank goodness for that," he laughed, "because it looks dreadful."

I must confess, I agreed with him. Having seen myself in the mirror I was quite shocked at how bad I looked, but I'd swallowed a few pain killers and didn't feel too bad.

Actually, I felt quite good. The last twelve hours had been pretty scary, but it also felt over.

"Here's some breakfast," he said, pouring me a mug of coffee and pushing the toast rack across the table.

"I've been thinking," Larry said, waving half a slice of toast at me, "about last night."

"Me too," I replied, "a lot."

"You really were there, weren't you?"

I nodded, "I got all these burns and bruises a hundred years ago, and they still show. Remember when we talked to old Colin a few weeks ago and he said someone had pulled Edward from the fire?"

"Yeah, that was you they saw, wasn't it?"

"Yes, it must have been. The story he told us wasn't quite the way it all happened but then he told it at least second hand, and he wasn't actually there."

"No, but it was pretty close."

"Yes, and I've been thinking. I had to be there because I was there."

"And you were there for a purpose; to save Edward's life."

"But in doing so, I killed William."

"You didn't, Seth Chambers, our great-grandfather, killed William. You saved Edward." He paused and looked at me. "You do realise that if you hadn't done that then I would never have been born?"

"I'll try not to remind you of it too often."

Cause and effect, I thought. We were living in a present that came about because I changed the past. I'm not sure I really understood that because nothing had changed, it was the past we had always known.

But Edward should have been the one who died that Christmas Eve a hundred years ago, no one else was going to save him. William was too far away when Chambers pulled the trigger and all the villagers had backed away in case they got hurt. It was my action, mine from 2018, that had changed what was meant to happen and history had taken a different course; one that included Larry.

What if ... Janet and my mum hadn't died in that car crash? Normally we would have arrived on Christmas morning, so I wouldn't have been there last night.

What if ... I hadn't been there?

"The last thing I saw," I said looking at Larry, "was Madea. She was kneeling at the altar. I think this has been all about her. About Beth, I mean." He looked at me. "Her disappearance was always a mystery, wasn't it?"

"And now we know."

"Yes, she was in the chapel, she was trapped in the vault."

"She must still be there."

"Yes, and we need to release her."

"She won't still be alive."

"I mean, get her out and give her a proper burial."

"Maybe. Do you think that's the final piece of the puzzle?"

"Yes. I hope so, anyway."

"Well, let's go and find out then, shall we?"

Wrapped up warmly against the freezing weather we trudged out into the beautiful wintry landscape. The sun had just risen; making the white

226

snow sparkle. The morning was still, and a few puffed up birds hopped along branches, tweeting their sweet songs.

The chapel door was bathed in sunlight, and I shuddered; memories of the last time I was in there were still fresh in my mind.

"Was it only last night," I muttered, looking up at the door, "or was it a hundred years ago?"

"It's hard to believe that so much happened here."

"Well, at least we now know how it caught fire."

The inside of the chapel looked as it always did, full of garden junk and other rubbish. We could clearly see the blackened walls and ceiling. The oak beams holding the roof were remarkably unscathed thanks to the actions of the villagers that night who'd set up a water bucket chain to try and dowse the fire until the fire brigade arrived to put it out.

To get to the altar we had to clear our way through and we moved a pile of wood, two rusting wheelbarrows, a lawnmower that hadn't been used in three decades and enough empty plant pots to start our own garden centre.

"There's a lot of junk in here," I remarked.

"I don't recall it ever being cleared out. Certainly, never in my lifetime and dad never did it, we only ever used to dump stuff in here."

"It's amazing the junk we keep, just in case."

"Maybe now's the time to be ruthless" he continued. "Mind you, we can clean up these pots and plant them with seedlings to give to the village. We could leave them at the gate and let people help themselves." He threw a pile through the open door where they landed in the snow. "We'll put them in the greenhouse in the kitchen garden later," he said.

It took us longer than expected to clear a path to the altar but eventually we were there. We went round the back and ran our hands over the stone looking for a switch or catch.

"I've pushed, turned and tweaked everything," Larry said, scratching his head in bemusement.

"Me too."

I crouched down and stared at it, hoping for inspiration. It was plain stone this side, unlike the front which was ornate with stone carvings. The only marking was an inscription 'Matthew VII:VII'.

"Look at this," I said, "do you think that's a clue or something?"

"I've no idea. What's Matthew VII:VII, anyway?"

"I think it's a verse from the bible."

"I guessed that, but what's the verse?"

"No idea, I didn't pay much attention when we did scripture at school. Look it up."

Larry pulled out his phone. "No bloody signal." He waved it about a bit then, holding it out in front of him he walked to the door. "Here we go," he said. "Right, 'Ask, and it will be given to you;'"

"That's not very helpful."

"Wait, it's still loading. Here, 'search, and you will find it;'"

"We are searching," I said, "we're just not finding."

"And, 'knock, and the door will be opened to you.'"

"Knock?"

"Go on," he said, "try knocking."

I knocked on the panel and nothing happened.

"OK," I said, "it looks like it's a bit more than simply knocking on the door."

"How about if you knock that bit where they did the carving?"

I tried that but again the panel remained stubbornly shut.

"Did you see it opening last night?"

"Yes."

"Can you remember how?"

I stood back, closed my eyes and tried to recall the sequence of events.

"Chambers held Beth over there," I said, moving to where I had seen him holding Beth. "Then he threw her, and she fell backwards against the altar like so." I demonstrated her falling. "Her elbow banged against the altar stone here." I banged my fist on the spot where I remembered her elbow hitting the altar side, but still it didn't open.

"Shit and buggery," I shouted in frustration, stamping my foot heavily on the floor. Something clicked.

"Aha," I exclaimed and crouched down on the floor.

"What is it?"

"I think I just released it."

"But it's not open."

"Maybe it's rusty."

Something was stopping the panel from springing open and I pushed against it. There was a muffled crash, and the panel sprang open, just as I'd seen it do last night.

I knelt there, staring into the black vault and instantly drew back, my experience of last night fresh in my mind. The foul smell of stale air wafted up from its depths.

"What's down there?" Larry asked, kneeling down beside me. He switched the torch of his phone on and shone it into the hole.

"Oh, my God," he cried, and rapidly pulled back.

"What is it?"

I took his phone and looked down.

An eyeless face looked back at me, and I recoiled in fright. It was covered in dried, blackened leathery flesh which had shrunk tightly against the skull, pulling tight around the mouth, pulling it into a rictus grin. The dark hair, which continued to grow after death, was long and wiry, spread out over the lifeless face. Elsewhere over her body the flesh had either dried on or rotted away. She looked as though she'd died mid scream clawing at the panel. One arm had fallen to the floor, probably when I forced the panel open.

"She ... she was still alive," I said, horrified, "I could have saved her."

"No Jim, you couldn't," he said, putting his hand on my shoulder, "you really couldn't."

"But ..."

"No. If you were meant to save her," he interrupted me, "you would have stayed in 1918 for long enough for you to do so, but you came back to your own time. It was out of your control. It was meant to be."

"Then why?"

"Because ..."

"Yes?"

"Because ... she has lain here for a hundred years and, in all that time, no one knew where she was. I think you were right; this is all about her. She was forgotten, and I reckon she led us here to find her, so we could give her a proper burial, remember her properly."

"Do you think so?"

"She's our great-grandmother, we are her descendants. We're the only ones who are likely to care. Come on."

"Where to?"

"Back to the house."

"And leave her here?"

"I think we have to Jim. We've just found an unidentified dead body. We have to alert the authorities."

"But we know who it is."

"We do, but they don't know that, and we can't tell them how we know either. We'll just have to tell them we suspect it's Beth. They'll do their forensic stuff on her to verify who she is and when she died. After that we can let her rest in peace."

We walked back to the house. While we had been in the chapel it had clouded over and had started snowing again.

"You know what?" Larry said as he put the turkey in the oven.

"What?"

We wandered through the to the smoking room and I poured us both a glass of whiskey.

"When Christmas is over, we'll clear all that crap out of the chapel and redecorate. Give it a bit of a facelift, and then we'll see if we can bury Beth in there. If not, then at least we can put in a memorial stone to her or something."

"I think that'd be a really nice tribute to her."

Larry held up his glass and smiled, "I propose a toast; to our great-grandmother, Beth Chambers."

We clinked glasses, "Beth Chambers," I replied, "may she, from now on, forever rest in peace."

At that moment a strong breeze blew through the room, ruffling through Larry's hair and I shivered. For a brief moment I thought I saw, standing by the fireplace, an apparition of Beth and I'm certain I heard her say 'thank you'.

"Jim?"

"Did you just see that?"

"Yes."

"I think she's gone now."

"Yes."

"Merry Christmas, Larry."

"Merry Christmas, Jim."

# Epilogue
## 25th September 2019

"Excuse me?" I said to the nurse sitting at reception. Her badge said she was Nurse MacDonald. "Where can we find Leanne Hilliard, please?"

"And you are?"

"I'm her father," I informed her.

"And I'm her father-in-law," Larry added.

"Down the corridor," Nurse MacDonald smiled and informed us, "second room on the right."

We trotted along the ward.

Leanne was sitting up in her hospital bed with barely a hair out of place. She smiled when she saw us. Harry, who was by her side, came over and hugged us both.

"Well?" I said, "where is she then?"

Leanne pointed to her tiny sleeping new-born, our third grandchild, who was tightly wrapped in a pink blanket in a plastic crib by the side of her bed.

"Have you decided on a name yet?" Larry asked.

Harry looked at Leanne who said, "We thought, in honour of the newly discovered branch of our family, that we'd christen her Elizabeth Gwendoline Violet."

I smiled.

"You couldn't have been given her a better name."

## Author's Note

As much as writing a book is a solitary business, numerous people have been involved in its production.

I would like to thank my good friends (and fellow pedants) Tony Sawford and Jan Moore, and my wife, Jane, for reading each section as I wrote it and pointing out the numerous spelling and grammatical errors, as well as ensuring that I kept the plot tight and relevant. Any outstanding errors are mine and not theirs. Also, Eileen and Lynne, for reading the final manuscript and deeming it readable, I hope you enjoyed it as much as they did.

I have tried, as much as possible, to ensure the historical events, though fictional, have some basis in fact. The battle offensives described actually happened and the dates on which they happened in Edward's diary are historically correct. My description of the events, however, are entirely my own and I am sure my depictions are nothing compared to the horrors of real life in the trenches.

The creation of King Rat in the trenches during the World War One by putting several rats into a sack and seeing which one survived, was absolutely true. The King Rat was tough, savage, and cannibalistic. It was a way of managing rat numbers, leaving the soldiers to concentrate on fighting the war.

The ship used in the Channel crossing to carry Captain Hilliard back to England really existed, as did the company that owned it, although I've no idea of its destiny beyond that.

Roehampton Auxiliary Hospital was opened by Queen Mary in 1915 and became one of the leading hospitals for the supply of prosthetics for our war heroes. Several prosthetics companies were set up in makeshift workshops in the grounds of the hospital, one of which was Critchley of Liverpool. Jumpy stump and phantom limbs are real and must be a dreadful phenomenon for the amputees who experience them.

Some of the doctors mentioned in Edward's diary also existed, look them up, some of them were pioneers.

In 1918 Spanish Flu spread across the world, killing more people in two years than had died during the war. Let's hope the pandemic of 2020 doesn't end up as brutal.

Early on in this book Jim suffers from a mental breakdown. In writing about his breakdown, I spoke to qualified Psychotherapists as well as reading up on the subject. Any mistakes in my description of its manifestation or the subsequent treatment of it are entirely my own.

Rosehip Hall does not exist so don't bother trying to find it and, while there are many fenland villages in East Anglia, Downham Fen is not one of them.

Finally, the Hilliard family, as portrayed in this book, does not exist. This is a work of fiction and any resemblance to any person living or dead is unintentional and coincidental.

Nor did they, are far as I know, have anything to do with the draining of the fens in the 18th century.

## About the Author

PETER CRUSSELL is the author of the internationally selling children's book series, *TALES FROM THE ENCHANTED FOREST*, which is also published by New Report Publishing. The series is listed in *'Brilliant Books List Yr6 – Essential Reading For Every Y6 Classroom'* and all the books in the series are available from Amazon.

He has also written a play, *Café La Madeleine*, a French resistance drama set in World War Two, and co-wrote with composer, Rowan Alfred, the family musical *The Owl and the Pussycat*, which is based on the wonderful poem by Edward Lear.

As a poet, he regularly supplies poems for anthologies and is also an accomplished lyricist. His most recent collaboration was with the German composer, Thomas Konder, supplying English lyrics for several songs on his critically acclaimed album, The Labyrinth.

*The Ties That Bind* is his first full length novel.

Printed in Great Britain
by Amazon

54715737R00133